MORE THAN A HUNCH

Book Two

In the

Ladies in Lab Coats Series

By

Sally Burbank

Sally Burbank

MORE THAN A HUNCH

Book Two: Ladies in Lab Coats Series

More Than a Hunch is a work of fiction. All characters and events in this novel are the products of the author's imagination. Specifically, there is no Banderbaxy Pharmaceuticals, or a chemotherapy drug named Taxotaphen.

Contact the author on her website for speaking engagements or to explore her other books at:

www.sallywillardburbank.com

ISBN 978-0-998-32064-9 (e-book)
ISBN 978-0-998-32065-6 (paperback)

Contact the publisher at:
Woodmont and Waverly Publishing
207 Woodmont Circle
Nashville, TN 37205

Cover Design: Najla Qamber Designs
Editor: Candie Moonshower

OTHER BOOKS
by
SALLY BURBANK

FICTION:

Can You Lose the Unibrow?

NON-FICTION:

Patients I Will Never Forget

The Alzheimer's Disease Caregiver's Handbook: What to Remember When They Forget

ANTHOLOGIES:

Chicken Soup for the Soul
~The Power of the Positive
~Hope and Miracles
~Miracles Happen
~Laughter is the Best Medicine
~Readers' Choice 20th Anniversary edition

DEDICATION

This book is dedicated to my two wonderful children:
Steven Burbank and Eliza Baker.
You are both the light of my life!

AUTHOR'S NOTE

We live in a global economy where 90% of all generic drugs are now produced outside the States. Due to their low employee wages, India and China manufacture the lion's share of these cheap drugs.

While we love the $4-per-month price tag of foreign generics, many of us are now sounding the alarm that these affordable drugs may not always be as pure and effective as we had assumed.

Increasingly, cancer-causing contaminants have led to massive recalls and subsequent shortages of common medications such as Zantac, (a heartburn medication), and Valsartan and Losartan, (high blood pressure medications). Other medications are recalled because they aren't strong enough. Are drugs that don't kill bacteria or thin the blood properly really a bargain?

How are these inferior-quality drugs making it onto the market? How often, and how carefully, are these Chinese and Indian factories inspected? Do we know with certainty the inspection results are trustworthy?

In her well-researched book, *Bottle of Lies*, Katherine Eban exposes the underregulated and slipshod manufacturing standards of some Indian and Chinese pharmaceutical companies. Because factories in India and China are often provided weeks of advanced notice about an upcoming inspection, they have plenty of time to clean up their acts and alter quality control reports before the inspectors arrive.

In my opinion, the FDA does not perform enough *unannounced* testing of the actual *drugs* — instead of just reviewing quality control *data* produced by the factory workers themselves. After all, quality control data can easily be altered or deleted. The analytics company FDAzilla uncovered that during a five-year window, 55% of Indian and 65% of Chinese pharmaceutical companies fudged their quality control reports to pass an inspection. Some companies committed outright fraud. As a consequence, substandard drugs are released to the unknowing public.

Pharmacists and insurance companies have brainwashed us to believe generics are just as effective as their brand-name counterparts, and 93% of the time, they are.

But what about the 7% that is substandard?

The consequences to the American consumer of insufficiently inspected foreign generics are chilling. People die when their antibiotic isn't strong enough to kill bacteria. They have strokes when their blood pressure medication releases all at once, instead of slowly, over twenty-four hours. They hemorrhage or form clots if their blood thinner varies in potency from one batch to the next.

In *Bottle of Lies*, Eban chronicles the disturbing cases of Cleveland Clinic heart transplant patients who did great — until their brand-name immunosuppressants were unknowingly replaced with an ineffective Indian generic. The net result? *They rejected their transplanted hearts!*

Do some online research of your own, and if you become as concerned as I have, contact your Senator and Congressman. Demand that the FDA begins yearly *unannounced* inspections of all foreign drug manufacturing facilities again.

In 2014, when the FDA *did* have a policy of performing *unannounced* factory inspections, the rate of serious violations uncovered by inspectors rose by 60%.

It is time we get rid of advanced warning and insist on impromptu inspections. This is the standard for American drug companies, so why should we use more lax standards in China? If China wants in on the thirty-one-billion-dollar-a-year generic drug profits, it needs to play by the rules. It is time we quit trusting the fox to guard the henhouse.

The COVID-19 pandemic has further exposed how outsourcing our critical medical supplies to China left Americans and Europeans woefully undersupplied with protective N-95 face masks and gowns. Ditto with antibiotics.

I was inspired to write *More Than a Hunch* after reading Eban's book and after researching the issue of foreign generic drug safety in more detail.

In brainstorming the plot, I asked myself, "What if an oncologist unknowingly injected tainted chemotherapy, and as a consequence, her patient nearly dies? What if the son of that patient is an attorney who regularly sues doctors for malpractice? What if the oncologist had a hunch the chemotherapy was somehow contaminated? Can she prove it before she gets sued? Will her patient survive?

I hope you enjoy *More Than a Hunch*. If you do, please spread the word to your friends and family and post a review on Amazon and Goodreads.

~ Sally Burbank, MD~

CHAPTER 1

Marcus Romano eyed his Rolex, turned to his mother, and sputtered, "If that doctor of yours doesn't show up soon, I'm sending her a bill—for one wasted hour of my life."

His mother glared at him over the top of her *Good Housekeeping* magazine. "Oh, get off your high horse. Libby will be here any minute." She wagged a scolding finger at him. "And when she does, I don't want you badgering her. She takes time with her patients, so it sometimes puts her behind. Trust me—she's an excellent doctor."

Marcus gripped the arms of his chair and snorted. "Excellent doctor? She dumped enough chemotherapy in you to kill an elephant. Look at you." He gestured toward Sophia's jaundiced eyes and complexion. "Sheer medical incompetence, if you ask me."

Sophia rolled up her magazine and whacked him on the thigh. "Well, nobody *asked* you, Smarty-pants, so quit bad-mouthing my doctor. I'm sure she'll have a perfectly reasonable explanation."

"Excuse, more likely," he muttered, unsuccessful in his attempt to block out the reek of antiseptic that permeated the stainless-steel exam room. Shifting his long legs restlessly in the undersized plastic chair, he added, "She's probably at the funeral of the last patient she poisoned."

Whack! Another hit to the thigh. "Be nice."

1

Unrepentant, he crossed his arms. "I'll bet she screwed up your chemo dose, and that's why you're yellow. If I'm right, she should pay for her ineptitude."

"Enough! No more of your highfalutin' lawyer threats, or I'll toss you out of here. Just because you're worried sick about me is no reason to act like a jerk. Remember, you're only here as my concerned son, not an obnoxious prosecuting attorney licking his chops to sue. Now settle down and give her a chance to explain."

Marcus sucked in a deep breath and conceded his accusations *were* premature, and he *was* unfairly jumping to conclusions. He needed to remain calm and give the doctor a chance to explain.

This isn't a courtroom, so retract your claws.

Sophia scrubbed her arms vigorously, leaving bright red streaks.

He grabbed her wrist like a vice grip. "Stop that! You'll give yourself a skin infection with all that scratching."

She yanked her hand free. "You have no idea how badly this itches. It's like a million chigger bites all over my body."

Before he could reprimand her further, he heard a knock on the door. Dr. Libby Holman dashed in carrying a laptop, which she placed on her computer workstation. She then sank into a chair facing them. "I'm so sorry for your long wait." She turned toward Sophia with a smile, and after one glance, her mouth dropped, and her eyes widened. "Sophia? You're positively yellow."

Sophia scratched her arms again and offered a weak smile. "From what I could dig up on *WebMD*, I think something's wrong with my liver."

"Evidently!" She patted the examination table. "Hop up and let me take a look at you."

While Dr. Holman obtained a thorough history and examination of Sophia, Marcus couldn't help but examine his mother's oncologist. Not the frumpy nerd he'd envisioned—not at all. Her thick auburn hair curled gracefully around her face and complimented her large turquoise eyes. Her toned physique suggested she did more in her free time than pour over medical journals. He forced himself to look away. Pretty or not, she most likely overdosed his mother's chemotherapy, so he expected a credible explanation or that comely face of hers would face him in court—for malpractice.

Oblivious to Marcus's inner rantings, Libby completed her evaluation and then extended a friendly hand. "Marcus, where are my manners? I should have introduced myself earlier. I'm Libby Holman. I've heard so much about you from Sophia over these last six months I feel like I already know you."

He forced himself to stand up and shake her hand. Even if she had nearly killed his mother, he would remain civil until she had a chance to explain—or until he could dig up clear evidence against her.

He tried to ignore the jolt in his chest when their eyes locked, and she smiled up at him with luscious full lips and beautiful teeth. He averted his eyes and flopped back into his chair.

Forget it! That beautiful face of yours will not distract me.

He was here for one reason and one reason alone: to get answers.

He cleared his throat and forced his voice to sound pleasant.

3

"Obviously, I'm worried about my mother. Is it possible you accidentally infused too much chemo this last cycle?"

Her spine stiffened, and she pulled back in her chair. "Of course not. I'm very meticulous with my dose calculations."

Uh-huh. Just what I expected – denial.

The woman had most likely overdosed his mother with her toxic brew but now claimed no responsibility for the dire outcome. Before he could stop himself, he snapped, "Are you positive, because *something* went wrong. Look at her!" He swept his arm in a Vanna White motion toward his mother. "She practically glows in the dark now."

Libby swiveled in her computer chair to face him head-on. "Let me reiterate. I infused the same dose as her previous five cycles, which, I might point out, shrank her lymphoma from the size of a cantaloupe to completely undetectable on last week's CT scan."

"Then why is she yellow?" he demanded.

His mother reached over and dug her claws into his arm. Ma may not appreciate his tone of voice, but *somebody* had to stand up for her. She was too nice for her own good—always volunteering at the homeless shelter and walking dogs for the Humane Society. He could picture her patting Dr. Holman's hand and cooing, "That's alright, dearie. I know you didn't mean to destroy my liver. I forgive you." Yes, as a Christian, he *was* called to love his enemies, but he couldn't forgive her if she didn't even 'fess up to her mistake!

His mother dug her nails in deeper. "Marcus, you won't find a more competent oncologist than Dr. Holman. I promise you—my liver failure is not her fault."

Marcus arched a defiant brow. "You don't know that for certain. *She* chose the chemo, calculated the dose, and set the infusion rate. Your liver didn't fail until immediately after this last dose of chemo."

"That doesn't mean Libby is to blame," Sophia retorted.

"Absolutely, and I'm not *accusing* her of anything. I'm looking for answers, so I merely raised the possibility of a dose miscalculation, that's all."

He turned back to Dr. Holman. "You said yourself her lymphoma is gone, so if cancer isn't causing her jaundice, what is? Could you have accidentally used *pounds* instead of *kilograms* in your dose calculation?"

Momentary panic crossed Dr. Holman's face.

Noting her alarm, he continued. "Just last week, I filed a lawsuit against a cardiologist who inadvertently killed a toddler. Turns out, he calculated the dose of a potent cardiac drug using pounds instead of kilograms. Poor kid received twice the recommended dose."

When her eyes widened, Marcus went for the jugular. "Physician error—I see it all the time. Busy, stressed-out doctors make careless mistakes, and then their patients pay the penalty."

She glared across the table at him. "There are many causes for jaundice besides physician error, you know," she snapped.

"Such as—." He gestured for her to continue.

"Viral hepatitis, autoimmune liver disease, a gallstone stuck in her bile duct, toxins, primary biliary cirrhosis and—."

He jumped to his feet and pointed at her computer. "You better not be putting cirrhosis in your differential diagnosis. Mom doesn't even drink."

She inhaled a deep breath and released it slowly—as though needing time to compose herself before blowing up at him. "Primary biliary cirrhosis has nothing whatsoever to do with alcohol intake."

His cheeks warmed at his idiotic behavior.

Way to look stupid, Marcus. Settle down—before you make an even bigger fool of yourself.

"Oh, sorry. I didn't know that," he admitted.

Her eyes narrowed. "Look, since I've completed medical school, residency, and a rigorous three-year oncology fellowship at Sloan Kettering, why don't you leave your mother's medical condition to me, and I'll leave legal affairs to you?"

His mouth dropped at her condescending tone.

Did she just tell me to mind my own business?

This *was* his business—his mother's life was at stake!

Crossing the room in a heartbeat, he leaned forward and gripped the arms of her computer desk, thereby forcing her to look up at him and give him her full attention.

She wanted him to buzz off and trust her?

Forget it, lady! I trusted you to cure Mom's cancer. Look where that got me. She's a regular walking banana now.

He growled out, with as much civility as he could muster, "I will not be summarily dismissed. I came here to get answers, and I'm not leaving until I get them."

6

He prepared himself for a biting retort. A snappy rebuttal. An impassioned insistence that she had *not* made a mistake and was more than qualified to diagnose his mother *without* his help, thank you very much. Instead, she started to shake from head to toe as though she'd been sitting in a meat freezer for an hour. Without warning, she stood, grabbed the trashcan, and vomited. Then she slunk back into her chair as though wilting.

Was this her idea of professional conduct—barfing in the middle of an office visit?

Her face blanched, and the next thing he knew, she crumpled over her computer table face down, arms dangling. She nearly landed her laptop on the floor.

Sophia jumped off the exam table and darted to Libby's side. "Look what you did to her!" she hissed at Marcus. "I told you not to bully her."

Ashamed that his aggressive behavior could have triggered such a visceral reaction, he lifted Libby into his arms and placed her gently onto the exam table.

His mother pointed toward the door. "Quick! Go find a nurse while I try to revive her."

CHAPTER 2

As Marcus rushed into the hallway, a nagging suspicion came to mind: Had Libby *faked* this passing out spell to avoid answering his questions? He saw this kind of bluffing maneuver all the time in the courtroom — criminals feigning seizures or heart attacks right in the middle of a trial to skirt out of his grueling cross-examination. Still...just in case her spell *was* legit, he bolted down the hall in hot pursuit of a nurse.

Not seeing one in sight, Marcus dashed back into the exam room, hoping Libby had perked up. No such luck. There she lay — a corpse — her arms hanging like limp linguini. No doubt about it — if this was a charade, the woman deserved an Oscar.

What if she'd dropped dead because of his badgering?

Adrenaline coursed through Marcus's veins, and he darted back into the hallway and pounded on every exam room door. "Hey! I need a nurse. Emergency in room three."

A nurse poked her head out of an exam room and promised to grab the crash cart and meet him in room three.

Marcus rushed back to Libby's side, but when he saw her still lying lifelessly, he raced back into the hall and hollered, "Make it snappy, or she'll need a coffin."

Marcus jostled her shoulder, hoping to rouse her. No response. He shook with increasing vigor. Nothing. Sweat beaded his brow. He was a lawyer, not a doctor.

Shoot! I don't know squat about resuscitation.

Remembering an episode of *Scrubs* he once watched, he placed a hand in front of her mouth and nose to feel for expired air, a sign that she was breathing. Wasn't that the first step of CPR?

A slight puff of warm air touched his fingers.

Thank God! She's alive.

Meanwhile, his mother grabbed her arm and palpated her wrist. "I can feel a pulse, but it seems awfully slow." Staring at her watch, she counted Libby's heart rate.

Just then, Libby stirred slightly and mumbled so softly Marcus had to bend down to hear her. "Ice water."

He promised to bring her some and charged toward the door.

What was taking that blasted nurse so long?

Just then, a frazzled, plump nurse with a nametag that read Melissa dashed toward the exam room with the crash cart, a damp washcloth, and a cup of ice water. After listening with a stethoscope, she placed a wet washcloth on Libby's forehead. She then yanked off an ammonia pellet taped to the side of the exam table, snapped it in two, and wafted it under Libby's nose.

Libby jolted and croaked out, "I feel sick."

Melissa snatched up a vomit basin just in time for Libby to hurl the remains of her lunch.

Marcus turned his head, so he didn't have to watch any more of the revolting display. This was why he had become a lawyer instead of a doctor—body fluids were not his thing.

Melissa wiped Libby's mouth and ordered her to sit up and sip some ice water.

When he dared to look, Marcus couldn't help but notice Libby's ashen face and trembling hands.

She hadn't faked her spell. He had actually intimidated her to the point of fainting. Wow!

His chest constricted as guilt about his boorish behavior washed over him. This was a medical office, not a courtroom, but in his angst about his mother's health, he'd resorted to his comfortable role as prosecuting attorney. While trying to advocate for his mother, he'd behaved like a pompous jerk. A schoolyard bully, even. Christians were supposed to care about people—not intimidate them to the point of passing out.

He hung his head in shame. Where was the calm, methodical, detached problem-solving approach he usually employed? Why had he been so quick to jump all over Libby and assume the worst? Clearly, he had become too emotionally vested in his mother's case to be rational. Or civil. The woman deserved an apology.

The nurse dipped the washcloth in ice water and wiped Libby's face. Worry lines etched his mother's forehead, and she gripped Libby's hand. "Is she going to be alright?"

"Oh, she'll perk up," Melissa insisted with a reassuring smile. "She always does."

Marcus's head jerked up.

Wait! She's done this before?

"Does she do this often?" he inquired.

Melissa's eyes narrowed with suspicion. "Only when she feels verbally attacked."

Sophia crossed her arms and glared at him. "See! I told you this was all your fault. You turned my doctor's appointment into one of your hideous courtroom interrogations."

Unable to suppress his defensiveness, Marcus retorted, "I was only trying to look out for you, Ma. I didn't mean to cause all this." He gestured toward Libby.

The nurse, no doubt wanting to diffuse the tension, said, "Libby suffers from vasovagal spells and dysautonomia. Extreme emotional upset triggers her vagus nerve, which leads to a sudden drop in blood pressure and heart rate. She then gets weak and clammy and sometimes passes out." Melissa reached for Libby's wrist and counted her pulse again. "It's up to fifty, so she'll be fine."

As if on command, Libby sat up, though still paler than a bowl of mashed potatoes.

"Dr. Holman, I'm truly sorry for my needless aggression. I'm afraid my worry about Mom brought out the litigator in me. I didn't mean to upset you. Please forgive me."

She offered him a weak smile. "I understand. And I apologize for my spell." She then averted her eyes, as though embarrassed. "I'm sure you didn't come here today to witness all this. I'm afraid I've never handled interrogation by attorneys very well. Truthfully, they intimidate me."

His heart momentarily stopped.

She'd been interrogated by attorneys before? Was it for malpractice? If so, how many cases had been filed against her?

He eyed her suspiciously.

Was Dr. Holman some quack with a malpractice record longer than Santa's naughty list?

Had she graduated dead last in her medical school class, or graduated from some sketchy medical college in the Cayman Islands?

Note to self: check out Dr. Holman's litigation record.

He pursed his lips, unsure of how to proceed. If he pushed too hard, she might faint again, and he'd get nowhere. He needed answers, so perhaps a more conciliatory approach was best. "Dr. Holman, let me make it clear I know you would never *intentionally* overdose my mother."

Sophia glowered at him then waved a dismissive hand. "Ignore him, Libby. Marcus is so worried about me that it's making him behave despicably." She patted Libby's hand. "Trust me, he isn't normally a rabid Rottweiler, I promise."

Rabid Rottweiler? Gee, thanks, Ma.

Marcus chose to ignore his mother's barb and said as calmly as he could, "Ma, I'm not *accusing* Dr. Holman of anything. I'm merely *suggesting* that perhaps she could have *accidentally* infused too much chemotherapy this last go-round, and that's why you're jaundiced. After all, we're all human and can make mistakes, right?"

Libby's jaw clenched before she informed him, "I did *not* make a mistake, Marcus. I always double and triple check my chemo doses. I even get my nurse, Melissa, to independently calculate it as an additional safety measure. If not dosed properly, these are potent, dangerous medications."

Marcus nodded approvingly. "I appreciate your extra precautions. Trust me, not all physicians are as attentive to detail as you are."

Noting her fisted hands and sour expression, he tried to reassure her.

"You don't have to feel defensive, Dr. Holman. Mom probably wouldn't let me sue you, even if you *had* botched up her dose."

Libby's back stiffened at his mention of the word 'sue'. Lawsuit: no doubt every doctor's worst nightmare.

Her eyes glinted in anger as though challenging him to a duel. "Marcus, I have infused Taxotaphen for over four years now, and I have *never* seen liver failure from it. Not once. Just because your mother is jaundiced doesn't mean I screwed up her chemo dose. I will do a thorough investigation with an ultrasound and blood work to uncover the cause."

"Okay, but in the meantime, while we wait on test results, how do we fix her?"

Libby sucked in a deep breath, as though bracing herself for his explosive reaction. "Honestly? There isn't a specific treatment until we know the underlying cause. Her liver will either heal, or it won't. Unfortunately, I can't speed up her liver's recovery." She must have registered his displeasure with her lame treatment plan, as she added, "I'll gladly arrange a consult with a hepatologist for a second opinion."

Silence permeated the room as this unsavory bombshell sunk in.

No antidote? No cure?

He wanted to punch a wall. "My mother could *die* from this, and there's nothing you can do to help?"

Sophia dug her claws into his arm again. "Marcus Daniel Romano! You apologize this minute! That was rude and uncalled for, and you know it!"

He shook his head defiantly.

His mother's life was on the line, and this doctor was no more help than the janitor.

Sophia reached for his arm and squeezed it. "Marcus, my life is in God's hands. If He wants to take me home, I'm not afraid to die and go join your father in Heaven. If God wants to heal me, He's powerful enough to do that, as well. Intimidating and insulting my doctor won't make my liver heal one bit faster." She clasped his hand in both of hers. "You need to accept that you're powerless over this. Turn it over to God and have a little faith that Libby can figure out what's wrong with me."

Just hearing his mother acknowledge she could die filled his eyes with tears. Hating to look like a crybaby, he turned his back to Libby and faced his mother. "I buried Dad less than a year ago. I don't want to lose you, too."

She gripped his hand. "I understand, but rudeness to Libby won't prolong my life or heal my liver. It just makes everybody tense. We need to be on the same team here, not attacking each other." She squeezed his hand. "Focus your angst into prayer—that's where the power is."

Marcus closed his eyes and let his mother's words soak in. She was right, of course.

Surliness cured nothing. Embarrassed about his insufferable behavior, he turned to Dr. Holman, ready to dish up a large slice of humble pie. "Dr. Holman, I'm usually detached and analytical when it comes to solving problems, but when it comes to losing my mother, I seem to lose all objectivity. My first inclination was to blame you. I apologize for implying you did something wrong when I had nothing more than flimsy circumstantial evidence to back it up."

She nodded, as though accepting the olive branch he extended. "I understand your anger more than you realize. My mother died of breast cancer when I was eleven, so trust me, I know firsthand what it feels like when you are powerless and full of rage." She smiled at him. "And please, call me Libby. Your mother has talked so much about you over these last six months that I feel like I already know you."

He nodded. "I know what you mean. If I have to hear one more time how smart and caring and pretty Dr. Holman is, I'm going to buy her a dog muzzle."

Sophia crossed her arms in mock protest. "One minute, you can't bear to lose me, and the next, you're fitting me with a dog muzzle?" She turned to Libby and smirked. "Is that your definition of how a son should 'Honor his mother'?"

Libby raised a hand in protest. "Whoa! I'm staying out of that one."

Marcus grinned. "Very wise of you. Trust me, with Mom, you can't win when she makes up her mind about something."

He shook his head and informed her, "You'll get a laugh over this. Mom's been on my case for months now to ask you out on a date."

She chuckled. "Yes, Sophia has offered on several occasions to introduce me to you, too. Claimed we would be perfect for one another."

"As can be seen from our chummy interaction today, right?"

They both laughed then turned to Sophia to gauge her reaction at being outed and the brunt of their teasing.

Hands on her hips, Sophia said, "I just want my only son happily married to a nice Christian girl before I meet my Maker. Is that so terrible?"

He rolled his eyes. "Ma, I'm perfectly capable of finding a nice girl without your meddling."

Sophia snorted. "Right. Like that awful Brittany woman you were so smitten with? I'd sooner you marry Jezebel than that greedy she-devil."

He felt his face flush. He could see Libby chomping on the inside of her cheeks to keep from laughing.

Swell. Now I've gone from schoolyard bully to laughingstock.

He released an exasperated moan. "Ma! That was more than a year ago." He cleared his throat and turned pointedly toward Libby. "Getting back to Ma's liver, what do you think caused the problem?"

After a long pause, Libby said, "I'm worried her chemotherapy somehow got tainted."

Marcus scratched the back of his neck as he considered her lame theory.

Tainted chemo? Seriously? How likely is that?

She went on to explain. "Taxotaphen, the chemo your mother received, went generic one month ago. Until this last dose, Sophia received only *brand name* Taxotaphen—made here in the United States by Oncolo Pharmaceuticals, a highly reputable drug manufacturer. This last dose was a generic *equivalent* produced in India."

Marcus pursed his lips, mulling over her theory. "So you think somebody in India *intentionally* added a liver poison to my mother's chemo—like that psychopath who added cyanide to Tylenol years ago?"

Libby shook her head. "No, I was thinking more of *unintentional* contamination caused by sloppy manufacturing standards at the factory. I have more than a hunch that some kind of contaminant or liver toxin inadvertently made it into Sophia's chemotherapy."

It seemed like a stretch, but Marcus would hear her out.

She continued her argument. "Unfortunately, it's not as unusual as you might think. There was an article in *Time* magazine a few months back about all the contaminated generic drugs coming into the United States from third-world countries. It seems as though every month, yet another generic drug gets recalled due to contaminants or carcinogens. I just finished reading Katherine Eban's book, *Bottle of Lies*, where the shady dealings at a major Indian pharmaceutical factory were exposed."

Come to think of it, he'd read that same article in *Time*. Poisonous baby food in China. Glass fragments embedded in an Indian cholesterol drug. Tainted anti-depressants and ineffective antibiotics.

Hmm. Maybe her hunch isn't so far-fetched after all!

He pursed his lips as he mulled over her theory. But wouldn't it be all over the news if an entire batch of Taxotaphen were contaminated? Wouldn't patients worldwide have developed liver failure? Surely the drug would have been recalled by now.

As if on cue, his mother said, "You know, now that you mention it, I thought something was a little strange with this last infusion. It felt different than the others."

Libby's head jerked up. "Different? How so?"

Sophia scratched her arms, leaving red streaks. "For starters, it burned a little going in this time."

Libby's eyes widened. "You should have said something. We could have diluted it more or slowed down the infusion rate."

Sophia raised a hand of protest. "No, it didn't burn enough to complain; I just thought it was odd when the other five infusions hadn't burned at all."

Libby typed Sophia's observations into her computer then glanced back up. "What else?"

Sophia tipped her head in thought. "I felt a little queasy and flushed." She raised her index finger. "Oh, and the next day I had diarrhea."

"Why didn't you call me?" Libby asked.

Sophia shrugged. "The drug hadn't caused a problem before, so I assumed I'd picked up a stomach virus or something. When my urine darkened, I wrote it off as dehydration from the stomach bug and made myself drink more water."

She shrugged. "Since my recent CT scan showed no cancer, I wasn't worried—until my eyes and skin turned yellow, and I itched like crazy."

Libby typed these last details into her office note, then glanced up and informed them that elevated bilirubin levels from drug-induced hepatitis caused tea-colored urine, yellow skin and eyes, and intense itching.

Sophia's brow furrowed. "Bilirubin? That sounds more like the name of a goat than a medical term."

Libby chuckled. "What happened next, Sophia?"

"I got itchy." She glared at Marcus. "Intensely itchy." She began to claw at her arms. Marcus grabbed her wrist. "Stop that!"

"Unfortunately, the itching will continue until your bilirubin comes down." Libby tugged a prescription pad from her lab coat pocket and scribbled out a script.

"This is a potent anti-itching cream. It should help." She handed the prescription to Sophia."

Marcus removed his hands from his mother's wrists so she could take the prescription, but he pointed a finger at her. "Stop scratching, or I'll put baseball mitts on you and adhere them with duct tape."

Sophia scowled at him. "That's even worse than your dog muzzle threat."

Marcus ignored her and turned to Libby. "There's probably no way to retrieve the chemotherapy bag so we could run toxicology tests and *prove* your contamination theory, is there?"

Libby brightened. "As a matter of fact, I *do* still have the bag. It's in the toxic waste container awaiting the monthly pick-up from the biohazards disposal company."

"Would there be enough chemo left in the bag to test?" Sophia inquired.

"If there's a Tablespoon or two in the bag or tubing, I'll bet they could run a comprehensive toxicity panel and find out if the drug was somehow contaminated, and if so, with what."

Sophia's face lit up. "That sounds promising."

Marcus nodded. "It would help eliminate contaminated chemo as the cause."

"I'll send off toxicology testing today." She turned to Marcus and added, "I'll also photocopy the label from the chemo bag so I can prove I did not miscalculate the dose."

Guess she's still worried about a lawsuit.

CHAPTER 3

"Shouldn't we notify the drug manufacturer so they can investigate things on their end?" Sophia asked. "If the drug was contaminated at the factory, they need to recall it—before more patients get poisoned."

Libby pointed at Sophia with her pen. "Good point. In fact, why don't I call them right now." She yanked her cell phone from her lab coat pocket, but after glancing down at her screen, her eyes widened, and her hands began to shake.

"Libby, are you okay?" Sophia asked.

So Mom noticed Libby looking frightened, too.

Libby frowned at her phone. "I hope so. Unfortunately, I've been barraged with a bunch of threatening phone calls and texts lately. Whoever it is, he just sent me another threat."

"Your caller ID can't tell you who it is?" Marcus asked.

Libby shook her head. "The police say he's calling from an unregistered pay-by-the-minute phone, so they can't trace him."

"That's disturbing," Sophia said.

Noting her trembling hands, Marcus inquired, "Any idea who it might be?"

Libby's eyes met his then quickly looked away, as though she had something to hide. "Oh, it's probably just some crackpot pulling a prank."

If it was just a prank, why did she abruptly avert her eyes—as though she was hiding something? Why did she look terrified?

"The police told me unless the guy makes a specific death threat or commits an actual crime, there isn't much they can do. They said they don't have the manpower to investigate every prank call."

As though uncomfortable dwelling on personal problems, Libby snapped the phone shut and placed it back in her lab coat pocket. "I'll call the drug manufacturer after our visit is over." Eying Marcus, she added, "No point wasting any more of your time. I'll research which toxicology company performs the most comprehensive testing, and then I'll get it sent off."

Turning to face Sophia, she added, "I'll get Melissa to draw your blood and set up an abdominal ultrasound. We'll follow up in a week to see how your liver is recovering."

She then reviewed the warning signs that should prompt Marcus to bring Sophia to the ER immediately: confusion, excessive sleepiness, hand flapping, or a swollen abdomen.

Marcus prayed it didn't come to that. He also prayed the nutcase harassing Libby would give it a rest. His mother's doctor didn't need any distractions right now.

* * *

Libby hurried back to her office and flopped into her chair, her vision blurring slightly—a telltale sign of an impending headache. She groaned and massaged her throbbing temples.

Darn it! I don't have time for a migraine.

21

She yanked her desk drawer open, pulled out a bottle of sumatriptan, and forced herself to swallow one, hoping she had caught it in time.

As an oncologist, she'd lost many patients to cancer over the years, but none because of a drug she had personally infused. What if Sophia's liver failure *was* due to a contaminated batch of chemotherapy? Would Sophia survive? Would that obnoxious son of hers sue her for malpractice? He might sue her even if Sophia recovered — just for sport. It was just her luck that the guy was an attorney who sued doctors for a living.

To think Sophia had repeatedly suggested setting her up with the guy. No way! Talk about an intimidating jerk. Sure, with his curly black hair and toned physique, he was easy on the eyes, but right now, she wanted to cram an IV pole down his know-it-all gullet. How had sweet Sophia produced such an insufferable bully?

When Libby first started practicing oncology four years ago, her colleagues cautioned her not to get overly attached to her patients. "If they die, you'll burn out," they insisted.

But she couldn't stop herself from loving Sophia Romano. She'd even become a surrogate mother of sorts to Libby. Despite facing cancer and chemotherapy, Sophia always wore a smile and shared uplifting reports from her work at the Nashville homeless shelter and Humane Society. She made a point of inquiring about Trixie, Libby's unruly, remote-control-chewing Labradoodle puppy, at nearly every office visit. Despite facing cancer, Sophia asked for prayer requests from Libby and her staff, claiming she wanted to put her hours of infusion time to good use by praying. One time, she even created a to-die-for tiramisu for the whole office.

Saving sweethearts like Sophia from the tentacles of cancer was what had first attracted Libby to oncology. True, she couldn't save everyone, but when she did cure someone, a wave of satisfaction flowed through her, and she knew she had found her God-given calling. If only someone had saved her mother...

Libby offered up a prayer for Sophia's quick recovery then reached for her cell phone. Time to call Banderbaxy Pharmaceuticals, the manufacturer of the new generic form of Taxotaphen.

Had any other complaints about liver toxicity surfaced? She also needed to research toxicology companies. She glanced at her watch, and her shoulders sagged. Fifty minutes behind schedule. She'd never get back on track at this rate. After keying in Banderbaxy's phone number and muddling through the endless phone options, she was dumped on eternal hold. She reached for her unread copy of the *Journal of Clinical Oncology*. She might as well put her time on hold to good use. Except... she couldn't read the fine print due to the swirling spots in front of her eyes, thanks to her migraine.

As she sat on hold, she relaxed her jaw and massaged her temples hoping to relieve her headache. She tried to dismiss the disturbing question spinning in her brain: Could the person who sent the scathing text messages threatening to "get you" and "make you pay" somehow have entered her office and poisoned Sophia's chemotherapy? It seemed preposterous — paranoid, even — but *someone* was sending those threatening messages. Had he now upped the ante and resorted to poisoning her patients as a way to punish her?

Don't be ridiculous. It's probably just some bored teenager who gets his jollies by tormenting random strangers.

She released a frustrated sigh. If only the police would track the creep down. Then it would eliminate her worst fear: Roger.

Could it be Roger?

Surely this many years after facing each other in court, he wouldn't be seeking revenge—would he? He told her that day in the courtroom she would someday pay for ratting on him to the cops.

Her stomach twisted.

Please, God. Don't let it be Roger.

Melissa knocked on her office door then popped her head inside to remind her Mrs. Somers was waiting impatiently in room two. She grinned and added, "Wow! Isn't Sophia's son a hottie? No wonder you fainted." She pretended to fan her face with her hand.

Libby scowled. Yes, the guy *was* drool-worthy, but no way would she admit that to Melissa—not after he'd practically accused her of malpractice. She flipped the page of her unread medical journal and feigned complete disinterest in Marcus. "Was he? I didn't notice."

Not taking the hint, Melissa barreled closer to Libby's desk. "Wait! Isn't Marcus the son that Sophia wanted to match you up with?"

Libby kept her eyes fixed on her magazine and said nothing.

Melissa smirked. "Too bad you vomited in his face. Not much of a first impression."

Rub it in, Melissa. Like I'm not embarrassed enough as it is.

Libby glared at her nurse and gestured toward the door. "Don't you have a bag of chemo to hang?"

"Touchy, aren't we!" Melissa said with an impish grin. She gestured toward Libby's phone. "Will you be much longer, or should I tell Mrs. Somers you'll be right in?"

Libby disconnected her call. "I give up. I've been on eternal hold, so I'll just have to call Banderbaxy later. Tell Mrs. Somers I'll be right in."

Melissa steepled her hands into a prayer gesture. "Thank you! You know how cranky she gets if we keep her waiting."

Libby stood, stretched, and rolled her neck—wishing she could rid herself of the jackhammers in her head, her worries that Roger was stalking her, and her fears that Marcus was going to sue her for malpractice.

Marcus. What an infuriating man.

He was already underwhelmed with her medical skills, and after he witnessed her nauseating display in the exam room, he probably found her as attractive as a used colonoscope. Not that it mattered, because it didn't. Not one bit. Why should she care what Marcus Romano thought of her? He was an overbearing JERK.

With a capital J.

CHAPTER 4

He should go to bed. At two in the morning, Marcus had no business conducting online research on liver toxins. For starters, despite her protests, he still wasn't convinced Dr. Holman hadn't miscalculated the chemo dose, especially since his mother noticed this last infusion burned and caused flushing and nausea when the other five hadn't.

Hadn't he read last week in one of his law journals about the volume of medical errors due to poor handwriting, distraction, and burnout? Thus, if the toxicology tests didn't disclose the cause of his mother's jaundice, an unintentional overdose on the part of Dr. Holman still topped his list of likely causes.

But it wouldn't hurt to research liver toxins just in case Dr. Holman's hunch that the chemotherapy had been tainted or contaminated at the factory panned out.

He had already scrolled through a dozen sites about liver toxins, but most pertained to toxins that were consumed or inhaled, not infused intravenously.

Stiff from hours of computer research, he arched his back and stretched his arms overhead, unable to suppress a weary yawn. He padded to the refrigerator and poured a glass of iced tea—anything to keep himself awake. If something had poisoned his mother, he intended to figure out what.

Dad was barely cold in the grave, so he couldn't bear to lose his mother, too. Despite her annoying tendency to meddle and matchmake, he adored her and would do anything to keep her around.

He swallowed a swig of tea and plodded back to his computer desk, his eyelids now heavy as law school tomes. Gus wandered over and insisted on a scratch behind the ears. "I'm in over my head," he informed his oversized Afghan wolfhound, as though Gus could understand his every word. Gus licked Marcus's hand then trotted back to his bed to gnaw on a bone.

When his head bobbed with exhaustion, Marcus admitted defeat and shut down his computer. He strolled to the bathroom and offered up a desperate prayer:

Lord, please heal Mom's liver and give Dr. Holman wisdom. If someone contaminated her chemo, help us uncover who's responsible and what the toxin is. Forgive me for bullying Dr. Holman today. Help me to work with her instead of against her when I'm still suspicious she botched up Mom's dose. I leave this whole mess in your hands. Amen.

After brushing his teeth, Marcus yanked back his duvet and crawled into bed, his mind re-hashing his mother's doctor visit. For months now, his mother had tried to match him up with Libby Holman. Dating his mother's oncologist? How weird was that? If they broke up, would his mother feel forced to find a new oncologist?

Or, what if his mother wanted to change oncologists, but he and Libby were still dating? Talk about awkward. And ill-advised. No, he needed to keep their relationship strictly professional. Never mix friendship with business.

Besides, if she proved guilty of overdosing his mother's chemo, the litigator in him might want to sue her, especially if Mom died.

If only he could get the image of Libby's luscious lips and thick auburn hair out of his mind. A guy could get lost in those huge, turquoise eyes. But no matter how pretty the face, dating a woman who might have poisoned his mother was out of the question. Hard to feel warm-and-fuzzy about a woman you might drag into court for malpractice.

Yawning, he set his alarm for six and turned out the light. Unfortunately, morning would come far too soon.

* * *

Libby flipped her pillow and punched it into submission. She needed sleep, or she'd be worthless tomorrow, but worries about Sophia and the possible causes of her jaundice swirled through her brain and made sleep impossible.

Thankfully, when she'd rummaged through the hazardous waste container — double-gloved — she'd found the empty bag of chemotherapy and IV tubing with Sophia's name on it. She'd sighed in relief when she noted the dose stamped on the bag was, in fact, the correct dose.

No, Marcus Romano, I did not calculate Sophia's chemo dose using pounds instead of kilograms. So there!

She couldn't wait to wave the chemo label in his face. "See — I've committed no malpractice, Mr. Know-it-all, Hot Shot Attorney." Well, okay, she wouldn't say it with those exact words.

Of all the occupations, why did Marcus have to be a prosecuting attorney? No doubt, he was already licking his chops and ready to slap her with a two-million-dollar lawsuit.

At least he didn't work for one of those sleazy law firms that advertised on buses and park benches begging people to "get the money you deserve."

Just what she needed—a malpractice suit to drag her name through the mud and onto the front page of *The Tennessean*. Her patients would all drop her, and all her years of schooling would flush down the toilet. She'd wind up leaving town with a paper bag over her head.

She recently witnessed a colleague survive the stress of a lawsuit, which, thankfully, he won, but not before his reputation tanked. The case dragged on for months, and poor Dr. Hamilton had aged ten years in the process. How she dreaded being dragged into court again.

Even though years had passed since she faced a judge and jury when testifying against Roger, just the thought of facing another intimidating attorney made her stomach roil.

She picked at a hangnail while mulling over her plight.

Why did this crisis have to happen? She meticulously double-checked her chemotherapy doses, returned patient phone calls, and explained the risks and benefits of every chemotherapy infusion. In addition, she'd never been sued before.

But she'd also never had a patient turn yellow after a drug she had personally infused.

She was doing all she could medically to diagnose and treat Sophia, so there was nothing more she could do except pray. And pray some more.

Please, God, heal Sophia's liver. And while you're at it, can you keep that obnoxious son of hers from suing me?

* * *

A week passed, and thankfully, Sophia survived the worst of her liver failure. When Libby entered the exam room, while Sophia's eyes still displayed a sickly yellow hue, and her arms still revealed the red lines of intense scratching, at least she was alive. Thank God she had not declined into fulminant liver failure.

When she saw Marcus sitting next to his mother, her stomach twisted into a knot.

Shoot! Why did he have to come?

Just the sight of the gorgeous know-it-all triggered her insides to shaking. Stir in his impressive Vanderbilt law degree—no doubt he filed lawsuits for entertainment the way she practiced Beethoven sonatas on the piano—and she was one step away from a full-blown panic attack.

How she hated in-your-face attorneys.

She offered up a quick prayer: *Please, God, don't let me faint.*

Marcus stood and extended his hand with a surprisingly friendly smile on his face. As she shook his hand and caught a whiff of his outdoorsy aftershave, their eyes locked, and her breath caught. She couldn't pull away, and she had to force herself to inhale.

Her heart hammered in her chest, but this time, it wasn't from the threat of a lawsuit.

Melissa was right. Marcus *was* hot—from his muscular forearms peeking out of his rolled-up white shirt, to his chiseled chin, dark chocolate eyes, and perfect smile. While had noticed he was handsome at the first visit, she'd been too distracted by Sophia's jaundice and Marcus's open hostility to register the whole package. Now, with their eyes locked, she could barely remember his name. Or hers.

After an awkward pause, she pulled away and ignored the thudding in her chest. "Hello, Marcus. Nice to see you again."

Liar!

She could feel her cheeks flushing redder than the scratch marks on Sophia's arms. After settling into her computer chair and wiping her perspiring palms onto her lab coat, she gave herself a pep talk.

You're an intelligent, board-certified oncologist. You've done nothing wrong, so don't let him intimidate you. Focus on Sophia's health.

Mentally fortified, she sat down and reviewed the previous week's ultrasound and blood results with them. Unfortunately, the tests uncovered no apparent cause for Sophia's liver failure. She tried not to gloat when she handed Marcus a copy of the label from Sophia's chemotherapy bag, along with a copy of the Taxotaphen package insert delineating the proper dose based on weight, age, and kidney function.

She forced herself to use a calm and professional voice when she informed Marcus this proved she had calculated Sophia's dose properly.

"I *knew* you'd done nothing wrong, but Mr. Cynical here," Sophia said, pointing her thumb at Marcus, "needed proof. I guess it's the litigator in him."

Libby turned to observe Marcus's reaction to his mother's snarky remark.

He offered a shrug and a sheepish smile. "I'm truly delighted it was *not* your fault, Libby. On the other hand, we're now left without a cause for the liver problem, correct?"

His gaze met hers, and once again, she had to force herself to breathe.

What was it about this guy? It wasn't as though she'd never seen or interacted with good-looking men before. Heck, she didn't even *like* the guy! So why was she reacting to him in this way?

Marcus leaned forward in his chair, fingers steepled. "Did you send off the chemo bag for toxicology testing?"

Of course! Did he think she'd drop the ball and forget to do it?

"I did," she muttered through clenched teeth.

She repeated her mantra: *You're a competent oncologist. Do not let him get under your skin.*

She forced herself to remain professional. "In fact, I even researched which facility performed the most comprehensive testing, and I mailed them the bag and tubing on Wednesday."

"Which place did you choose?" he inquired, eying her with maddening confidence.

Her hands trembled, and no amount of self-talk made them stop. She may as well wear a sandwich board emblazoned with: *You make me nervous as a cat in a bathtub, Marcus Romano.*

"Toxicology Incorporated. Why do you ask?" she said.

He pulled out his Smartphone and scrolled with his finger until he located a specific screen. "Good. That's the same company I came up with as the best choice."

Before she could stop herself, she sputtered, "You researched the toxicology companies?"

"Of course. The results are critical to us uncovering what's wrong with Mom, so I wanted to make sure we sent it to the best possible company."

She clenched her teeth. Did he think she'd purposely pick a second-rate facility to cover up a mistake?

He raised a hand in defense. "I know what you're thinking, but I wasn't second-guessing you, Libby, I promise."

Like I believe that!

When she crossed her arms and must have looked unconvinced, he added, "I just thought if we both came up with the same company after each of us performed independent research, it would confirm we selected the best company."

Right! Do I look stupid? You were checking up on me!

Thank God she'd selected the same company he had, or he might accuse her of purposely picking a half-baked facility.

She inhaled a slow, cleansing breath.

Remain calm and professional. You have done nothing wrong.

"Did you see on their website that results can take up to three weeks to come back?" Marcus asked.

"Three weeks?" Sophia said, shoulders sagging. "Why so long?"

"I considered going with a company that promises results in three days," Libby said, "but they didn't test anywhere near as comprehensively as Toxicology Incorporated. Since we only had a small volume left in the bag and tubing, I thought we needed to be thorough the first time."

Marcus nodded. "I agree."

Sophia piped in. "So by the time I'm dead, we'll finally get the results and know what killed me? Wouldn't it be easier to just wait for the autopsy?"

Marcus and Libby simultaneously turned and stared at Sophia with mouths agape. Marcus straightened in his chair and cleared his throat.

"Ma, that wasn't funny. You need to leave comedy to professionals."

Sophia slapped his arm playfully. "Oh, loosen up! If you can't change your circumstances, you may as well lighten things up with a little humor. You know what they say: 'Laughter is the best medicine.'"

Marcus rolled his eyes with a chuckle. "See what I've put up with my whole life?" He gestured toward Sophia. "A mother who thinks she's a stand-up comedian."

"At least you *have* a mother," Libby retorted.

As soon as the words escaped her lips, she clamped a hand over her mouth. "I'm sorry. That was inappropriate." She stared into her lap, wishing she could crawl into the red Sharps container and escape their stares. Even pokes from contaminated needles beat the pity that radiated from their eyes.

Sophia reached forward and patted her hand. "That must have been a terrible loss for you. Didn't you tell us you were only eleven when your mother died?"

Libby nodded, too embarrassed to say more...or make eye contact.

"Is that what sparked your interest in oncology — your mother's death?"

Even now, anger bubbled up inside her against the cruel disease that left her mother emaciated, gasping for breath, and in terrible pain. The breast cancer hadn't responded to anything, and as Libby witnessed her mother's slow, agonizing demise, rage against this emperor of all maladies consumed her.

She raised her eyes to Sophia's. "I decided at my mother's funeral that I would do everything in my power to keep other families from suffering the way my family had."

Marcus leaned forward with a surprising amount of compassion radiating from his eyes. "I was devastated when my father died last year, and I'm thirty-four. I can't imagine what that was like for you at age eleven. I'm so sorry, Libby."

Eyes pooling, she turned back to her computer, mortified to have wasted so much of their office visit lugging in her own emotional baggage.

Get it together, Libby. Change the subject before you start to cry.

"Getting back to you, Sophia, I'll call tomorrow with the results of today's liver blood tests. We'll keep our fingers crossed that your levels are down. As soon as the toxicology report arrives, I'll notify you both of the results."

When they stood to leave, Marcus clasped her hand in his, his eyes penetrating hers like a laser beam.

"Thanks for your time today, Libby. I'm glad we're on the same page about the toxicology lab." He squeezed her hand. "I apologize again for my overbearing behavior last week."

She forced herself to look away. Where was the angry, intimidating guy who was so easy to despise? The bully she wanted to throttle. Who *was* this gorgeous guy who made her heart skip and her breath catch? Today, he was almost...nice! She forced herself to meet his gaze.

"Apology accepted, Marcus."

He nodded and released her hand. "I appreciate all you're doing to help Mom."

After Sophia and Marcus left, a wave of loneliness washed over her. Somehow Marcus's gentle touch and kind words reminded her of how long it had been since anyone had touched her.

Yes, she'd been successful in her career, and she had several close girlfriends, but in truth, she was very much alone.

Losing both her parents and breaking off her engagement with Colin had left a gaping hole in her heart. Sophia had unwittingly become her surrogate mother. Perhaps that was why her liver failure weighed so heavily on Libby's heart.

Even now, there was no guarantee Sophia would survive.

She was doing everything she could to save Sophia.

But was it enough?

CHAPTER 5

After Marcus drove his mother home, he sped to his house and changed into running gear. It would be dark in an hour, so he needed to hoof it. Gus paced in the living room more than ready for their three-mile jaunt in Percy Warner Park.

As they dashed up and down the trails, Marcus couldn't get his mind off Libby Holman. The image of her tearful turquoise eyes and vulnerable posture tugged at his heart. Knowing that she, too, had prematurely lost a parent to cancer drained his venom against her. Their shared grief forged the possibility of an unlikely kinship.

He rounded the corner to his favorite spot on the trail—a Nashville vista peeking out between the oak and white pine trees. Gus trotted next to Marcus, his tongue lobbing sideways from his mouth and his bangs flopping haphazardly across his eyes. Marcus stopped to admire the panoramic view and to scratch Gus behind the ears.

He knew from his mother that Libby was unmarried and didn't have a boyfriend. Why, he couldn't imagine, as she was pretty enough to attract any guy she wanted. Her face had flushed crimson on several occasions during the office visit today. Perhaps she was shy. What must it be like for her to faint when she became upset? Talk about embarrassing! Vasovagal—wasn't that the term the nurse used?

"She pursued her dream of curing cancer despite her weakness," he informed Gus, stroking the dog's shaggy neck. "That's pretty admirable, don't you think?" Gus gazed up with adoring eyes.

Marcus tugged on Gus's leash and picked up his pace. "Come on, buddy. We've got another mile to go before dark."

* * *

Libby felt a weight the size of her grand piano fall from her shoulders as she stared at the laboratory report. Sophia's liver function tests had improved by twenty percent since last week. This meant Sophia's liver had survived the worst and was on the slow road to recovery. Over the next eight to ten weeks, her liver should hopefully return to near normal.

As Libby entered Sophia's exam room, she tried to ignore her surprising pang of disappointment that Marcus hadn't come to the appointment.

"He had an important deposition today and couldn't make it," Sophia explained.

Libby handed Sophia the comparison lab report and pointed out the declining SGPT and Bilirubin levels. "See? This proves your liver is on the mend."

Sophia's response shocked her. She snapped her fingers and sputtered, "Shucks! Now I'll have to head up that fund-raiser for the homeless shelter. Think of all the work I could have escaped if I'd died." This was followed by a howl of laughter.

Libby played along. "I could always give you another round of tainted chemotherapy if you're desperate to get out of your fund-raising hassles."

Sophia chuckled. "No, I'll pass on the chemo dessert platter, thank you." She wiped the tears from her eyes. "I know I sound delirious, but when I thought I might die from this, I wrote out a list of all the reasons death could be a *good* thing. Getting out of chairing a huge fundraiser and filing my taxes rose to the top of the list."

"I guess there's a silver lining in everything, even liver failure, huh?"

As Libby rose to exit the exam room, Sophia gripped her arm. "Call Marcus for me. He'll bombard me with a million questions I won't be able to answer." She grinned. "Besides, I need to head over to the funeral parlor and cancel my casket order." Another peal of laughter.

Libby couldn't help but smile. She'd never met a patient who found such humor in her own mortality.

* * *

After work, Libby sipped on a mug of decaf and watered her wilting office philodendrons — anything to procrastinate calling Marcus. She completed two disability forms and renewed a subscription to *People* magazine for the waiting room. When she ran out of excuses, she dried her perspiring palms on her lab coat and rehearsed the exact words she would say to him. After all, everything she said could be used against her in a courtroom, despite his claim that he didn't intend to sue her. She prayed just hearing Marcus's voice wouldn't catapult her into stammering — or unconsciousness.

Using the office landline, she dialed the phone number Sophia provided her, secretly hoping Marcus wouldn't answer.

With any luck, she'd get away with leaving a voice message. Unfortunately, on the third ring, he picked up.

She parroted her memorized spiel about Sophia's improved liver function, proud of herself for not getting tongue-tied. She then reviewed the expected course of his mother's recovery, if all went well. She felt comfortable enough to share his mother's joke about canceling her coffin order and being disappointed she had to follow through with chairing a charity fund-raiser.

She heard Marcus release an exaggerated sigh. "I'd like to blame it on the chemo, but truth be told, Mom has always had a dreadful sense of humor. The worst part? *She* thinks she's hysterical."

"It's her way of coping with her fear of dying." Libby curled the phone cord around her finger, enjoying the rich timbre of his voice. He probably had a great singing voice. Before she could stop herself, she blurted out, "Are you a singer, Marcus?"

He responded with a laugh. "Wait! What? One minute we're talking about my mother's sense of humor, and now you want to know if I can sing? Did I miss something here?"

Her cheeks burned. What had possessed her to ask such a personal question? But it was too late now—she had to say something. "I couldn't help but notice your rich speaking voice, so I thought maybe you could sing. I'm a musician myself, so I notice these things. I didn't mean to pry."

"You're not prying, and as a matter of fact, I *do* sing. You, my dear, are blessed to be speaking with a baritone in the Nashville Symphony choir."

He cleared his throat and broke into a few measures of "Un Amore Per Sempre," an aria she recognized from the CD of a famous classical singer.

He was surprisingly good—a nice rich baritone and not a single sour note.

"Musical talent dripping out my ears, huh," he said, with a self-deprecating laugh.

"Absolutely, and opera, no less! I'm impressed. A man of hidden talents, I see."

"A regular Renaissance man, right?" He chuckled. "You cannot tell *anyone* I love opera, or I'll be forced to chop you up and toss your remains in the dumpster. Brittany had no use for opera. She claimed real men listen to Led Zeppelin or the Stones."

Libby's interest piqued. "Brittany—isn't she the woman your mother referred to as that she-devil?"

He chuckled. "Afraid so. Mom was definitely *not* a fan. She thought Brittany was a shallow gold-digger. Unfortunately, Ma turned out to be right."

"Oh, dear. What happened?" Libby couldn't stop herself from prying.

"Long story short? Brittany used my name and credit rating to fraudulently obtain six credit cards, which she promptly maxed out."

Libby gasped. "Ouch! No wonder your mother can't stand her."

"I sure know how to pick a fiancée, huh?"

Libby sipped her decaf and leaned back in her leather chair, legs propped on her desk with her ankles crossed, surprised at how relaxed she felt talking to Marcus.

Maybe he wasn't the ogre she'd made him out to be, after all. "How long had you two been dating when she pulled that stunt?"

"A year or so. And the pitiful part? I met her at church, and we'd just gotten engaged."

"Oh, wow!" Libby let the unsavory news sink in. "How disillusioning. Did you press charges against her?"

"I didn't want to because I'd look like a gullible sucker in front of the judge, but my mother insisted Brittany would never learn her lesson if I didn't. Plus, I had to press charges once I knew who committed the fraud or the credit card company wouldn't erase the balance."

"So you had to take your own fiancée to court? How dreadful."

He released a snort. "Tell me about it. I'd rather tour a nuclear dump."

Libby's call waiting notified her of an incoming call. When she glanced down at her phone and saw an unlisted number, her breath caught.

Is it my stalker again?

The creep had already called six times this week, and each time he'd left messages threatening to "up the ante." A cop wrote up an incident report and promised to "look into it," but since the cop got paged out to investigate a murder in the middle of their interview, Libby doubted he'd invest much time on her disturbing phone calls, especially since the call was made from an unlisted Tracphone.

While heading out the door, the cop had merely advised her not to answer her phone if it was an unknown or unlisted number.

"This is all a game to these punks. They get their thrills by frightening innocent people. If you refuse to play along, they'll look for someone else to harass."

He made it sound easy, but as a doctor, Libby *had* to answer unfamiliar phone numbers. It could be one of her chemotherapy patients with a fever. It could be the ER or a colleague wanting to discuss a patient.

By law, she was required to be available 24/7 to her patients. Thus, ignoring phone calls was not an option.

As the call waiting continued to vibrate, Libby ended her call with Marcus and braced herself for the voice message awaiting her. She pushed the button, and her heart turned to ice as an ominous voice growled, *"I know where you live and where you work. I'm watching you, and you will get what you deserve."*

She gripped the arm of her chair and forced herself to suck in slow, deep breaths.

Was it some punk kid who'd chosen her number at random, as the cop suggested, or was this a serious threat? The voice sounded familiar, but she couldn't pin it definitively on Roger — or anyone else she knew.

She tried to talk herself out of a panic attack. Maybe he was all bark and no bite. After all, he'd been threatening her for over three weeks now without actually doing anything.

But try as she might, Libby didn't believe it.
She tried to suppress her growing worry that Roger was seeking revenge for her role in ensuring his lengthy prison stay.

If it *was* Roger, she was in trouble.

Deep trouble.

CHAPTER 6

Sophia and Marcus were bent over a crossword puzzle when Libby walked into the exam room for Sophia's follow-up appointment a month after she first turned yellow. Thankfully, Sophia looked noticeably less jaundiced, and her arms were no longer streaked with red scratch marks. Marcus glanced up and asked Libby, "Where were the 1994 winter Olympics held? Eleven-letter word. Begins with the letter L."

Libby pursed her lips in thought. "Try Lillehammer."

Sophia stared at her blankly then wrote the letters into her puzzle. "It fits!" She turned to Marcus and whacked his arm. "See—I told you she was smart."

Rubbing his arm, he retorted, "Did I ever say she wasn't?"

Libby ignored the playful banter and took a seat at her computer station. She clicked into Sophia's record and scrolled to the appropriate page.

"How do my liver tests look this week?" Sophia asked.

Libby clicked to the lab results screen and smiled. "Your SGPT has dropped more than a hundred points since last week, and your Bilirubin is down, as well."

"That sounds promising," Sophia said.

"It means the worst is behind us, and your liver is healing nicely. That's the good news. Now the bad news."

Sophia's head jerked up. "There's worse news than I've got lymphoma and nearly died of liver failure? Oh, goody! I can hardly wait." She rubbed her palms together in mock glee. "Is it a brain tumor this time?"

Libby smiled. "No brain tumor, but I just received the report from Toxicology Incorporated."

Sophia gestured with her hand for Libby to continue. "And..."

Libby handed a copy of the toxicology report to Sophia and Marcus. "Just as I feared, your chemotherapy *was* tainted. With aflatoxin, a potent liver toxin."

Marcus's eyebrows furrowed, and he rubbed his chin. "Aflatoxin? But that's usually found in rotting grains and peanuts."

Right! Why did it not surprise her Marcus had researched liver toxins?

"Most reported cases do occur after eating or inhaling contaminated peanuts or grains and not after IV infusions."

Sophia pursed her lips. "Then how did aflatoxin make it into *my* bag of IV chemotherapy?"

Sophia and Marcus stared at her as though expecting a credible explanation.

Libby lifted open palms. "Contamination during the manufacturing process — that's my best guess."

"As in a contaminated vat at the factory?" Marcus asked.

Libby pointed at him. "Exactly. I performed an advanced Medline search about the drug company that produced Sophia's generic Taxotaphen. Banderbaxy Pharmaceuticals is based in Paonta Sahib, India, and the research was eye-opening — and disturbing — to say the least."

45

She handed Marcus and Sophia a copy of her research. "Here's what I found."

They flipped through the report then looked up for her to summarize and explain the findings.

"When the patent for brand name Taxotaphen expired two months ago, Banderbaxy sucked up most of the business since they are the world's leading producer of generic drugs. I tried to get a prior authorization from Sophia's insurance company to use brand-name Taxotaphen, but they turned me down because the generic is cheaper."

Marcus scowled. "It won't be cheaper if they're stuck paying for lawsuits and liver transplants."

At the mention of lawsuits, Libby's chest tightened. She had hoped he'd dismissed the idea of suing since Sophia was improving, but unfortunately, contaminated aflatoxin now added *proof* that Sophia had not received standard of care medical treatment. Sophia nearly died from a drug Libby personally infused — a drug laced with a potent liver toxin.

Oblivious to Libby's inner turmoil, Sophia crossed her arms and fumed, "In my book, a drug that poisons people is no bargain."

Marcus raked a hand through his hair. "I thought the FDA regulated this kind of thing to keep our drugs safe."

"Exactly. My pharmacist insists generics are just as good as brand-name drugs," Sophia said.

"Most of the time they are," Libby reassured them. "But unfortunately, the FDA seems to be more *re*active than *pro*active when it comes to *foreign* drug manufacturers."

"What does that mean?" Sophia asked.

"What I mean is, if they find less than ideal manufacturing conditions, they'll write a scathing letter demanding the factory shape up, but they don't have the legal authority to shut down a factory located in another country."

"They don't? Then how can they ensure drugs coming in from India and China are safe?" Sophia demanded.

"Once a problem is uncovered, the FDA will recall the drug and slap their hand with a hefty fine, but they don't do the number of *unannounced* factory inspections in India and China and other countries that I'd like to see done. Frankly, they don't have the manpower or budget to police every pharmaceutical company in the world."

"I suspect the language barrier doesn't help," Marcus added.

Fuming, Sophia crossed her arms. "This drug needs to be recalled before more patients get poisoned. How do we make that happen?"

"I spoke with someone at Banderbaxy yesterday," Libby said.

"Were they receptive? Did they agree to recall the drug or immediately inspect the factory?" Marcus asked.

No, they hadn't. In fact, Libby's blood was still boiling from their cavalier attitude. They'd brushed her off by claiming they would write up an incident report and look into the matter. But would they? If so, when?

While she was ninety-nine percent certain Banderbaxy was responsible for Sophia's contaminated chemo, Libby didn't feel comfortable *accusing* them just yet—not when her stalker could potentially be behind the tainted chemo.

Sure, it was a long shot, but *whoever* he was had been threatening to ruin her for days now. Plus, she couldn't risk Banderbaxy suing her for libel if the aflatoxin later proved to have been added by her stalker—or some deranged employee at the Atlanta distributing company.

"Why didn't Banderbaxy recall the drug immediately?" Sophia demanded.

"Banderbaxy said there's no proof *their* product caused your liver problem. They claimed your liver failure could have been caused by overuse of pain medications, a virus, heavy drinking, or a suicide attempt with Tylenol."

Sophia slapped the arm of her chair. "Suicide attempt? If I wanted to die, I'd have just let the lymphoma do me in! Why would I subject myself to six months of chemotherapy if I wanted to die?"

"That also doesn't explain the aflatoxin this toxicology report documents," Marcus said, tapping the report with his index finger.

Libby raised a hand. "In fairness to Banderbaxy, I just received this toxicology report an hour ago. They didn't know about the aflatoxin. They just knew Sophia developed severe liver damage after an infusion of their drug. I tried to call them a few minutes ago but got stuck on eternal hold. After twenty minutes, our call got disconnected."

She glanced from Sophia's jaundiced face to Marcus's livid one and suddenly felt overwhelmed.

How was she supposed to make a pharmaceutical giant in India recall its tainted product, especially when they wouldn't even answer the phone?

48

Worse, how many other cancer patients might needlessly die or suffer liver failure while Indian bureaucrats dubbed around writing incidence reports and pocketing their profits?

She turned to Marcus. "I've never faced anything like this before. Other than calling the FDA and Banderbaxy with the results of this toxicology test, what more should I do? I can send out a warning to every oncologist in Tennessee not to use generic Taxotaphen, but would a threatening letter to Banderbaxy Pharmaceuticals from you — a prosecuting attorney — hold more weight?"

Marcus's hands fisted. "We're about to find out. Like you, I've never gone up against a massive pharmaceutical giant." He stood up and paced slowly across the room, rubbing his chin. "I'll have to research how to do it properly, but when I'm through, all guilty parties *will* be held accountable."

Libby's heart jolted.

He's going to sue me.

Since *she* had chosen and administered the contaminated chemotherapy, she could be held partially liable.

She leaned back in her chair and inhaled a deep breath, willing herself not to panic.

Focus on healing Sophia. That's all that matters.

Marcus turned toward his mother. "Come on. Let's get you home. I've got work to do to get this thing solved."

Before they left, Marcus obtained a copy of Sophia's medical record and Libby's phone number. "In case I have medical questions."

Libby grudgingly supplied the records and phone number, knowing she had just handed Marcus her seal of doom—all the evidence he would need to sue her for malpractice. While Banderbaxy would bear the lion's share of culpability, because Libby had chosen and *administered* the drug, state law would hold her partially liable, as well.

Malpractice court? Please, God, no!

CHAPTER 7

When Libby pulled into the parking place in front of her townhouse, her best friend and next-door neighbor, Brandy, dashed out to greet her before she even had time to shut her car door. Pointed to her head, which displayed cornrows styled into an elaborately braided bun, she spun around grinning. "What do you think?" Before Libby could respond, she insisted, "You *better* like it, because it cost me a fortune."

Brandy prided herself on staying one step ahead in hair trends and fingernails that were polished in three colors and adorned with intricate stencils. To look at her, you'd never believe she was a math whiz who taught high school AP calculus. Perhaps because her mother and sisters owned and operated five popular hair and nail salons in the Nashville area, Libby shouldn't be surprised with Brandy's weakness for cute nails and stylish hairstyles.

Libby circled her friend to take in the full effect. "I love it! It brings out your cheekbones and eyes."

While the two women strolled to their mailboxes to retrieve their mail, Brandy enthused, "I don't mind saying, I look good, and before this month is through, I'm going to find me a man. A decent man, this time."

Unfortunately, Brandy's track record — like Libby's — for finding a decent man — left a lot to be desired. Brandy seemed to be a magnet for emotionally and financially needy men.

Brandy's last boyfriend, a likable guy she'd met online, sat around watching sports and playing video games half the day when he should have been out looking for a better paying job than his current part-time barista position.

For six months, Brandy encouraged him, poured through help-wanted ads, and even forked over money one month to help him pay his rent. After he turned down a fabulous job offer because, "They expected me to travel all over the South and work one Saturday a month," Brandy broke it off.

"I'm not wasting any more of my time with someone who isn't a hard worker. He doesn't have to be rich, but I don't do lazy."

"I'm with you on that," Libby agreed. "We've both worked too hard to get where we are to put up with slouches."

The two women had then gone out to dinner and a movie to commiserate on the slim pickings for decent men these days.

Libby unlocked her mailbox and tugged out an assortment of bills and ads, along with the latest oncology journal. On the top of the pile sat a small, indiscrete cardboard box. Bank checks, maybe?

Except, there was no return address.

As they sauntered toward the front door of Libby's townhouse, Brandy gestured toward the unopened box. "Inquiring minds want to know. Open it."

After Libby ripped off the tape and tore open the box, the sudden stench of a decaying animal carcass overpowered her. Her heart jolted at the sight of a dead rat. She gasped and nearly dropped the box. A note was affixed with a string to the rat's neck. With trembling hands, Libby forced herself to read the message aloud. *"It takes one to know one."*

Brandy's hand flew to her mouth. "OMG! I'll bet it's that stalker dude. Now he knows where you live?" Her eyes widened with concern.

Libby leaned against her front door and tried not to panic.

It has to be Roger. Who else would accuse me of being a rat?

But Roger wasn't due to get out of prison for another six months. Weren't authorities supposed to notify her when he was released?

Could they have released him early on parole? Maybe he bribed some depraved friend to mail her the package even if he himself was still in prison.

Who else could it be? Libby wracked her brain to come up with anyone else who might have it in for her. Nada. She circled back to Roger.

Brandy pulled out her mobile and keyed in the phone number for Metro police. "This has got to stop. Stalker-dude now knows where you live. It's time for twisted brother to cease and desist."

Hands too shaky to unlock her front door, Libby allowed Brandy to open the door and let her in. She sank onto the couch and forced herself to inhale slow, calming breaths.

Oblivious to the crisis in Libby's life, Trixie leaped onto the couch, circled madly, and licked Libby's face. Libby forced herself to pat her animated puppy. She then took Trixie outside to do her business while they waited for the cops.

Within minutes, a bald, muscular, bespeckled cop named Julius arrived and wrote up Libby's complaint. Libby shared her suspicion that it might be a man named Roger Anderson. She didn't provide details on *why* Roger might be harassing her because she had never divulged her past with Brandy — or anyone else, for that matter. She chose instead to merely tell Julius that Roger was "an abusive man from my past."

She couldn't make herself share the full story — even to her best friend. That horrible chapter of her life was one she chose to avoid, and until the harassing phone calls started, she had become skilled at cramming all the painful memories into a dusty corner of her brain and forgetting about them. She told herself it was all in the past and best forgotten. A life lesson she need not dwell on — until now.

Julius would learn the truth as soon as he entered Roger's name into the police databank. Libby desperately needed to know if Roger was still in prison, or if he had been released on parole. If he was now free, where was he living? She prayed it wasn't Nashville.

After tugging on Latex gloves, he snapped photos of the dead rat, the handwriting on the box, and the accompanying note, then carefully tagged and bagged the evidence. He promised to investigate and get back to her.

He wagged a stern finger at Libby.

"I want you to promise you'll call me if you get any more threatening messages."

He handed Libby a business card, though she noticed his eyes were glued on Brandy as he spoke. "And Brandy, don't hesitate to call me if Libby doesn't. Keep your doors locked and your cell phones charged and handy."

"Cell phones?" Brandy said derisively, placing her hands on her hips. "I'm buying pepper spray—and a baseball bat. Better yet, you got a taser we could borrow?"

Julius chuckled. "Wow! Remind me never to cross you in a dark alley. If you like, I could show you both a few self-defense moves." With eyes fixed solely on Brandy, he added, "It would be my pleasure."

"I'd love that. A girl can never be too careful," Brandy said demurely. They arranged a time to get together for their first lesson, then Julius packed up his evidence and left.

Brandy clapped her hands in glee. "Girl, did you see how he was looking at me?"

Libby couldn't help but smile. "He was definitely checking you out."

"It's my new hairdo, isn't it?" she enthused, touching her bun.

"That and your crack about the baseball bat and taser. He likes your spunk."

Brandy chuckled. "Self-defense moves, my eye! He wants to make the moves on me."

"He seemed trustworthy and hard-working. I liked him."

"Uh-huh." Brandy inspected her nails. "Julius is my kind of man—hunky, smart, gainfully employed."

"Breathing," Libby tossed out sassily.

Brandy whacked her arm. "Hey, just because *you* choose to live like a nun in a convent doesn't mean I have to. That boy is fine, and I intend to make him mine."

Libby laughed. "You sound like a Motown hit." She extended her arms in a dancing gesture and gyrated around the living room.

"Joke all you want, but while you're sitting around playing your dullsville Chopin and Beethoven, I intend to show Julius what's missing in his life—me." She admired her rainbow-stenciled nails and added, "Julius was hot, don't you think?"

Honestly? He was a tad chunky for Libby's tastes, but not wanting to demoralize her friend, she said, "He has a cute face. I hope he's not married."

"He wasn't wearing a ring. I checked." As though reading Libby's mind, she added, "I know he may be a little beefy, but I *like* a man with some meat on his bones, and in my book, that Julius is one superior cut of sirloin."

Libby laughed, grateful her best friend had diffused her stress. That's what she liked most about Brandy—she was loyal and made Libby laugh.

Right now, she needed all the laughter she could get because someone was out to get her.

CHAPTER 8

Marcus stood up from his computer workstation and stretched before wandering to the kitchen for a snack. He chomped into a Granny Smith with a vengeance. He had investigated Banderbaxy online for three hours straight, and he already felt overwhelmed by the international conglomerate. The company produced thirty percent of the world's generic drugs. Thirty percent! How was he supposed to go up against a ten-billion-dollar-a-year behemoth drug company when he still had law school loans to pay off?

Marcus Romano vs. Banderbaxy Pharmaceuticals. It sounded like a David and Goliath matchup, except Marcus wasn't skilled with a slingshot! No telling how many millions of dollars the company could hurl out in legal defense if Marcus slapped them with a lawsuit.

The more he researched Banderbaxy, however, the more he *wanted* to slap them with a lawsuit. The unsuspecting public was being contaminated regularly because of the company's sloppy manufacturing and quality control standards.

Marcus sank into his chair, grabbed the pile of incriminating documents, and highlighted in yellow the most egregious problems. The FDA had recently cited them for improper medication handling, unsterile production lines, fudging quality control reports, fungal spores.

The list went on and on. But what was the punishment? A measly letter and a laughably small fine. No shutting down of the factory. Just a slap on the wrist and an admonition to "shape-up." Nothing in his research documented the FDA had followed through with an unannounced factory inspection to ensure all the manufacturing violations were corrected. Anger burned in his belly.

No wonder his mother's chemo was contaminated. After skimming Banderbaxy's last scathing inspection report, he wondered if the company did *anything* right — besides raking in billions of dollars in profit each year. The report implied the factory practically swept dirt off the floor and tossed it into the medicine vats for good measure.

Why was the FDA *allowing* such dangerous products into the United States? If it was their job to protect the American public from weak or contaminated drugs, why weren't they issuing stronger sanctions against Banderbaxy? Or shutting down the factory altogether?

How often did FDA inspectors fly to India to perform impromptu inspections? Since there were four hundred languages and dialects spoken in India, they would need translators and special permission before barging into a foreign factory unannounced. But if Banderbaxy *knew* the actual date and time of the FDA inspection, wouldn't they get their act together for the inspection — similar to the massive house cleaning his mother did if she knew guests were coming for a visit?

The whole process was a farce — like a policeman who only issued tongue-lashings instead of hefty speeding tickets. Who's gonna slow down for that?

But what could *he* do about it? He had no authority, no big name, and even less money to mount a proper legal attack.

He glanced down at his watch then pulled out his phone on impulse. He punched in Libby's number to ask her if they could get together for an hour or so. He wanted to discuss his research findings with her and develop a game plan. Since she was more medically inclined, she could verify that he wasn't overreacting. He couldn't share his results with his mother, as they would only upset her.

"You can provide an unbiased medical perspective," Marcus explained to Libby as the reason for his call.

He had no other motive for wanting to meet with Libby. None. After his disastrous relationship with Brittany, the last thing he needed right now was a girlfriend. Why risk another budget wrecker and heartbreaker? Yes, he hoped one day to find his soulmate, but truthfully, after the Brittany fiasco, he was still too shell-shocked to jump into the shark tank of dating again.

Fortunately, Libby hadn't sounded put off by his request. She even offered to drive to his house with some upsetting research discoveries of her own. His shoulders sagged.

How much worse can it get?

With a sudden jolt of adrenalin, Marcus glanced around the living room and ran for the vacuum. The couch where Libby would sit was covered with dog hair.

Thanks to shaggy Gus, the carpet looked like the place hadn't been vacuumed in a year.

After sucking up all the fur from the carpet and furniture, he paraded around the room spraying Febreze to remove any "doggie" odor. He carted outdated newspapers and law journals—piled a foot high on the coffee table—to the recycling bin. He loaded a dirty glass and dinner plate into the dishwasher and took a final look around. While the place would never grace the cover of *Southern Living*, at least it was clean.

He brewed up a pot of decaf and tried to suppress the wave of anxiety coursing through his veins.

Chill! It's not a date. Your relationship with Libby is purely professional.

Maybe so, but he couldn't stop himself from darting into the bathroom to scrub the toilet and wipe down the mirror. When the doorbell rang, it startled him so much he dropped the toilet brush into the commode. He quickly extracted the toilet brush, flushed, then washed his hands. Glancing into the bathroom mirror, he groaned. His unruly hair had always had a mind of its own, but tonight it looked positively wild, no doubt from the umpteen times he'd run his hand through his hair in angst. In a desperate attempt to restore some semblance of order, he ran a comb through his hair then hustled to the door.

He opened the door and couldn't drag his eyes away from the shapely beauty standing in front of him.

Lord Jesus, help!

Dressed in skinny jeans and a fitted turquoise top, she sure didn't look like any doctor he'd ever visited. Stir in auburn hair flowing to her shoulders and huge eyes that matched the color of her top and his breath caught. Out of her lab coat, he had to pinch himself to remember she was his mother's doctor.

He invited her in and followed her into the living room, trying not to admire her shapely backside as she walked.

Get a grip!

Keeping this a purely professional relationship wasn't going to be as easy as he had hoped.

As she settled onto his black couch, Gus padded up and sniffed her straight in the privates. Marcus groaned and yanked on Gus's collar. "Gus! Stop that!" He pulled the uncultured beast away. "You'll have to forgive him — he seems to think he's a drug-sniffing police dog."

Libby leaned over and scratched Gus behind his furry ears. "Too bad he wasn't an aflatoxin-sniffing pooch; Banderbaxy could sure use him."

After she won Gus's heart with her cooing and pats, Marcus offered her a mug of decaf. As they sat on the couch and sipped coffee, Marcus showed her the scathing letter from the FDA to Banderbaxy, as well as all the disturbing factory inspection reports. The warmth of her thigh nestled against his unnerved him, and he found it difficult to focus on contaminated drugs.

Marcus shared all of his research findings, then Libby dropped her bombshell: "Over two hundred people have died in the last eight years because of contaminated drugs produced by Banderbaxy."

She lifted her index finger. "And that doesn't include people like your mother who were merely harmed but not killed."

Marcus's heart stopped. "Two hundred people? How'd you find that out?"

Libby pulled out an inch-thick packet of research. "I got the medical librarian at our local hospital to perform an advanced Med-line search about Banderbaxy."

"And..." Marcus gestured for her to continue.

"She faxed me documentation about all their production violations." She handed him her paperwork. "I thought these might prove useful for your letter to the company."

He skimmed through them, periodically stopping to circle a key fact and to star an important statistic. His lips thinned. "As far as I'm concerned, these people are murderers."

Peering over his shoulder, she concurred. "My thoughts exactly."

He glanced in her direction, and their eyes locked. Somehow, she had changed from a doctor he wanted to sue to an ally. And a beautiful one at that. In fact, right now, he wanted her to be a whole lot more than his ally. He found himself unable to pull his gaze away from her luscious lips, which were trembling slightly.

Does she feel the chemistry between us, too?

A sharp woof from Gus shattered the moment. He moseyed over and stuck his nose between them, staring up with a soulful gaze. Marcus patted the top of Gus's head. "Does someone feel neglected? Go find your elephant, Gus."

The furry pooch happily complied, carting back a bedraggled elephant with one missing leg and a tattered trunk. He dropped it on Libby's lap

She giggled and reached for the slimy toy, but Marcus grabbed her hand. "You don't want to touch that nasty thing. There's dog slobber all over it."

He grabbed the elephant and heaved it into the hallway. He turned back to Libby with a sheepish smile.

"I'm afraid with me gone all day, Gus expects attention when I get home."

"Hey, trust me, Gus is a saint compared to Trixie."

"Trixie?"

"My Labradoodle. She's still a puppy, and her dog obedience training isn't going very well."

"How bad is she?" he asked, engaging in a tug-of-war with Gus over the elephant.

Libby scrunched her nose. "Let's just say, she's chewed through three remote controls in the last five months I've owned her."

He laughed. "That'll teach you not to leave your remote control on the coffee table." He hurled the elephant into the hallway again. "Getting back to business, did you report the aflatoxin contamination to Banderbaxy?"

Her shoulders slumped. "I tried, but I can't get through to them. I've left message after message with my name and phone number, and I've even said it was life-threatening." She raised her palms. "No response whatsoever, and I've called every single day. Twice on some days."

Marcus shook his head in disgust. "There's no excuse for such shoddy customer service."

He grabbed the elephant and held it high, forcing Gus to jump up and grab it. "Banderbaxy needs to be held accountable for their sloppy manufacturing practices."

"They need to recall the drug," Libby agreed.

Tired of fetching, Gus rested his chin on Libby's lap with beseeching eyes, the ridiculous elephant hanging from his mouth. Libby scratched Gus's neck and patted his head.

"What a good boy," she cooed. Gus flopped his front paws onto her lap and then rested his head on them, gazing up at her with abject adoration.

Marcus eyed his bewitched pooch. "Now you've done it. He's going to expect VIP treatment every time you come over."

As soon as the words exited his mouth, his cheeks heated. He just implied she'd be coming over regularly — like a girlfriend or something. Which she wasn't. Thankfully, Libby didn't seem to notice, or if she had, was too polite to mention it.

She scratched Gus's neck and he released a contented sigh. "You like that, don't you, boy. You're nothing but a big, old baby," she cooed.

Marcus crossed his arms with feigned outrage. "So much for loyalty. I feed him, take him for a daily run, give him heartworm medicine, and toss him slobbered-on elephants until I need a rotator cuff repair, but a little pampering and petting from you, and he'd trade me in for a dog chew."

Libby grinned. "I think Daddy's jealous, Gus. He thinks you like me better."

Gus responded by crawling into her lap, tummy-side up with his stocky, hairy legs pointing heavenward. They eyed the overgrown pooch perched like an upside-down piano bench and burst into laughter. She rubbed his tummy before Marcus pushed him off.

"Crazy mutt! Get down! How can we come up with a game plan against Banderbaxy with you demanding all our attention?" He pointed toward Gus's bed. "Go chew on your bone."

Gus slunk to his bed and gnawed on a bone.

"I'm afraid I've spoiled him. He was my father's dog, but after Dad got sick, he was so big and lively that Mom didn't think she could handle him, so I offered to take him."

Libby grinned. "Hey! I love that dog. I haven't had a male so eager for my affection in a long time."

He noted her cheeks flaming at the blunt admission. "No boyfriend, huh?"

She released a sigh. "Afraid not."

Before he could stop himself, he blurted, "That's hard to believe. You're smart, beautiful, compassionate—what more could a guy want?"

An unexpected look of sadness crossed her face. "When they get to know me—really know me—things don't work out."

What was she talking about?

She suddenly looked uncomfortable and glanced at her watch. "I should probably be going. It's after eleven, and I have to work tomorrow." She stood and strolled toward the door.

Marcus escorted her. "See if you can get through to Banderbaxy tomorrow, and I'll contact the FDA and convince them to investigate."

She nodded. "Will do."

She exited the house then turned around to say good night. As she gazed up at him with those huge, mesmerizing eyes, the strongest desire to kiss her grabbed hold of him.

On impulse, he leaned forward, ready to indulge in the magnetic pull of her lips.

Unfortunately, Gus chose that very moment to barge between them and demand a goodbye pat from Libby.

Whoever said dogs were a man's best friend should be shot!

Secretly though, he was relieved. Hje had no business kissing her. She was his mother's doctor — as in off-limits no matter how inviting the lips.

Libby released a nervous giggle and squatted down to pat Gus. She tucked a loose curl behind her ear with a trembling hand and avoided eye contact.

She knows you were about to kiss her.

Was she relieved — or sorry — when Gus interceded?

He forced himself to focus on Banderbaxy. "How about we get together in a couple of days to share what we can drag out of Banderbaxy and the FDA?"

"Sounds good." She raised her eyes to his, and their eyes locked. He swallowed a lump the size of Rhode Island and found he couldn't move. All thoughts of contaminated pharmaceuticals disappeared.

Did she have any idea how hard he was struggling not to pull her in his arms and kiss her?

Libby offered a polite goodnight and strolled to her car. He couldn't stop himself from staring as she climbed into her car and backed out of his driveway.

Good thing she's leaving, or I'd be a goner.

CHAPTER 9

As Libby drove home, she couldn't get Marcus out of her mind. His eyes—warm and sensitive when tearing up about his mother, crinkling at the corners when he laughed, and black with rage when discussing Banderbaxy—were growing on her. She could barely remember the jerk she met that first day in her medical office.

Initially, she only agreed to go to his house to appease him—in case he still harbored thoughts of suing her. After all, if she collaborated with him, he'd be less likely to turn on her and include her name in his lawsuit, right? By the time the evening was over, however, she found herself daydreaming about raking her fingers through those thick black curls of his.

Which was out of the question when he was the son of a patient, and toying with suing her!

She needed to extinguish such fantasies from her mind immediately. After all, he only called her to glean medical expertise and support in their fight against Banderbaxy. To Marcus, she was nothing more than his mother's oncologist.

Although...she could have sworn he almost kissed her tonight—twice, in fact. And the scary part? If Gus hadn't intervened, she wouldn't have stopped him. She would have—

Enough! He's off-limits.

As she parked in front of her townhouse, she smiled at the image of Gus—a hairy overgrown oaf—belly side up in her lap, begging for a pat. What a sweetie!

As she reached to unlock her front door, she suddenly felt something underfoot on the welcome mat. She glanced down and gasped at the sickening sight of a bloodied, dead squirrel sprawled across the mat. She yanked her foot away with adrenaline coursing through her veins.

She bent over and lifted the squirrel by the tail, holding it as far away from her body as possible. She trekked toward the dumpster, but when she lifted the squirrel to heave it inside, its head flopped unnaturally to the side, as though hanging by a thread.

Somebody had slit its neck! She stared at the gruesome carcass and forced herself to breathe, trying to ignore the pounding in her chest. This was not the work of a stray cat or coyote; this was deliberate.

What kind of sicko slaughters defenseless squirrels and leaves them on someone's doorstep?

She then noticed the small note attached to the squirrel's ankle that read, **You're next.**

If it was Roger, he wasn't just acting creepy—he was downright depraved.

Her eyes darted to the nearby shrubs and parking lot, half expecting him to jump out.

She carried the squirrel—evidence of the madman's latest shenanigans—back to her townhouse and left it outside the door. Her hands shook so badly she could barely get the front door unlocked.

Once inside, she slammed the door and instinctively engaged both locks. She leaned against the door, her knees jelly, and her breath ragged.

Surely it was Roger. Who else could it be?

She located the business card Julius gave her, but her call went straight to voice mail. She dialed the nearest police station and asked to speak with Julius since he was familiar with her case.

"He's not on duty tonight," the dispatcher said. "Would you like to speak with someone else on the force?

Libby released a frustrated sigh. No, she *didn't* want every cop in Metro knowing about her past!

"No, but please have Julius call me as soon as he's back on duty." She provided the dispatcher with her phone number and ended the call.

Julius promised he'd investigate whether Roger was out on parole, and if so, where he now resided. Why should she divulge her deepest darkest secrets to yet another officer?

Except she hadn't heard a word from Julius since the dead rat incident two days earlier.

Maybe he was busy investigating murders, or robberies, or true emergencies.

Face it—dead rats rate pretty low compared to dead humans!

This can wait, she told herself, ignoring her thudding heart. She glanced out the window and noticed no lights on at Brandy's.

How she craved Brandy's support right now. She glanced at her watch—nearly midnight. She couldn't wake her up at this hour—Brandy had to be at work at seven. Besides, what could Brandy do?

She'd just have to tough it out tonight and give Julius a call first thing in the morning.

She packed the slit-throat squirrel in a large Tupperware container and put it in the freezer since Julius would need the evidence. She didn't want some feral cat or fox dragging off her evidence from the welcome mat.

She wandered through the townhouse restlessly, knowing she'd never fall asleep. Every crack of the walls and hum of the air conditioner made her heart jolt. As though sensing her fear, Trixie traipsed behind her tail between her legs as Libby went from room to room, turning on every light.

She'd let Trixie sleep with her tonight since Trixie's bark might scare off an intruder.

Grabbing a cast iron frying pan and a sturdy umbrella to use as weapons, she locked herself in her bedroom and pushed a dresser in front of the door. She forced herself to lie down on the bed.

Trixie pounced on top of her, tail wagging, tongue lapping, a happy glint in her eyes, all fear now forgotten. Libby hugged her animated pooch, tears filling her eyes. "I don't feel as scared when you're here, girl."

Trixie circled on the bed, then finally settled down next to Libby.

"Dear Jesus, keep me safe," she whispered as she set her alarm clock with trembling fingers. Not that she needed an alarm clock with Roger — or some other creep — lurking around.

Sleep? Fat chance of that.

CHAPTER 10

Libby jolted every time she heard a noise. She must have dozed off at some point because her alarm clock jarred her out of sleep at six a.m. Stiff and achy from her rotten night, she dragged out of bed, showered, and trudged off to work.

Which was a disaster — the last thing she needed after her sleepless night. For starters, her trusty RN, Melissa, called in sick with a stomach bug and couldn't make it into work. The temporary agency sent over a substitute nurse, but the woman proved useless. She didn't know how to draw blood or start IV's, and she knew nothing about chemotherapy or flushing Port-a-caths.

In short, Libby had to do everything herself except for rooming the patients and taking their vitals. Adding further to her stress, her computer — fresh from an upgrade — left her staring at the "blue circle of death" with every other click.

One patient became so nauseated from a chemo infusion no amount of IV Zofran or Phenergan would suppress the vomiting. The net result? A revolting mess on the floor to clean up. Twice. The worthless nurse refused to clean it up, blandly informing Libby, "I don't *do* vomit. It's not in my temp agreement."

You don't do much of anything, Libby muttered to herself as she mopped up the disgusting mess.

Then a patient with six adult children all showed up to discuss their mother's pancreas cancer treatment. Normally, this would be a welcomed discussion, but the McDaniel clan was something else. Libby had to referee a near brawl between the six siblings when they disagreed vehemently about how aggressively they should treat their elderly mother's advanced cancer.

Three wanted to throw in the towel and consult hospice, and three insisted on trying experimental chemo. Words like "murderer," "delusional," and "heartless" flew back and forth like ping pong balls between the quarreling siblings.

When two brothers leaped up, fists clenched and ready to have it out, Libby jumped between them. "Stop that right now, or I will call security and have you both thrown out. Your mother deserves better than this from both of you."

They stood in fighting posture, each waiting for the other to back down until their poor emaciated mother stood up feebly and scolded them. "I'm ashamed of you! This is my decision, so sit down and be quiet."

Well, then... The two brothers slunk to their chairs, arms crossed, and eyes eviscerating each other with venomous glares.

Yes, it was *that* kind of day.

Unfortunately, with all her added nursing duties, Libby ended up with no time to contact Banderbaxy about the contaminated chemotherapy or Julius about the slit-throat squirrel.

Was Marcus having any better luck with the FDA?

Surely an American agency, whose sole responsibility was to ensure the safety of pharmaceuticals, would jump all over this.

Marcus texted her, asking if she would like to take the dogs for a walk after work. "We can share our progress while Gus and Trixie get acquainted," he said. She wanted to decline since she'd gotten nowhere with Banderbaxy today. He might think she hadn't cared enough to make calling them a priority. Besides, after her sleepless night and horrendous day at work, she was exhausted — physically and mentally. She'd need toothpicks to keep her eyelids open long enough to drive home. Plus, she looked like the dickens with dark circles under her eyes and frizzy hair. She might even reek of vomit!

Not that it mattered when this was only a meeting to discuss Banderbaxy, she reminded herself.

She should at least go and support his progress with the FDA. Maybe then he'd see her as an ally and refrain from suing her.

She suppressed a weary sigh and agreed to meet him at Percy Warner Park to hike the three-mile loop with the dogs. She prayed Trixie would behave herself.

* * *

Libby pulled into a parking place at the entrance of the park and waved to Marcus, who was stretching his hamstrings against a tree. Gus stood nearby sniffing and digging at a rabbit hole. Libby hooked a leash onto Trixie's collar, but before she could even slam her car door, Trixie bolted toward Gus, nearly dislocating Libby's shoulder.

After a tug-of-war with Trixie, Libby managed to close and lock her car door. She could see Marcus chuckling at her rambunctious pooch.

"She's a feisty one, isn't she?" he hollered, jogging toward them.

Her cheeks burned in humiliation as Trixie lunged toward a chipmunk. Her half-baked attempts at dog training had proven a colossal failure. She noted strangers snickering and pointing at her unruly canine.

What had possessed her to get a puppy?

The two dogs sniffed and circled each other, then Gus crouched as though ready to pounce. They darted around in circles making a comical display—a boisterous small puppy and a huge Afghan wolfhound. The net result of their frolicking? Two retractable leashes tangled up and intertwined, and two dogs leaping at each other like bucking broncos at the Calgary Stampede.

Marcus laughed while attempting to disentangle the leashes. "On a positive note, they seem to like each other."

Libby countered, "On a negative note, they'll probably have us tied to a tree before this hike is over."

Libby tried to force Trixie into compliance, but the rowdy beast refused to obey.

"Let me try," Marcus offered, reaching for Trixie's leash and handing Libby Gus's leash.

Thankfully, Marcus seemed more amused than annoyed by Trixie's playfulness. "Whoa," he said, tugging on the leash. Trixie leaped and darted, her tail wagging like a flag in a hurricane.

Eyebrow arched, Marcus inquired, "What do you feed this creature? Red Bull and Ritalin?"

She laughed. "She probably *needs* Ritalin; I think she has ADHD."

He smirked. "You think?"

Is there a cave nearby where I could hide?

"I've been meaning to sign her up for dog obedience classes," she offered lamely.

Marcus's eyes bulged. "This wild thing in dog obedience school? You thrive on public humiliation, do you?"

Her shoulders slumped. "You think she's a lost cause?"

He shook his head. "Not at all. She just has lots of energy. How old is she, anyhow?"

"Five months."

"Ah, that explains it." He squatted down to scratch the side of Trixie's neck. "A mere puppy, and an adorable one, at that."

"Thanks," she said, somewhat mollified by the compliment.

"Don't worry. She'll settle down with age." Meanwhile, Trixie leaped up onto his thighs and nearly knocked him down.

"When?" she asked, unconvinced.

Marcus grinned. "Age ten, when she develops arthritis?"

Despair filled her. *"Ten?"*

He laughed at her wilted expression. "I'm just yanking your chain, pardon the pun. Gus is four now, and he's settled down a lot this last year." He reeled in Trixie's leash like he was fighting a catfish on the end of a fishing pole.

"What an energizer bunny like Trixie needs is a fast run. Wear her out." He held Trixie's leash taut and dashed up the stone steps leading to the trailhead. "Let's go."

Gus stayed at Libby's side, the perfect gentleman. Meanwhile, Trixie crisscrossed the trail in front of them, nearly tripping her on several occasions.

When Libby finally landed in a heap of ferns because of Trixie, she sputtered, "I am one step from taking Trixie to the Humane Society and trading her in for a geriatric dog with a bad hip."

Marcus reached out a hand and helped her up. Trixie suddenly circled their legs, slamming Libby and Marcus together. Marcus grabbed hold of Libby's shoulders to steady her. Trixie ran around them in circles as though tying a villain to a tree. Their eyes met, and before she knew it, they were laughing so hard tears rolled down their cheeks.

"I hope you have good health insurance because I see crutches and orthopedic surgery in your future," Marcus teased, wiping the tears from his eyes. He lunged for Trixie's collar to pull her into control, but instead, he landed himself—with Libby pinned underneath—into a clump of ferns. Their legs were so entwined they couldn't move. Stunned, she remained transfixed and pressed against Marcus. He reached to stabilize her.

When their eyes met, all laughter ceased. As though in a spell, Trixie and Gus and the ridiculousness of their circumstances vanished.

The crazy notion that she had somehow found her soul mate—a man who would love and accept her—even with her checkered past and wild dog—pelted her heart with such magnitude, she gasped.

Their eyes locked, and she felt his breath—warm and intimate—dance across her face. He gently caressed her cheek, and she held her breath.

Don't let this moment end.

A desire to run her fingers through his thick curls and to feel his lips against hers surged through her. She longed for his kiss more than oxygen itself.

He must have sensed her need because his face slowly descended over hers, narrowing the space between them. His hands cupped her face, and his lips hovered mere inches from hers, as though longing, but hesitant to make contact. Throwing caution to the wind, she parted her lips, longing for his kiss.

"Libby," he croaked, his eyes probing hers, his fingers grazing her cheek. His lips descended toward hers — until Trixie pounced straight on top of them. It appeared this was nothing more than a game of cops and robbers to the ill-mannered pup.

Spell broken, Marcus grabbed Trixie's collar and gained the upper hand. He disentangled the leashes and helped Libby up.

Marcus brushed the ferns and leaf fragments off his backside. "It appears I may be sitting next to you in that orthopedic office." He wagged a scolding finger at Trixie. "I will teach you to mind if it's the last thing I do. And with your energy, it might well *be* the last thing I do."

Libby felt her face heat. "Marcus, I am so sorry. I clearly shouldn't have brought her. She isn't fit to be out in public yet."

"Nonsense! She's never going to learn to behave unless we teach her." Marcus held Trixie next to his side with a short tight leash. "Besides, she needs exercise to use up her energy." He squatted down and rubbed Trixie's head. "I can't help it if I have lots of energy, Mama," he said, as though speaking in a singsong voice for Trixie.

He glanced up at Libby. "Trust me, Gus was a total menace when he was a puppy. But I've got experience now. Man versus beast, and I intend to win." With a show of bravado, he pointed to his chest with his thumbs.

Trixie, eyeing a squirrel behind Marcus, leaped forward and knocked him flat on his rear.

Libby burst into laughter and tucked a strand of hair behind her ear. "My bet is on the beast. I'm telling you, she's incorrigible."

Marcus jumped up and dragged Trixie back to a heel position. "Trixie, meet your new trainer." He eyed the animated pooch sternly and added, "And I'm warning you, when I make up my mind to do something, I don't quit."

Marcus retracted the leash and only allowed a few inches of lead. "I'll bring treats next time. Dogs need rewards as much as discipline," he informed her. He eyed the trail ahead of them. "Let's sprint until we wear her out."

Libby suppressed a groan, exhausted from her sleepless night and tiresome day at work. Before she could protest, however, Marcus was off.

Since Marcus was forced to bodily drag Trixie back into a heel position every few feet, he was no doubt more worn out than the fully charged pup.

After running until Libby wanted to crumple into a heap and die, Trixie settled down and began panting so hard, Marcus was forced to stop.

Thank God!

Not wanting to look like a wuss, she'd forced herself to run, but her legs now shook with fatigue. She bent at the waist and sucked in deep gasping breaths. Once their breathing recovered, they resumed a leisurely walk.

Maybe now they could tackle Marcus's interaction with the FDA—the real reason for today's meeting! "Fill me in on your conversation with the FDA," Libby said.

"I located someone directly responsible for investigating bad drugs. I'm pleased to say the agent, Scott Marina, seemed to take my complaint seriously, especially after I faxed him the results proving Mom's liver was injured and the toxicology report confirmed aflatoxin contamination."

Since Libby had retrieved the IV chemo bag out of her red bag hazardous trash, Marcus was even able to provide the FDA with a specific lot number for the drug. Scott promised to investigate immediately.

"Did he say when he'd get back to you?"

Marcus shrugged. "He just said 'in a timely manner.'"

"Hmm. Bureaucrats aren't known for doing anything in a timely manner."

"No telling how many cancer patients could die while they diddle around writing reports instead of actually recalling the drug."

"Exactly."

"Well, I intend to keep on them, and they *will* recall the drug—if only to shut me up."

"What should we do next?" Libby asked, jumping over a puddle in the middle of the trail. She tried to usher Gus around it since Marcus wouldn't appreciate a mud-drenched dog dirtying up his passenger seat.

"If more cases show up, a class-action lawsuit against Banderbaxy will get their attention." He smiled wryly. "Of course, I can't file a class-action unless more than one case shows up, but I can *threaten* to sue them if more cases turn up. That ought to make do something."

Libby inwardly groaned as they approached a steep section of the trail. She forced her weary legs up the steep incline to her favorite spot on this trail—a stunning view of Nashville. Between panting breaths, Marcus said, "If other cases do show up, I'll have to confer with colleagues, as I've never filed one before." He grinned. "Truthfully, when it comes to class-action lawsuits, I'm all bark, as I've never taken a single bite."

"Don't class-actions take a lot of time and money?" She chuckled. "I only know that from reading a John Grisham novel."

"I'm sure they do, and unfortunately, I've still got twenty grand in law school loans to pay off."

"Hey, maybe you could offer to let the big guys who advertise on TV do all the dirty work, and you could just dig up the cases." She grinned. "That's what the lawyer in the Grisham novel did." She whacked his arm playfully. "Just think! You could pay off all your law school loans *and* your mortgage by suing Banderbaxy."

A flash of anger crossed his face. "I'm not trying to get rich off the backs of poisoned cancer patients, Libby. I am only doing it to make Banderbaxy stop producing contaminated drugs. Contrary to popular opinion, not all attorneys are money-sucking low-life."

She stopped dead in her tracks, wishing she could take back her words. Why had she uttered such a tasteless remark? She'd bruised his pride and touched a sensitive nerve. No doubt Marcus, like all attorneys, hated lawyer jokes.

She grabbed his arm and forced him to look at her. "Marcus, I'm sorry. I was trying to be funny, and like your mother, I obviously need to leave comedy to professionals. Please forgive me."

He glanced away clearly embarrassed at his overreaction to her flippant comment. "No, it's not you. It's me. I'm just really edgy these days." He raked a hand through his hair. "I barely got Dad buried when Mom got diagnosed with lymphoma. Then stir in the Brittany fiasco and my credit rating tanking." His eyes pooled with tears. "Over the last couple of weeks, I thought..." He finally choked out, "I thought I was going to lose Mom, too."

Libby instinctively pulled him in for a hug. His shoulders heaved, and he released his pent-up angst with a sob. She whispered, "Let it out, Marcus."

Too distraught to talk, he clung to her like a child clinging to his mother in a thunderstorm. His watery eyes then met hers with such vulnerability, she felt her own eyes well up. "Tell me honestly, Libby. Is Mom going to make it?"

Her heart shattered. "Yes. The worst is behind us." She wrapped her arms around his waist and held him close. She rubbed slow, soothing circles across his back. After several minutes, he turned away and mopped his eyes with his T-shirt. "Sorry for the waterworks. I didn't mean to fall apart like that. I haven't cried since my father's funeral. I guess all the stress finally caught up with me."

She caressed his face with her fingertips, hoping her full acceptance of his vulnerability shone through. "Marcus, I'll do everything in my power to help your mother pull through this. But ultimately, her life is in God's hands, isn't it?"

He reached for her hand, and they silently hiked the last stretch to the summit. After such a steep jaunt, the two dogs flopped onto a patch of grass next to the trail.

Marcus and Libby gazed at the Nashville skyline, with the two peaks of the Batman building silhouetted against the first sign of a sunset. Streaks of fuchsia and orange painted the skyline behind a backdrop of skyscrapers. Marcus stared at the vista with his fingers still intertwined with hers. "It's been a rough couple of years. I keep wondering what's going to hit me next."

Libby brushed a tear from his cheek with her index finger and smiled. "Trixie landing you in the ER with a broken neck?"

He glanced over at Trixie, gnawing on a stick, and chuckled. "The way my luck's holding up, you're probably right."

"You didn't get a chance to fully grieve your father's death before Brittany broke your heart and betrayed you with the credit card theft."

Marcus nodded..

"If I know your mom like I think I do, she stood by you through the whole ordeal, didn't she?"

"She did, despite grieving for my dad herself. Even though we squabble sometimes, Mom and I got really close after Dad died and Brittany betrayed me. We were there for each other, and now, I need to be strong for her."

She squeezed his hand. "You *are* strong, Marcus. She thinks the world of you."

His eyes suddenly pulled out of their trance-like stare and met hers. "So help me, I will fight Banderbaxy and keep them from poisoning any more patients."

"And I'll do everything in my power to help you."

His eyes never wavered from hers, and he gripped her shoulders. "I'm grateful for your support, Libby."

He released his grip, and they wandered closer to the clearing so they could soak up the panoramic vista painted across the sky. They said nothing as they drank in the vibrant colors of the sunset.

"I like to come here when I feel overwhelmed. It reminds me that God stays the same, no matter what happens in my life," Libby said.

Marcus nodded. "Sunsets connect me to God in a way that Bible studies and sermons just can't."

"Maybe because we *see* God's power and constancy instead of just reading or hearing about it."

"Talk is cheap," Marcus agreed. "Brittany claimed she loved me but then betrayed me."

"I know what you mean," Libby concurred.

Mesmerized by the sunset, she blurted out without thinking, "I once had a relationship where I thought someone loved me, but his actions proved very differently."

"What happened?" Marcus asked.

Dare she tell him about Roger? Or Colin? Would he bolt if she shared about her past?

She bent down to stroke Trixie—anything to avoid eye contact with him.

Better not risk it—especially with his Mom so sick. He didn't need anything else to upset him right now.

"I, um, I don't think I'm ready to talk about it yet," she mumbled, praying he wouldn't pressure her to 'fess up.

"I understand," he said. "I didn't mean to pry."

She breathed a sigh of relief.

No doubt wanting to break the sudden awkwardness between them, Marcus roused the dogs. "We better get a move on before it gets dark."

They powerwalked the last mile until they reached the trailhead. Their conversation reverted to less intimate topics — Trixie's obsession with remote controls, Marcus's large geode collection, Libby's recent splurge on a used Steinway piano, and a fantastic performance of *La Boehme* that Marcus recently attended.

Once they reached her car, Marcus helped Libby load Trixie into the passenger seat. He walked around to the driver's side of her car and opened her door. "I'll pester the FDA 'til we see results."

"Maybe we should *both* call Banderbaxy until one of us can get through to a live human being."

Marcus snorted. "Who will no doubt be some punk kid in Bangalore who claims his name is 'Bruce' or 'Charles' even though he can barely speak English."

Libby cocked a brow. "What? You aren't fluent in all four-hundred Indian dialects?"

"Not unless ordering Chicken Tandoori and Naan bread counts."

She closed her car door, rolled down her window, and latched on her seatbelt. "Well, there's always Rosetta Stone."

He chuckled. "Somehow, I don't think aflatoxin, jaundice, or liver toxicity will be in Sanskrit 101."

She shoved an errant strand of hair behind her ear. "Probably not." Their eyes met, and after an awkward pause, she said, "Should we touch bases later this week to review our findings?"

He glanced at Trixie and leaned until his face was mere inches from Libby's. "If we're going to turn that rogue beast of yours into something more than a boon for the local orthopedics, she'll need *daily* lessons."

"You're willing to endure Trixie again? She tied us up and landed us flat on our backs."

He winked and grinned devilishly. "I rather enjoyed that part—being tied up with you."

Libby instinctively jerked back, suddenly triggered by a distasteful memory with Roger. Before she had reported Roger to her father and the cops, he had mentioned wanting to tie her up and introduce her to womanhood. The flashback so jarred and repulsed her she instinctively recoiled.

You're Sophia's doctor, not some slut desperate to be tied up with a man you barely know!

Despite knowing Marcus's comment had been said in jest, she began to shake, triggered by her frightening flashback with Roger.

Why had she let things advance so quickly with Marcus? She barely knew the guy, but she'd been ready to kiss him. Had she learned nothing from trusting Roger and Colin so easily?

She turned the key in her car's ignition with trembling hands. She glanced up, hoping he couldn't tell how much his flippant comment had rattled her.

A hurt, then embarrassed, expression crossed Marcus's face. He held up an apologetic hand. "I'm sorry, Libby. I didn't mean to offend you, honest. I was totally kidding." He looked away and raked an agitated hand through his hair. He stepped back from the car and said stiffly, "I'll call you later this week for your update about Banderbaxy, okay?"

He made no mention of further dog obedience training, and too unnerved to bring it up herself, Libby nodded and said nothing.

*I may as well nip this attraction between us in the bud —
before I get hurt again.*

She kept her eyes locked on her steering wheel and
forced herself to say, "Sounds good." She shifted into
reverse and hightailed it out of the park before he could
see the tears streaming down her face.

CHAPTER 11

Gus jumped into the passenger seat of Marcus's Mini-Cooper, and Marcus bee-lined out of the parking lot. Was he delusional to think Libby *wanted* him to kiss her when they became entwined together in the ferns? Their eyes locked, their lips almost touched, and he could have sworn a soul connection developed between them.

After that tender moment, he felt safe enough to share his deepest fears about losing his mother. Now he felt like a fool. A total, idiotic, wishful-thinking fool. Her repulsed response to him when they reached her car could not have been more obvious. Here he'd gone out on a limb and told her he wanted a repeat performance of their tumble in the ferns, and she may as well have snapped, "Forget it, buster!"

He merged onto Belle Meade Boulevard with Gus panting at his side. He had previously resolved that his mother's oncologist was strictly off-limits. Why had he ignored his better judgment?

Because it felt wonderful to be held by Libby.

Over a year had passed since he held Brittany in his arms. He missed the tender caress and caring words of a woman. Not that Brittany had been sincere, but he hadn't known that at the time.

He sped through a yellow light and tried not to dwell on how wonderful it felt to hold Libby in his arms and see the concern radiating from her eyes.

That she was beautiful, with her bouncy auburn hair reflecting the afternoon sun, certainly hadn't helped his resolve to resist her. When she smiled, her whole face lit up. And those huge, expressive turquoise eyes of hers — they glowed with happiness when she laughed.

Strangely, even her inability to make Trixie behave tugged at his heart and made her all the more appealing.

But she clearly didn't return his feelings. His notion that she was attracted to him was nothing more than wishful thinking. She was just kind-hearted.

No doubt his blubbering like a baby turned her off. A man shouldn't bawl his eyes out in front of a woman he's only met four times in his life. Marcus hadn't cried after he uncovered Brittany's betrayal. Instead, he stuffed his hurt and anger because he had to — by then, his mother was fighting lymphoma. He'd stayed strong for her and never grieved any of his losses — until today. Now he felt like a fool. Libby was his mother's oncologist, not some shrink for the emotionally unglued.

He made a right turn onto Harding Road, still mulling over his embarrassing breakdown. She probably thought he was unbalanced and in need of intense counseling. Or anti-depressants. Or electric shock. Or whatever it was doctors did for unhinged people these days.

He shook his head. How could he face her after this? Did she see him as a mental case, or worse yet, some *Fifty Shades of Grey* pervert who wanted to tie her up and have his way with her? What had possessed him to crack such a tasteless joke?

Maybe his sense of humor had become as dreadful as his mother's.

Ahead of him, the light turned red, and he slammed on his brakes to keep from plowing into the car in front of him.

Red light. Stop now.

That was what he needed to do with his feelings for Libby. Stop now. Nip them in the bud.

He turned to Gus. "She's not interested, buddy." He gripped the steering wheel and mumbled, "No doubt talking to a dog proves I'm mental."

The light turned green, and he sped the rest of the way home, planning how to proceed with Libby in the future. Strictly professional. No more sobbing like a baby who'd dropped his pacifier. He would focus solely on Banderbaxy and his mother's health. He would push for a recall of Taxotaphen, and he'd force the pharmaceutical giant to raise its manufacturing standards. When he was through, maybe Libby would once again esteem him as a competent attorney.

Decision made, he informed Gus, "It's just you and me again, buddy. Trixie's history."

CHAPTER 12

Libby slammed her car door and trudged toward her townhouse. What a disastrous end to an already lousy day. All she wanted to do now was grab a bite to eat and crawl into bed. The sooner this day was over, the better.

As she unlocked the front door, Brandy dashed out from the adjacent townhouse holding a colorful gift bag. "Hey, look what somebody dropped off on your welcome mat."

Libby froze, already dreading what she would find in the bag.

What would it be this time? An eviscerated opossum?

Brandy extended her arm holding the gift bag and shook it. "Come on, open it! I'm dying to see what's in there." She grinned. "All right, I confess. I already took a teeny tiny peek through the tissue paper, and you'll be relieved to know it is not a dead animal." She leaned toward Libby and whispered, "I think it's lingerie." She grinned, as though Libby had some secret lover.

Fear surged through her veins, both chilling and numbing. It had to be her stalker. She stared at the bag, not wanting to open it.

Hand on her hip, Brandy admonished, "Girl, you been holding out on me? Who's the mystery man?"

Libby's shoulders sagged. "Trust me, as of twenty minutes ago, there's no mystery man."

"Open it," Brandy insisted, forcing the bag into her hand.

With shaking fingers, Libby rifled through the red tissue paper then pulled out racy, black lingerie with a matching garter belt...except the lingerie was slashed and torn almost beyond recognition, and the garter belt was bloodied. Inside a typed note read, "We won't be needing these when I see you next."

Heart pounding, Libby crammed the lingerie back into the bag and tossed it away from her, as though it contained a bomb.

"What kind of a sicko sends a gift like that?" Concern etched across Brandy's brow.

Suddenly faint, Libby crumbled onto the welcome mat and hung her head between her legs, forcing herself to take slow deep breaths.

Brandy squatted next to Libby. "Whoever sent this bag is a total pervert. I'm worried about you." She pulled out her cell phone. "I'm calling Julius."

"No!" Libby extending her hand like a stop sign. "He's already looking into it. I told Julius who I thought was responsible, and he said he's investigating."

Brandy crossed her arms and stared at Libby with narrowed eyes. "Who, exactly, is this Roger Anderson, anyhow?"

Libby averted her eyes and picked at a hangnail. "He's just someone I jilted a few years ago," she offered evasively, not ready to reveal the full story to her friend.

Brandy reached for the tossed gift bag and tugged out the shredded lingerie again. She clicked her tongue and displayed the tattered garment in front of her.

"Anybody twisted enough to send something like this is bad news." She shook her head." Downright dangerous."

"Don't you think I know that?" Libby snapped. "I've called the cops on multiple occasions, and Julius is the only one who has taken me seriously. He said he's looking into it, so what more do you expect me to do?"

Brandy frowned. "Hey! I'm not the bad guy here. You don't have to snap my head off."

Libby pushed fingers to her throbbing temples. Between the slaughtered squirrel, her sleepless night, her rotten day at work with Melissa out sick, and her rift with Marcus, her nerves were frayed to the breaking point. Now this horrifying gift bag. Still, Brandy didn't deserve the brunt of her foul mood.

She released a weary sigh. "You're right. I'm sorry, Brandy. I meant to call Julius today to see how his investigation is coming along, but my nurse was out, and I was an hour behind schedule, and I didn't even find the time to eat lunch, let alone call Julius."

Brandy punched Julius's phone number into her phone. "I'm calling him right now. He would want to know about this latest installment. No more dilly-dawdling with Larry-the-Lingerie-Loser lurking around."

Julius answered on the second ring. Brandy filled him in on the contents of the gift bag. He promised to come right over.

The two women entered Libby's townhouse, and ten minutes later, a white police cruiser parked out front. Julius hurried inside, which set Trixie on a barking frenzy.

"I hadn't forgotten about you," Julius insisted, handing Trixie a dog biscuit he pulled from his pocket. He grinned at Libby. "Dog biscuits. A trick of the trade I learned early on in my career to avoid getting bit in the rear."

Libby settled Trixie onto her dog bed with a chew toy and apologized to Julius for her disruptive canine.

"Hey, I've dealt with worse. Chihuahuas — nippy, nasty little buggers. At least Trixie doesn't bite, right?"

"No, she doesn't bite — she just chews up remote controls." She reached for and displayed Trixie's latest shenanigans."

Julius clucked his tongue then squatted to rub Trixie's neck. "You've been a very bad girl, haven't you! Do I need to arrest you for destruction of property?"

Trixie's tail wagged as though he had promised another dog chew.

Brandy brought out some glasses of iced tea and handed one to Julius. "I want to know what you've discovered about the guy who's been harassing Libby."

Julius settled onto the couch and swallow a swig of tea. "Turns out, Anderson *is* out on parole now."

"Parole?" Brandy's mouth dropped. "Roger Anderson has been in prison?"

Libby gripped the arms of her chair, too stunned to utter a word. The words ricocheted in her mind.

Roger is out on parole.

"I called his parole officer twice," Julius continued, "but I had to just leave messages for him to call me back. So far, he's completely ignored my calls, so I have no idea where he's living."

Libby stared at him in stunned silence.

Roger is out on parole. My worst nightmare.

"If I don't hear from the parole officer by tomorrow morning," Julius said, "I'm calling the Chief of Police in Chattanooga to investigate further."

Brandy's eyes grew large. "Parole officer? So not only has creepy stalker dude been in prison, he now has a parole officer, too?" She turned to Libby with accusing eyes. "I thought you said he was just some old boyfriend you ditched."

Julius cleared his throat and feigned the excuse of needing to use the restroom, obviously not wanting to be the one to divulge Libby's secret to Brandy.

Even though Brandy was her best friend, Libby had never wanted to share about her past with Roger. In fact, she had done her best to forget the whole sorry chapter and move on with her life. But clearly, she still carried baggage the size of Kansas, or she wouldn't be so secretive about it — especially to her best friend.

So much for my years of counseling.

Counselors had rightfully insisted she was not to blame, that she had nothing to be ashamed of, and she was just a child.

Blah, blah, blah. Libby *knew* all that in her heart. So why the secrecy?

Other people didn't get it. In school, classmates asked, "Why didn't you just say no?" or "Why didn't you report him to the police sooner?" or, "Why didn't you tell your father what he was doing to you?" Even Roger's defense attorney accused her of "seducing" his client until the judge banged his gavel and insisted the comment be stricken from the court record.

But the damage was done. She could see jurors turning to stare at her, each secretly wondering if she was a tease who had come on to Roger. A regular Lolita.

The final straw? Her fiancé, Colin. After Libby finally trusted him enough to open up about her past, he blamed *her* for not telling her father and the cops sooner. "You must have secretly *liked* what he was doing to you, or you would have spoken up sooner."

Right! Blame the victim. I was twelve, Colin! Twelve! And too terrified to speak up.

The more Colin implied *she* was partially to blame, the madder it made her. Finally, she broke off their engagement. She'd been victimized by Roger as a child, but no way would she tolerate verbal abuse from Colin as an adult!

The ignorant reaction of many people—like Colin— left her angry and defensive. Thus, she learned to keep her mouth shut. Besides, it was no one else's business, anyhow!

On the other hand, she was sick to death of living in secrecy and hiding her past. Plus, now that Roger was released on parole, it wasn't just her past. It was her present and her future.

She glanced over at Brandy.

What will she think of me when she learns the truth?

Would their friendship be permanently marred because Libby had chosen to hide the truth? She picked at a hangnail, trying to decide what to say.

Taking a leap of faith that Brandy would stand by her, she forced herself to blurt out, "Roger has been in prison for twenty years—for pedophilia. He did inappropriate things to me when I was twelve, and I testified against him in court."

Brandy raised a hand to her mouth, his eyes wide with shock.

The room fell silent. Libby stared at the floor and refused to make eye contact with Brandy, fearful of what she was thinking.

Brandy scooched closer on the couch and wrapped her arms around Libby's shoulders. "Oh, Libby, I'm so sorry you went through that. You know I'm here for you, no matter what, right?"

Libby brushed tears from her eyes and leaned onto Brandy's shoulder, still unable to speak.

Julius re-entered the room and cleared his throat, pulling them back into the present. "I found out Roger has been out on parole for two months now. He was released five years early for good behavior in prison."

"Weren't they supposed to notify me before he was released?" Libby protested.

Julius nodded. "Yes, but the report says they *tried* to reach you at the last address and phone number you gave them. Apparently, you did not update your demographics when you moved into your townhouse."

Libby hung her head in shame. Why had she neglected to update her online data?

"They sent a certified letter three months ago to your old address," Julius continued, "but it was returned to sender. The authorities in Chattanooga didn't know how else to reach you since your phone number had also been disconnected."

She chewed her lower lip before confessing, "I got rid of my landline two years ago to save money. I just use a cell phone now."

She probably hadn't stayed on top of it because, psychologically, she'd wanted to pretend the whole thing never happened. Just forget Roger and live in a bubble where he would never be released from prison.

Stupid, stupid, stupid. What had she been thinking?

On the other hand, if she'd known he was about to be released on parole for "good" behavior, what would she have done about it—other than fret?

Julius continued. "The Sex Offender Registry shows Anderson rented a place in Chattanooga and has a restraining order against contacting you or any of the other girls he molested."

Brandy's eyes bulged. "*Other* girls? My gosh! This guy is a monster."

As Libby let the unsavory news settle in that Roger was out on parole and could thus potentially be her stalker, Brandy inquired, "How do we know he hasn't left Chattanooga and come to Nashville?"

My thoughts exactly!

Brandy eyed Julius skeptically. "Just because he had good behavior in prison doesn't mean he won't try to track Libby down once he's released."

"If he does, he goes back to prison," Julius pointed out.

Brandy snorted. "If stalker-dude has it in for Libby, it may be too late by then. Do you know for a fact he's actually living in Chattanooga and not Nashville?"

Julius averted his eyes. "Truthfully? No. Since his parole officer hasn't returned my call, I *don't* know for certain he hasn't skipped town and come to Nashville." He pointed toward the bag of lingerie. "That convinces me he probably has."

"It doesn't take a rocket scientist to figure out this Roger Anderson is now in Nashville, and he's terrorizing my friend." She snorted. "Good behavior, my eye! If he was a law-abiding citizen, he wouldn't have spent twenty years in the slammer for molesting children."

"Plus, research shows pedophiles can't be rehabilitated, so why was he let out five years early?" Libby demanded.

Julius shifted his weight and shrugged. "Good question. I guess the judge is hoping with a restraining order Roger will stay away from Libby and the other victims, if only to avoid more time in prison."

"Seriously?" Brandy sauntered over to Julius with hands on her hips. "Julius, honey. My best friend here could be assaulted or murdered, and you're dawdling around trying to contact some absentee parole officer? You can do better than that. Now we both know twisted brother here is pestering my friend and needs to go back to prison before my friend gets hurt." She jabbed a finger in Julius's chest.

His eyes widened.

"I want you to track down that sleazebag's sorry hide, drag him back to his cell, lock him up, and throw away the key," Brandy insisted.

"I'm doing all I legally can," he responded, swallowing and backing away from Brandy.

Brandy smiled and placed a manicured hand on his arm. "Julius, you know what I see when I look at you? I see a man with strong, virile muscles bulging from his shirt." She then stroked his forehead. "I see an intelligent, cerebral brow. A very capable man more than competent to crack this case and land that felon back in the slammer."

Libby suppressed a smirk.

What a flirt!

Brandy ran her fingertips down Julius's face. "I'm off work tomorrow, and I think you and I should take a little trip down to Chattanooga and personally find that parole officer and check out where this Roger Anderson is supposedly living. See if he's there. Talk to this parole officer in person. No more telephone tag. News flash: It isn't working."

Julius shrugged. "Well, I am off duty tomorrow."

"All the better," Brandy insisted. "I *want* to be off. It's a teacher training day." She rolled her eyes. "Like high school calculus is going to change. What a waste of time. I'll gladly get out of it, and we can make a day of it in Chattanooga. I'll even treat you to the best pork barbecue in all of Chattanooga, plus a movie at the 3-D cinema once we're finished our spy work."

Still attempting to maintain a professional veneer, Julius pushed up his glasses and cleared his throat. "I suppose it wouldn't hurt to do some on-the-scene investigation. How about I pick you up here at eight?"

Brandy's face lit up. "We'll be like Sherlock Holmes and Watson."

Julius smiled then collected the bag of lingerie for evidence and left. Brandy danced around the room with gyrating arms. "Girlfriend, that boy is all but mine."

Libby brewed up a pot of decaf, and the two women settled onto the couch sipping, deep in thought. Finally, Brandy broached the pink elephant in the room.

"Libby, why did you hold out on telling me about Roger?"

Libby hung her head and stared at her feet.

"I *should* have been honest with you." She paused grappling to find the words. "What happened with Roger is a chapter in my life I'm not proud of. I know in my head and heart that I was a victim and not responsible for what happened, but after enough people implied that I was partially to blame for not telling my dad or the cops sooner, I learned to keep quiet. I wasn't a little kid when it happened. I was twelve, so a part of me, despite all the counseling, still occasionally accuses, 'You should have spoken up sooner.'"

She sipped her decaf with shaky fingers, her eyes filled with tears. "I knew what I was letting Roger do to me was wrong, but he convinced me no one would believe me if I reported him because he was a church youth group leader."

"What a low-life!"

Libby nodded. "Sadly, I lacked the emotional maturity to know how to handle it, so I did nothing and just put up with his demands. I was afraid to speak up."

Brandy reached for Libby's hand and squeezed. "That's why you're still single, isn't it? You're afraid to let people in. To trust. To be vulnerable. To risk being judged for your past. You're afraid to let someone know the real you — the one that comes with a little baggage."

Libby snorted. "Try an entire luggage store full of baggage."

Brandy smiled. "But if you want people to love you, really love you, you have to let them know you — the good and the bad."

Libby clenched her teeth and slammed her coffee mug onto the end table. "That's easy for you to say. When I told my previous fiancé, Colin, about my past, he couldn't handle it."

"How so?"

"He said I must have enjoyed it, or I would have spoken up sooner. So much for full-disclosure and allowing people in! All it led to is heartache and a broken engagement. Trust me, I'm better off saying nothing."

Brandy grabbed Libby's hand and squeezed it again. "If Colin couldn't handle that you were a victim of pedophilia at age twelve, he's a total douchebag, and you're better off without him."

"Maybe so, but you can see how it would make me hesitant to open up again. I mean, how do I know who I can trust, and who is going to judge me? I sure don't want to lose my heart to another Colin."

Brandy pursed her lips in thought. "I suppose you take the relationship slow and pray a lot."

"Hmm. That's actually good advice."

Brandy grinned. "If only I practiced what I preach. I tend to dive into relationships headfirst and then discover I don't know how to swim."

Libby chuckled. "We're a pathetic pair."

"No wonder we're both still single."

As though sensing Libby's desire to move away from her past, Brandy changed the subject. "You carrying that pepper spray I bought for you from the Army-Navy store? Take it everywhere you go."

Libby patted her purse. "Right here."

Brandy glanced around the room. "Maybe you should purchase one of those security systems that makes a racket if someone tries to break in. One that immediately notifies the cops."

Libby smiled and gestured toward Trixie.

"Hey, I've already got a security system that makes a racket. Trixie barks her head off any time someone comes to the door."

Brandy snorted. "If Roger came bearing dog treats like Julius just did, Trixie would probably lick his hand and wag her tail."

Libby chuckled. "You're probably right."

"What does this Roger Anderson look like, anyhow? I'm going to be on the look-out for him after his last shenanigans."

Libby conjured up her last courtroom image of Roger. "Well, I haven't seen him in twenty years, but back then, he was tall, blond, and extremely good-looking. Your classic surfer beach boy look."

"I'll keep my eyes out for him."

"If you see him prowling nearby, text me a warning so I won't come home."

Her eyes bulged. "Text you? Girl, if that sicko gets anywhere near me, I'm clobbering him on the head with my cast-iron skillet."

Libby chuckled. "Just make sure it's not the UPS delivery man before you go clobbering people over the head with heavy pans. Lord knows I don't want to bail you out of jail for assault and battery."

CHAPTER 13

As Marcus perused the research Libby obtained about Banderbaxy, acid boiled up his esophagus. The average Indian generic drug factory was only inspected every ten years. Worse, the Indian equivalent of the FDA, called the CDSCO, was corrupt. Even the Indian Parliament accused the agency of accepting bribes.

He skimmed several more pages. Ninety-three percent of the drugs coming out of India *were* of acceptable quality.

But what about the other seven percent?

Patients were unknowingly taking antibiotics too weak to kill bacteria, blood thinners that didn't prevent strokes, and blood pressure pills contaminated with carcinogens.

He raked a frustrated hand through his hair and tugged out his cell phone to call Scott, his contact at the FDA's Office of Crisis Management.

Luck was on his side, as the receptionist connected him straight through.

"Marcus, I've reviewed the data and toxicology report you sent me, and I put in a call to our counterpart organization in Mumbai. They assured me they would inspect the factory and issue sanctions if they are indicated."

"Are you talking about the CDSCO?"

"Yes," Scott said, sounding surprised Marcus had heard of the organization.

"If their track record is any indication, the inspector will be more likely to accept a bribe than issue a recall or perform an unannounced factory inspection."

"You must have done your homework," Scott commented.

Marcus shifted the phone to his other ear. "Enough to know the CDSCO is often corrupt."

"That was more than two years ago," Scott reassured him. "We've done a lot to ensure the safety of Indian generics since then."

Marcus's jaw clenched. Right! "If they were doing such a stellar job, my mother wouldn't be jaundiced from aflatoxin-tainted chemotherapy, now would she?"

He stood up and paced his office, feeling like a caged cougar. "According to my research, two-thirds of Indian and Chinese pharmaceutical factories have *never* been inspected by the FDA. Not even once. Is that true?"

Dead silence greeted him on the other end of the phone line. Obviously, Scott was not expecting him to come to the table spouting facts.

Marcus continued. "So, tell me, Scott, when was *this* particular Banderbaxy factory in Paonta Sahib, India last inspected?"

Another dead silence.

Just as he expected—his mother was poisoned due to inadequate oversight of a foreign pharmaceutical company. He gripped his phone so hard he could have crushed it.

Scott finally confessed, "To be honest, I don't know when it was last inspected."

"Why?" Marcus demanded.

"These are Indian generics, so it's the job of the CDSCO to ensure the safety and purity of their medications, not ours."

Marcus pounded the wall. "But it's the job of the FDA to ensure drugs purchased by American consumers are safe and effective, am I correct? At least that's what your mission statement claims," he snapped, unable to suppress his sarcasm.

"Mr. Romano, I'm beginning to feel defensive. *I* didn't add aflatoxin to your mother's chemotherapy, and I'm trying to *help* you, so I'd appreciate you not attacking me."

Marcus would not be shushed. "If it's the job of the FDA to ensure all drugs sold in the United States are safe, how can you *not* keep records of when this factory was last inspected and whether or not it passed its last inspection? How can you *not* insist on performing unannounced inspections of your own, since the CDSCO has a track record of corruption and bribery?"

"We have! We do! Just last year, the federal budget provided funding for new inspectors in Mumbai and New Delhi."

Marcus turned the corner and continued his pacing. "Yes, I read that—five whole inspectors for a country with 1.27 billion people. I also read that *none* of the inspections are performed *unannounced.*

"What's your point?" Scott asked.

"The factories are conveniently given several weeks of notice before the inspection, which gives them ample time to clean up their act before you arrive."

Scott released a patronizing sigh.

"Mr. Romano, when we are in a foreign country, we cannot simply barge into a factory unannounced and demand they let us inspect."

"Why not?" Marcus demanded. "That's what you do to American brand-name drug companies."

"Well, for starters, they need time to locate interpreters. Second, they have to get their documents in order before we go flying half-way around the globe to perform an inspection."

Unconvinced, Marcus retorted, "If India wants our American dollars badly enough, they should allow unannounced inspections — unless they have something to hide."

Scott's voice took on a pinched and angry tone. "*That's* the job of the CDSCO. We don't have the resources and manpower to police the entire world."

Marcus gripped the phone with whitened knuckles. "In other words, you're trusting the fox to guard the henhouse?"

Another patronizing sigh. "Mr. Romano, ninety-three percent of the pharmaceuticals out of India and China meet all the safety and purity standards set forth as a standard of excellence for the industry. Your implication that we allow boatloads of toxic drugs into the country is untrue and highly offensive."

"And the seven percent that *isn't* pure? The seven percent that poisoned my mother, or doesn't kill bacteria, or lower cholesterol properly?"

He was only getting started, and he had no intention of letting Scott off the hook until he was through.

"Oh well? That's the price we pay for living in a global economy?" he accused in the phone.

Is that what you're saying, Scott?"

"We investigate and issue a recall any time one is indicated. I find it extremely problematic that your mother's is the *only* case of aflatoxin toxicity reported."

"How so?"

"If an entire vat was contaminated with aflatoxin, why haven't more cases shown up? Until we receive reports of other patients with liver toxicity after receiving Banderbaxy's generic Taxotaphen, we can't prove it wasn't some crackpot on this side of the Atlantic."

Marcus stopped dead in his tracks. "You're going to wait for *more* cases to crop up before you recall the drug?"

"In a word, yes. One case does not an epidemic make. Quite frankly, I'm suspicious the aflatoxin was added locally. After all, the drug didn't go straight from the Indian factory into your mother's veins. It was transported across the ocean on ships or planes, and it was stored in a distributing facility in Atlanta. A trucking company then delivered it to your mother's doctor, where it was stored until the day of infusion. Even then, a nurse or doctor would have measured and mixed it. All of these places provide a port of entry for the aflatoxin. We need to investigate things *this* side of the pond before we go accusing the CDSCO of not doing its job."

Marcus inhaled a deep breath then exhaled slowly dismayed there were now *more* possible sources for the toxin than just the Indian factory. As much as he hated to admit it, Scott was right.

If the entire vat was contaminated at the factory, there *should* have been other cases reported by now. His fear of losing his mother had, once again, made him lose the calm, detached, investigative approach he usually employed. And once again, he allowed his emotions to control him. He groaned.

Once again, he'd sounded like an out of control idiot. He sucked in a deep breath.

Might as well get the humble pie over with.

He sank into his desk chair, exhausted from his frantic pacing. "You know what, Scott? You're right. Because of their lousy track record, I *did* jump to the conclusion Banderbaxy had imported a shoddy product. But I see now there *are* other possibilities. And more cases *should* have surfaced by now."

"Keep in mind, when an Indian manufacturing plant causes an international scandal, it tarnishes the reputation of their entire generic market. The CDSCO does not want scandal, if only for financial reasons."

Marcus drummed his fingers on his desk. "So, what's our next step?"

"I've already contacted the CDSCO and the Mumbai branch of the FDA. They will coordinate an inspection at the Paonta Sahib factory. If aflatoxin is found, we will issue an immediate recall."

"What if Banderbaxy passes the inspection?"

"I'll send inspectors to the Atlanta distribution center where your mother's batch of Taxotaphen was stored."

"And if *they* pass the inspection?"

"The local police would then need to look for an inside job—a disgruntled employee at the doctor's office or even a psychopathic doctor or nurse or janitor."

Marcus's mouth dropped. "Libby would never do something like that."

"Libby?"

"Dr. Holman—my mother's oncologist. She's the one who ordered the toxicology test."

"Don't let appearances fool you," Scott warned.

"I'm telling you Libby would never do something like that."

"Sometimes the people you'd least expect are the very ones who are guilty. Since you are no doubt familiar with your mother's will, it would behoove you to investigate who would stand to benefit if your mother died. Could *that* person have somehow tampered with her chemotherapy?"

Was Scott implying someone—maybe even Marcus himself—had added poison to his mother's chemotherapy just to obtain money from her will?

His shoulders sagged. "This is even more convoluted than I imagined."

"Very convoluted indeed," Scott agreed. "Unfortunately, international drug manufacturing opens up even more routes for contamination—both deliberate *and* unintentional."

Marcus rolled his neck and massaged the tight muscles in his right shoulder blade. "I'm sorry I attacked you, Scott. I shouldn't have been so quick to jump to conclusions."

"I understand. You nearly lost your mother from a tainted drug. It's only natural you'd want this case solved—yesterday. That's why I'm in this business. I want to keep our drugs as safe and pure as you do. Unfortunately, these investigations take time, especially when there is only one reported case."

After Scott promised to provide updates, they ended their call. Marcus slumped back in his chair, arms dangling.

What a can of worms!

CHAPTER 14

Despite his awkward last encounter with Libby, Marcus decided to take off from work to escort his mother to her doctor's appointment, as it would provide a neutral, professional environment in which to discuss the aflatoxin investigation with Libby. He needed to broach the subject of any disgruntled or mentally ill employees who might work for her who could have added the aflatoxin to the chemotherapy.

During the car trip to Libby's office, he'd also casually ask his mother about the contents and beneficiaries of her will. Hard to imagine anyone would kill her for the few measly dollars she likely had left in her retirement savings after all the recent medical bills and funeral expenses, but it never hurt to ask. Since his mother had hired a family friend—an estate attorney from their church—to update her will after Marcus's father died, Marcus had no idea how much, if anything, she had left.

After his father died, Marcus had offered to re-write her will for free, but she'd declined. "You work too hard as it is, Marcus, so I hired Bernard to do it."

As Marcus pulled into his mother's driveway, he couldn't block the disturbing, and hopefully unwarranted, worry that Brittany was responsible for poisoning his mother. She was the only person Marcus could think of who might have a vendetta against his mother.

Brittany blamed Sophia for her incarceration. When Marcus first discovered Brittany had stolen his identity and charged twenty thousand dollars on fraudulently obtained credit cards, he'd wanted to write it off as a life lesson learned. Frankly, he didn't want to humiliate himself in front of a local judge and passel of attorneys by revealing he'd chosen a gold digger for a fiancée. Talk about embarrassing.

At the time, it seemed natural to help Brittany out. She didn't make much as a first-year kindergarten teacher, and besides, they *were* engaged.

In hindsight, however, he'd ignored all the warning signs—like the time he walked into the kitchen and caught her rifling through his wallet. "What are you doing?" he asked. She startled, her face wide-eyed and guilty. She quickly recovered and responded, "Oh, I was just checking out the picture on your driver's license. I wanted to see if you looked like a bank robber." She giggled, but her laugh sounded nervous, and her hand trembled.

It should have been a warning, but because he trusted her, and perhaps because he didn't *want* to see the truth, he ignored his gut. Other warning signs should have alerted him, as well. Namely, how did someone making a first-year teacher's salary afford handbags designed by Louis Vuitton? Or exorbitantly priced shoes by Chanel? How did she afford her silver BMW?

Every time they got together, she wore a new outfit from Neiman-Marcus. He'd stupidly played along and told her how stylish and beautiful she looked. Little did he know his flattery only egged on her shopping addiction.

Nor did he know *he* was footing the bill for her shopping sprees!

When he'd inadvertently discovered the bills of six maxed-out credit cards with *his* name on them at Brittany's apartment one night, she tearfully confessed what she had done and begged him to forgive her.

Unfortunately, the credit card companies were less forgiving and refused to write off the balances unless he pressed charges against her since he *knew* who the thief was.

His mother insisted Brittany needed consequences. "If you let her get away with credit card fraud, you'll re-enforce her bad behavior. She'll never learn she can't use her feminine wiles to manipulate men."

Marcus pointed out it wasn't very Christlike of him to not forgive her. He should let her slowly pay him back — or forgive her outright. Sophia disagreed. "If you won't do it for yourself, do it for all the other unsuspecting men out there."

Turns out, Sophia was right. Brittany had pulled the same stunt on another man in the church single's group shortly before she started dating Marcus. Like Marcus, Rodney thought the Christian thing to do was forgive her and hope she learned her lesson. Not wanting to shame her, he kept the identity theft to himself.

When he heard through the grapevine why Marcus called off his engagement, he decided to speak up. Brittany had apparently learned nothing — except that she could exploit men with her beauty and get away with it. The woman needed consequences.

Sophia agreed. "This isn't about forgiveness — it's about Brittany learning from her poor choices. Yes, you *are* called to forgive her and pray that God uses this experience to change her, but she won't grow in maturity if she's not held accountable."

"What if she ends up in prison?" Marcus asked, fearing the worse. "After all, this is a second offense."

Sophia shrugged. "If she looks hideous in hot orange, too bad."

Marcus prayed diligently about his decision and sought the counsel of his pastor, who agreed Marcus should press charges. "She needs tough love, Marcus. This is the *second* time she's financially exploited men she is dating. Plus, *you* shouldn't be lopped with her credit card debt."

In the end, Marcus did exactly what his mother, Rodney, and Pastor Jamison advised. Brittany never forgave him. Instead, she blamed *him*! In the courtroom, she twisted things around and claimed because Marcus had occasionally offered to buy her a couple gallons of gas or a box of cereal and milk to tide her over until payday, he had led her to believe he wanted to help her out financially, and therefore, it was *okay* to obtain new credit cards in his name to cover her expenses.

She glared across the courtroom at him, a hurt expression plastered on her face. "We were *engaged*," she said, wiping a tear from her cheek with a perfectly manicured finger. "Marcus always complimented me on how beautiful he thought I looked." She gazed up at the judge with her tear-stained puppy dog eyes.

"I bought all those attractive clothes to look nice for *him*. And now he's turning on me."

She burst into tears and blew her nose, milking her attempt to look pitiful.

Thanks to Brittany, his credit rating nose-dived, and it took a year of time-consuming legal maneuvering to clear his name. But in the courtroom that day, you'd have thought *he* was the villain—*he* had mistreated Brittany!

The final courtroom scene, with Brittany screaming at him for betraying her, would be locked in his brain forever. After Brittany lambasted him in court for "turning on me," she pointed a finger in Sophia's direction and screamed, "This is all *your* fault, Sophia Romano! Marcus would *never* have pressed charges against me on his own. He's too much of a Mama's boy to defy you."

The judge banged his gavel. "Silence in the courtroom," he commanded. But Brittany would not be silenced. She screamed at Sophia over the rapping gavel, "You claim to be a Christian? What happened to all that forgiveness crap you preach about? Didn't Jesus say to forgive seventy times seven? You're nothing but a hypocrite, Sophia Romano! A hypocrite!"

He'd never forget his mother's ashen face and shaking hands when Brittany spat out, "The only hesitancy I *ever* had about marrying Marcus was *you*. Who wants a mother-in-law who's always yapping about the Bible? I was sick to death of your preaching already, and Marcus and I weren't even married yet."

An audible gasp echoed across the courtroom, and everyone turned to stare at Sophia. The outraged judge banged his gavel. "Order in the court."

When she still didn't pipe down, he threatened to charge her with contempt of court and lengthen her sentence. That got her attention, and she said nothing further. The judge sentenced her to three months in prison since this was her second time of engaging in credit card fraud. She would also be required to make restitution to the credit card companies for her financial debt.

Even then, Brittany demanded the last word. As she passed Sophia on her way out of the courtroom with the bailiff, she glared at Sophia and hissed, "You'll pay for this, Sophia Romano. Just you wait!"

The words shuddered through him now. Brittany had been released from prison nine months ago, and Marcus hadn't heard a peep out of her. But could she somehow have heard about Sophia's cancer, gotten ahold of the chemotherapy, and added poison out of revenge?

He tried to dismiss the idea. How would Brittany get into Libby's drug closet to taint the chemotherapy? And where would she get aflatoxin? How would she know who his mother's oncologist was, or which bag of chemo to contaminate? Besides, surely Brittany wouldn't be revengeful enough to poison his mother — would she?

He chewed on his bottom lip. He hadn't thought her capable of identity theft or spewing such hateful comments to his mother in the courtroom, either.

Still mulling on whether Brittany might be culpable, Marcus pulled into his mother's driveway and saw her peering out the window watching for him.

Within a minute, she locked the front door, climbed into his car, and snapped on her seatbelt. To Marcus's relief, her skin and eyes looked considerably less jaundiced, so maybe she'd survive this nightmare after all.

After backing out of the driveway, he informed her of Scott's suspicion that the aflatoxin was added locally and with malevolent intent.

Her mouth dropped. "The chemo wasn't contaminated at the factory?"

He kept his voice calm as he explained that since no other cases had been reported to the FDA, it was more likely an inside job.

Sophia's brow furrowed. "Are you saying somebody specifically singled *me* out to poison?"

"You *do* tell dreadful jokes," he quipped, doing his best to keep a straight face.

She whacked his arm. "That wasn't nice."

He continued. "Scott says it could be someone wanting to punish Dr. Holman or you. Or, it could be some sociopath at the Atlanta distributing center who gets his jollies by poisoning complete strangers."

They rode in silence for several blocks pondering the possible culprits until Marcus voiced his worst fear. "Mom, do you think Brittany would stoop to poisoning you?"

Her head snapped sideways. "Brittany? How would she get into Dr. Holman's drug closet?"

Marcus shrugged. "I have no idea, but she's the only person I can think of who has it in for you. She *did* threaten you in the courtroom, remember?"

Sophia crossed her arms, a scowl on her face.

"I know I'm supposed to forgive my enemies, but I have to pray every single day where that one is concerned. The things she said to me—and in a public courtroom, no less!"

"Brittany was a shopaholic. Her whole self-esteem revolved around looking good and earning compliments. Ironically, every time I told her how beautiful she looked, I fanned the flames of her addiction."

Sophia turned and stared at him wide-eyed. "You're right. I never thought of it that way before. Shopping *was* an addiction for her—like a gambler who can't stop himself from ringing up credit cards at the casino."

He nodded. "Exactly. I'm praying she develops confidence in who *God* says she is, so she doesn't need to gain her self-esteem from fancy clothes and compliments."

Sophia folded her arms across her chest. "I knew the minute I met that materialistic she-devil that she was as shallow as my jelly roll pan."

Marcus groaned.

Here we go again.

"So you've told me, Ma. More than once, in fact."

Sophia shook her head. "Other than her looks, I never could figure out what you saw in that woman."

Marcus gripped the steering wheel and reminded himself not to disrespect his mother. "That's because you're not a guy. I was flattered such a gorgeous woman gave me the time of day. With her looks, she could have snagged up any guy she wanted, but she wanted *me*."

"Or your credit cards," Sophia retorted.

118

Marcus couldn't help but chuckle. "Now who's being snarky? I may be delusional, but I honestly think Brittany loved me—as much as she was capable of love as an addict."

"Maybe, but she sure loved fancy clothes and shoes more."

Marcus gazed into his rearview mirror as he merged into traffic. "Trust me, I learned my lesson. I'll never date a woman like that again."

"So instead, you shut yourself off completely. That's no better, Marcus. How long has it been since you asked a girl out for a date?"

He shrugged and gripped the steering wheel, offering no response.

"Isn't it time you got back in the saddle? You're not getting any younger, and I want grandchildren."

He inhaled a deep breath and released it slowly, contemplating her words. "Truthfully, I think I'm too shell-shocked to try. When it comes to women, I don't trust my own judgment anymore. Brittany claimed to be a Christian, and I honestly thought she loved me. Look how that turned out."

"Oh, Brittany could talk the talk, and she could even quote Scripture when it suited her purposes, but you have to look at the fruit—her actions. If you'd feasted your eyes on her actions instead of her surgically enhanced bust line, you'd have seen that everything she cared about was superficial."

"I suppose you're right," Marcus said, putting on his blinker to pass a dump truck.

"Now Libby, on the other hand..."

Marcus groaned. The humiliation of his last encounter with Libby burned in his memory. "Don't go there, Ma. As far as Libby is concerned, I'm just the son of a patient. Nothing more."

His mother stared at him. "How do you know that?"

He eyed his speedometer and pulled his foot off the accelerator. Just the mention of Libby's name, and he'd stepped on the gas and hit eighty. "Trust me, Libby made it very clear I should give up any thought of pursuing a relationship with her."

Sophia waved him off. "Oh, pooh! You've just misread her. Libby is shy. Just because she's not a pathological flirt like Brittany, doesn't mean she's not interes—"

"Drop it!" Jaw clenched, he white-knuckled the steering wheel. Then, feeling guilty for snapping at his mother, he forced himself to lower his voice. "Ma, there's no future there. She's not interested."

"Fiddlesticks! How could she *not* be interested? You're handsome, smart, gainfully employed, and most important? You have a witty, likable mother. What more could a girl want?"

He rolled his eyes. "How about a mother who doesn't meddle in my affairs?"

"I'm not meddling, I'm merely looking out for your future."

They rode in silence before Marcus decided to break the tension.

"According to Brittany, I was *too* nice to you. I was a Mama's boy." He turned to her and smirked. "Maybe I should shove you off a cliff. That way I'll never be accused of that again. Might help my dating prospects considerably."

"Ha, ha, ha. If you were a Mama's boy, you wouldn't have gotten engaged to Brittany. You knew I couldn't stand the woman."

He chuckled. "Fair enough."

"Besides, I wouldn't go threatening to toss me off a cliff, or I might write you out of my will." She wagged an index finger in his face. "Then, wouldn't you be sorry!"

Marcus snorted. "Right! After all the recent medical bills and Dad's funeral expenses, you'll probably leave me with a bunch of overdue utility bills and a maxed-out credit card."

Hands on her hips, Sophia fumed, "I'll have you know, Mr. Smarty-Mouth, that even though your father was just a lowly minister and not some hot-shot lawyer, he squirreled away over a million dollars in his retirement portfolio before he died. Not to mention the million-dollar life insurance policy I cashed in last year."

What? Mom is a multi-millionaire?

He jammed on the brakes to keep from slamming into the car in front of him and admonished himself to focus on his driving.

Sensing his shock, Sophia explained. "You know how much your father loved his Apple computer. Well, he invested a huge chunk of his retirement portfolio in Macintosh stock nearly forty years ago—long before the I-pad and I-phone craze." She grinned at him. "I guess I can thank Steve Jobs for my financial security."

Marcus shook his head, still in shock. "I assumed you didn't have enough money for a shopping spree at Goodwill on half-price Saturdays."

She arched a brow. "Just because I buy my clothes at thrift stores instead of strutting around in designer jeans and fancy boots like that she-devil Brittany, doesn't mean I'm destined for the poor house, you know. I'm just frugal."

Marcus had to smile. It appeared his mother was incapable of saying Brittany's name without adding the words she-devil. "Mom—you're called to forgive her. I have, and *I'm* the one whose credit rating she ruined."

Sophia raised a hand in defeat. "You're right, but when she hurt my son, she brought out the she-bear in me."

Marcus snickered at the thought of his pint-sized mother as a she-bear.

As Marcus exited the interstate, he asked, "Getting back to my original question, do you think Brittany would be capable of plotting to poison you?"

Sophia tipped her head in thought. "Much as she disliked me, I can't imagine she'd go so far as poisoning me." Her lips thinned. "But with Brittany, you never know."

CHAPTER 15

Just seeing Sophia Romano's name on today's schedule of patients sent waves of trepidation in Libby's stomach. Would Marcus come with her? If so, how would he act? Hostile? Pouty? As though nothing happened? Brandishing a malpractice lawsuit?

Ever since her dismissive closure to the hike, Marcus had not called or contacted her in any way. Not even a text. While her brain told her she should be glad, she replayed their brief near kiss in the woods more times than she cared to admit. She rehashed all the intimate things he'd shared with her at the vista. She felt such a connection with him, and then she'd blown it with her stiff goodbye. He thought she was rejecting him.

But I wasn't. I had a flashback and got scared.

With any luck, Marcus would have a court case today, and she wouldn't have to face him. Perhaps she could obtain his e-mail address from Sophia and shoot off a brief note summarizing Sophia's progress.

Nerves calmed, she strolled into Sophia's exam room shoulders back and head held high. Her confidence shriveled like impatiens in an August heatwave when there sat Marcus looking gorgeous as ever. "Hello, Marcus," she said, feigning a calm she did not possess.

She wished the Rapture would take place right now and spare her this awkward encounter.

He stood and reached for her hand. "Nice to see you again, Libby," he mumbled politely, then quickly dropped her hand and took a seat.

His tousled curls and chocolate eyes triggered memories of their jaunt in the park. Hard to believe a few days ago, she was tangled up with him in the ferns. Now, he seemed more remote than the Fiji Islands.

Focus on Sophia.

She sat down and swiveled her computer chair to face Sophia. "I'm pleased to see your complexion and eyes are considerably less jaundiced today."

Sophia nodded. "I'm not clawing myself to death anymore, either."

"I'll bet your liver blood tests will show a sizable drop." Still rattled by Marcus's presence, she swiveled her chair a bit further until she didn't have to see him at all. Maybe now she could pretend he wasn't there. She silently repeated her mantra.

You are a professional. Marcus is Sophia's son, and nothing more.

Unfortunately, Marcus would not stay silently huddled in the corner. When she had completed her evaluation of Sophia, Marcus insisted on discussing what the FDA investigator told him.

She could hardly believe her ears when Marcus informed her, "He thinks the perpetrator could be an employee at the Atlanta distribution center or even a disgruntled employee of yours."

Libby crossed her arms in disgust. "What? That's ridiculous! Did he accept a bribe from the Banderbaxy CEO to say that?"

"That was my first reaction too, but Scott pointed out no other cases of aflatoxin contamination have shown up, and if an entire vat of chemotherapy was contaminated, dozens of cases should have cropped up by now. He thinks since Mom's is the only reported case, it is most likely an inside job."

She felt the blood drain from her body.

Inside job? Did Marcus think she, or one of her staff, intentionally poisoned his mother?

Why would they do that? Was he saying this out of spite — because she'd spurned him in the park? If so, would he sue her? He was a lawyer, so what better way to seek revenge than with a hefty lawsuit? After all, he hadn't been above taking his ex-fiancée to court — why not her?

She instinctively gripped the arms of her chair, as though already in the courtroom facing an intimidating judge and prosecuting attorney.

Please, God. Don't make me face a courtroom again.

She forced herself to look Marcus straight in the eyes. He might be a hoity-toity attorney, but no way would she go down without a fight!

You've done nothing wrong. Don't let him intimidate you.

She sucked in a deep breath then swiveled her chair until she faced him head-on. "So, this Scott from the FDA thinks just because your mother's is the only reported case *so far*, that proves someone in *my* office tampered with Sophia's chemo?"

Shoot! That came out sounding way too defensive.

She wiped her perspiring palms onto her lab coat and admonished herself to stay calm, professional, and above board.

Marcus's eyes widened, as though surprised at her hostility. "Not at all! Scott merely suggested we look at *all* the possibilities. Remember, it could have been contaminated at the distribution facility in Atlanta, but as of right now, unless another case of aflatoxin poisoning shows up, he's concerned the contamination occurred locally."

"As in my office."

Silence permeated the room as Libby chewed on this disturbing morsel. Could Roger have somehow gained entry into her office and poisoned a bag of chemo? Julius *had* informed her Roger was out on parole. Could he have traveled to Nashville, broken into her office, and contaminated a bag of chemo to punish her—all between visits with his parole officer in Chattanooga?

"What's our next step?" Sophia inquired.

Marcus turned to his mother. "We need to investigate every person who has had access to Dr. Holman's chemotherapy or who might want to harm you or Dr. Holman. We'll have to trust the FDA to investigate the factory in India and the distributing center in Atlanta."

Libby made the mistake of glancing up. Her eyes locked with Marcus's, and she couldn't breathe. She forced herself to lean over in her chair. Whether it was from the shock of finding out the pharmaceutical giant may not be to blame, or the fear Marcus suspected her, or someone in her office of foul play, or just the emotional strain of seeing him again, her head began to swim.

She grabbed onto the arms of her chair and forced herself to suck in a deep breath.

Relax. Do. Not. Faint.

Marcus reached over and touched her arm. "Libby? Do you need to lay down?"

Before she could answer, she felt herself slumping forward into near unconsciousness.

Not again!

As though in a tunnel, she heard Marcus yell into the hall for the nurse to bring ice water, and she felt him scoop her up into his arms and placed her onto the exam table. He snatched the ammonia pellet taped onto the side of the table, snapped it in two, and wafted it under her nose, just like he'd seen Melissa do.

The noxious fumes jarred her, and she jolted into full consciousness. After sipping the ice water Melissa provided, she perked up. "I'm so sorry," she said, her cheeks burning.

So much for my, "You are a professional" mantra!

She released a frustrated sigh. *What must he think?*

Marcus gripped her hand. "Libby, I'm sorry if I made you feel defensive. I'm just trying to get answers. No one's blaming *you* for the poisoned chemotherapy, okay?"

Sophia chimed in. "Of course not! Poisoning her own patients would hardly be good for repeat business!"

Something about the spunky little woman voicing such an obvious statement triggered Libby's funny bone, and she began to smile. Then chuckle. Then howl with laughter. Soon Sophia and Marcus joined in, and the three of them laughed so hard tears streamed down their faces.

Sophia reached for a tissue and wiped her eyes. "Medical Marketing 101. Lesson One: If you want repeat business, don't poison your patients." The three of them were off again, grabbing their sides in stitches.

Marcus tossed out, "Gosh, Mom, maybe you should write a book. It's bound to be a bestseller."

Sophia raised a finger. "I know! I'll call it *Marketing for Dummy Doctors.*" She roared at her own wit.

Libby couldn't help herself. "*Marketing for Dummy Doctors.* Lesson Two: Don't vomit and pass out at every patient visit."

No doubt remembering he had more important things to focus on than Medical Marketing 101, once they settled down, Marcus asked, "Libby, do you have any disgruntled or recently fired employees who could be seeking revenge?"

Libby pursed her lips in thought. Her staff had all worked for her for the four years she'd been in private practice, and they were like family. Plus, they all thought the world of Sophia—especially on the days she treated them to homemade cinnamon buns and Starbuck's coffee.

Cynthia.

The name ricocheted in her brain like a pinball. Her heart sank.

How had she forgotten Cynthia?

CHAPTER 16

Libby had fired Cynthia three months ago for stealing. The woman had only worked for Libby four months when money began mysteriously disappearing from the petty cash. Libby proved Cynthia was the thief by indiscreetly marking all the five-dollar bills in the petty cash drawer with her initials in red ink.

Later that day, Libby confronted Cynthia and proved four red ink-marked five-dollar bills had found their way into Cynthia's wallet. When Cynthia showed no remorse and even accused Libby of framing her, Libby fired her on the spot. Since Cynthia had stolen more than three-hundred dollars in her four months of employment, Libby called the police and showed them the subtle red initials she'd used to prove Cynthia was the thief.

A police investigation uncovered Cynthia had a past record of theft in Virginia, which is apparently why she hightailed it to Tennessee — to start over.

Libby heard through the grapevine that Cynthia hadn't found a job since her termination. When several prospective employers called Libby hoping for a glowing recommendation, all Libby would tell them was, "Cynthia is ineligible for rehire." Any doctor with an IQ higher than his pulse rate could read between the lines.

But from Cynthia's warped perspective, it was Libby's fault she could not obtain another job.

Even worse, since Cynthia worked in their office for four months, she knew exactly when housekeeping came to clean the office. With a shot of adrenaline, Libby remembered Cynthia never returned her key to the office. Libby had called her landlord three times to change the lock to her front door, but he never followed through.

As weeks passed with no word from Cynthia, it slipped Libby's mind to call the landlord a fourth time — which meant Cynthia still owned an office key, allowing her full access to Libby's office.

Since Cynthia had managed the front desk, she would know all the computer passwords. She could easily check the appointment schedule and even what kind of chemotherapy Sophia received.

She'd shown no remorse for her stealing, but would she sneak back into the office and inject poison into Sophia's chemo out of spite? Since Libby barely knew the woman, she had no idea.

Libby had told Cynthia she viewed Sophia Romano as a mother figure, so if Cynthia were vengeful, Sophia would be the patient to target.

Cynthia would have to have entered Libby's office, logged into the computer, tracked down which chemotherapy drug Sophia was receiving and when, and then poisoned that specific bag of chemo sometime in the week before Sophia's scheduled infusion.

It seemed unlikely she'd stoop so low, but what better way to punish Libby for firing her than by poisoning a favorite patient and making Libby face the consequences?

Libby gripped the arms of her chair and closed her eyes.

Marcus's eyes widened. "Libby?"

Reluctantly, she shared her suspicion about Cynthia.

Sophia shook her head. "This thing is getting as many suspects as a game of Clue."

"Well, at least we've solved the weapon—aflatoxin. And the room, your office," Marcus commented.

Libby turned to Sophia. "What do you mean? What other suspects do we have besides Cynthia?"

Marcus and Sophia made eye contact, and Marcus shared his suspicions about Brittany.

Sophia piped in, "And then there's a possible sociopath at the distribution center in Atlanta."

And Roger.

Libby drummed her fingers on her workstation. "We still haven't excluded Banderbaxy Pharmaceuticals in my mind. Unless all the other doctors in the world ran toxicology tests, they might not have figured out the chemotherapy was contaminated with aflatoxin. They might have falsely concluded the patient became jaundiced due to alcohol, or pain meds, or an allergic reaction to Taxotaphen."

"True," Marcus said, standing up and ambling across the exam room. "It *could* still be Banderbaxy's fault, and the other cases just haven't trickled in yet."

"Stir in all the inspectors open to hush money, and we now have *more* suspects than a game of Clue," Libby said.

Marcus ran a hand through his hair. "So to summarize, the possible culprits are Cynthia from your office, my ex-fiancée Brittany, some deranged distribution center employee in Atlanta, or the Banderbaxy manufacturing plant in India. Have I left anyone out?"

Sophia smiled. "Colonel Mustard and Miss Scarlett?"

Libby knew she should reveal her suspicion about Roger, but that would require confessing her whole checkered past. When Julius and Brandy returned from Chattanooga, she'd have a better idea of how viable a threat Roger really was. If there was no evidence that he'd left Chattanooga, he would not be a suspect, and there would be no reason to add his name to the list.

No point airing my dirty laundry unless I have to.

* * *

After the appointment, Marcus asked to speak with Libby privately while Melissa drew Sophia's blood and scheduled a follow-up appointment. Libby's heart hammered as she ushered him into her office and closed the door.

What does he want?

She sank into her leather chair so she could use her large mahogany desk as a barrier between them.

Marcus sat stiffly in the Queen Anne's chair facing her desk. After an awkward pause, he said, "Like you, I assumed Banderbaxy contaminated Mom's chemotherapy, but if there's any chance someone local did it, don't you think we need to notify the police and get them involved?"

She froze.

The police? Already?

Marcus was right, of course. Police expertise *would* prove helpful, but she couldn't ignore her abject terror the whole ordeal would end up plastered on the front page of the *Tennessean*. Her career would be toast.

After all, what cancer patient would choose an oncologist who infused poisoned chemotherapy? She'd end up as scandalized as those pain center doctors who inadvertently injected cortisone contaminated with black mold spores. Lawsuits, public humiliation, bankruptcy—their lives were ruined.

And yours will be, too.

Libby swallowed the lump in her throat. She had to do the right thing, even if her career and reputation ended in shambles. Patient safety took precedence over her reputation.

"Libby?"

Her cheeks flushed. She'd been so lost in her own swirling thoughts she never answered his question. She met his eyes across her desk, and with as commanding a voice as she could muster, she said, "Yes, we should notify the police." She quickly turned her head so he couldn't see the tears brimming in her eyes.

As though sensing her fear, Marcus leaned forward and reached across her desk and gripped her hand. "Libby, you're not in this alone. You'll get through this with God's help."

His comforting words and caring touch unleashed an embarrassing torrent of tears, and before she knew it, she was sobbing—shoulders heaving, emotions raw—similar to Marcus's breakdown in the park.

He rushed around the side of her desk, squatted, and cradled her in his arms. He held her close and tucked her head into his neck, as though comforting a distraught child.

Libby clung to him, as the fear of what could lay ahead racked her body. "I'm so sorry this happened to your mother."

"I know," he murmured. "It's not your fault, Libby. No body's blaming you, okay?"

Somehow with Marcus's arms cocooned around her, the future seemed less daunting. She could smell the faint scent of his aftershave—woodsy and with a hint of spice—and strangely, it soothed her.

Slowly, her tears abated, but she found herself wanting to bask in the warmth of his arms and to soak in all the tenderness and protection he offered. To no longer feel alone. She'd forgotten how good it felt to be wrapped in the arms of a caring man. Four years had passed since she and Colin broke up. Four long years without a single tender caress. No wonder she wanted to cling to Marcus.

She glanced up, and his eyes gazed into hers, concerned yet gentle. He forked his fingers through her hair and pulled back the damp strands that clung to her cheek. He cradled her face in his hands, and their eyes remained locked. She couldn't help but gasp as a crushing desire to feel his lips pressed against hers overpowered her. She gazed back into eyes that radiated concern and... desire?

He still wants me!

All thoughts of professional conduct and long-term consequences evaporated.

She pulled his face toward hers, insistent and needy. Their lips merged with the slightest of pressure. She longed for more—for every drop of tenderness he could give. She tugged his head closer so she could explore his lips fully.

Marcus responded with an intensity that left her breathless.

She couldn't help but giggle when he marched a row of soft kisses first on her cheek and then on her neck. Their eyes met again, and she smiled shyly, all tension between them gone.

"I didn't mean to fall apart like that. Thanks for, um, comforting me," she said, suddenly feeling shy.

A slow grin spread across his face. "My pleasure."

He caressed her face with gentle fingertips. "We're in this together, Libby."

She smiled, grateful for his reassuring words. Marcus was everything she wanted in a man. But would he want her once he learned about Roger? If Sophia thought Brittany wasn't good enough for her son, what would she think if she knew about Libby's past?

Marcus's hands slid down her arms, and he gently squeezed her hands. "I'll give the cops a call and fill them in. They'll likely want to come by and investigate."

She swallowed the golf ball-sized lump in her throat, already dreading police interrogation. But it had to be done. "We have to do what's right, even if my reputation ends up in the toilet. Lord knows it won't be the first time."

Marcus's brow furrowed. "What do you mean, it won't be the first time?"

She wanted to slap herself. Why had she blurted that out?

She wasn't ready to tell Marcus the details of her relationship with Roger.

His eyes probed hers patiently, waiting for an answer.

You should tell him. Marcus deserves to know.

She inhaled a deep breath and forced herself to speak.

"After my mom died, my father started working crazy long hours to escape his grief. Consequently, I felt abandoned and furious with God."

He gripped her hands but said nothing, as though waiting for her to proceed.

She stared at their entwined hands, unable to make eye contact. "I-I got involved in something terrible. Something I deeply regret ever happened. I..."

Sophia barged into the room. "Okay, they drew my blood, and my follow-up appointment is sched..." She stopped short and stared at their two startled faces. They abruptly pulled apart.

"Well, well, well! What do we have here?" A knowing grin spread across her face.

Libby considered crawling under her desk to escape the embarrassing encounter. "You can come in. We're all done our discussion."

"Discussion?" Sophia smirked. "From the looks of your hair and flushed face, there was a whole lot more than discussing going on in here."

Okay, now she wanted to jump out the window and run away.

She opened her mouth to piece together a plausible explanation.

Before she could, Sophia flounced out of the room, calling over her shoulder, "Take your time. I'll be in the waiting room."

Silence permeated the room thick as Smoky Mountain fog.

Marcus offered a chagrined smile. "Right now, I feel like I'm back at a junior high dance getting busted for kissing my girlfriend behind the bleachers."

Libby giggled. "Me, too."

He leaned forward and tucked a strand of hair behind her ear. As his face merged inches from hers, she held her breath, wondering if he would kiss her again.

She forced her eyes to meet his, and he gently fingered the side of her cheek.

"Just so I can be sure I'm reading you right this time, can I assume after what happened earlier in here that you're no longer repelled by me, and we're starting a relationship?"

She swallowed, grappling to find the right words. Failing miserably, she merely mumbled, "Um, I think we are."

He reached for her hand and squeezed it, a huge grin on his face. "How about we get together tonight to finish the conversation my mother so rudely interrupted. I want to hear your story, Libby."

"Sounds good. Plus, you can update me on what the cops say."

"Maybe we can take the dogs for a walk while we brainstorm ways to better secure your office," Marcus suggested. "And Lord knows Trixie needs more obedience training."

After Libby volunteered to prepare dinner for him, Marcus planted a quick kiss on her cheek and left.

The second he left her office, however, fear and endless questions pummeled her. Would the cops squeal to reporters about the poisoned chemo? Had Julius and Brandy tracked down Roger in Chattanooga? Was Roger her stalker? How would Marcus handle her confession about Roger? Most importantly, who poisoned the chemotherapy?

Libby glanced at her watch and groaned. She was forty minutes behind schedule — again.

Why could she never stay on schedule? She released a frustrated sigh. She'd have to ponder all these pressing questions when she didn't have a waiting room full of cancer patients to see.

She smoothed out her lab coat, brushed her hair, and headed toward the exam rooms.

Time to get back to work.

CHAPTER 17

Libby changed clothes three times before settling on khaki shorts and the turquoise top that always triggered compliments about her eyes. Looking attractive made her less nervous about facing Marcus again. She flipped her head over and brushed her hair again to add extra body. While coating her mouth with cherry fusion lipstick, the doorbell chimed.

Dread and excitement churned in her stomach as she strolled toward the door. What if their conversation meandered back to where it had left off when Sophia barged into the room? Would Marcus insist she tell all? If so, would she? Why did he have to know this early in their relationship about her past? But if she kept secrets from him, how could their budding romance progress? On the other hand, if she told him the truth, would he view her as damaged goods?

Marcus had confessed his own embarrassing past with Brittany, so surely, he could recognize her past for what it was—the past. Plus, she'd only been twelve—a child—and, she'd recently lost her mother. Just because Colin couldn't understand, didn't mean Marcus wouldn't, right?

He didn't let Brittany off the hook.

That's different, she reassured herself. What Brittany did was criminal and committed as an adult.

Plus, Brittany also claimed to be a Christian the whole time she forged Marcus's signature all over town. Surely Marcus would grasp Libby was a victim and had done nothing wrong.

She headed to the hall and unlocked the front door, still wrestling with her decision. Did she know Marcus well enough to share such a private thing?

To tell, or not to tell...

Her safest bet? Say nothing. After all, why did Marcus need to know about her past? Why was it his or anyone else's business? She should wait until she learned what Brandy and Julius found out. If Roger was not her stalker, Marcus didn't need to know.

She opened the front door, her decision made. Bottom line? She didn't want to lose Marcus. With all the stress in her life right now, she couldn't handle him blaming her for Roger's behavior, nor did she have the stomach for a break-up. Confessing this early in their relationship might prove risky. Been there, done that. Look what happened with Colin.

* * *

Marcus felt like a child on Christmas Eve waiting for Santa to come and fill his stocking. He shuffled his feet on Libby's welcome mat and stroked Gus's head, eager to begin his date with Libby. Okay, not a date exactly, but come on! She couldn't have kissed him with such passion earlier that day if she wasn't attracted to him. And this time, *she'd* initiated the kiss! Even now, the memory of her lips hungrily seeking his triggered such a surge of anticipation he knew he was grinning like a fool.

At the sound of Libby's footfall padding toward the door, Marcus drummed his fingers on the doorframe and suppressed his nagging worry that Libby was hiding something from him. If only his mother hadn't barged in on them when Libby was about to tell him something important. She said she'd done something terrible.

How terrible? Had she committed some heinous crime—like murdering her mother and then claiming the woman died of breast cancer?

No, with the compassionate bedside manner she displayed toward his mother, she sure didn't seem like the murder-your-mother-in-her-sleep sort, but what did he know about women? Heck, he'd proposed to an identity thief!

He released a frustrated sigh. He had no intention of bullying the details out of Libby, but until she opened up, he'd better guard his heart. Secrets made for dangerous soulmates. Hadn't he learned that with Brittany?

When Libby opened the door and Marcus drank in her warm smile and captivating eyes, all thoughts of Libby-is-a-murderer flew out of his head. He couldn't stop himself from staring as he followed her shapely legs into the living room. He dragged his eyes away.

Stop it! Christian men do not ogle women.

Any inappropriate thoughts were immediately eliminated when Trixie pounced onto the scene. The unruly beast leaped and bucked as though she were a wild stallion resisting a bridle. Trixie and Gus sniffed each other, and Gus wagged his tail.

When Trixie responded by attempting to pounce on Gus, Marcus glanced over at Libby, and they burst into laughter.

"Are you *sure* you want to help me train her?" Libby asked.

"Trust me, it's going to take both of us to contain this wild thing."

Libby put both hands on her hips. "Hey! I'll have you know I've trained Trixie to sit since our last hike. Watch this." She turned to Trixie and commanded, "Trixie, sit!"

Trixie responded by tugging on Gus's ear.

"SIT!" Libby commanded in an authoritative voice. The ill-behaved pup made no effort whatsoever to rest on her haunches. Instead, she barked uproariously and landed her front paws on Marcus's thighs.

"Impressive," Marcus said with a wink. "You've really reformed her."

Libby fumed. "Come on, Trixie. We *worked* on this. SIT!"

Trixie stared up at Libby, her tail flapping like clothesline laundry in a windstorm.

Marcus pulled a dog bone out of his pocket and waved it in front of Trixie's nose. "Sit."

Eyeing the reward, Trixie leaped two feet in the air for the prize. Marcus yanked his arm overhead and snapped, "No sit, no bone." He then turned to Gus. "Sit." Of course, Mr. Perfect Pooch immediately complied and was rewarded with the coveted bone. Marcus then pulled out another bone and waved it in front of Trixie. "Sit," he commanded. No response. "SIT."

Okay, this mutt is not the smartest canine in the kennel.
Marcus pushed with all his might on Trixie's haunches until she was forced into a sitting position. He rewarded her with a bone. He continued the routine a few more times until finally, Trixie learned to sit.

Libby watched the dog training with fascination. Marcus remained firm with Trixie but then lavished her with praise when she finally grasped the concept. To keep Gus from getting jealous, Marcus rewarded him with bones and praise, as well.

"You'll make a fantastic father," Libby commented. Her cheeks flushed crimson, as though embarrassed to have uttered such a presumptuous remark.

Marcus squatted down eyeball-to-eyeball with Trixie and rubbed her neck. "A fella has to find the right woman before he can *be* a good father, doesn't he, Trixie?"

Libby released a nervous laugh. To salvage her pride, Marcus suggested they begin their walk.

* * *

After traipsing the streets surrounding Libby's townhouse for an hour, Trixie could heel—sort of—unless a squirrel, chipmunk, rabbit, neighbor's cat, leaf, or piece of floating trash distracted her. Despite munching through all the dog treats, she gazed up at Marcus with eager expectation. Perhaps he should transfer his retirement accounts into Purina dog bones. The way Trixie scarfed them down would make the stock soar as much as his dad's Apple stock.

Unfortunately, Trixie proved so disruptive that any semblance of a meaningful conversation about securing Libby's office from intruders was out of the question. When they arrived back at Libby's townhouse, she invited him to join her for lasagna and spinach salad.

The two dogs flopped next to each other in the living room, finally worn-out from their vigorous walk. While Libby microwaved lasagna and assembled salad in her tiny kitchen, Marcus took a seat on the couch and sipped the iced tea she offered him.

He spotted a scrapbook on the coffee table. Curious, he leaned forward and opened the cover. The first page revealed an adorable, chubby-cheeked baby Libby. He thumbed through the pages noting pictures of Libby with her mother and father at Disneyland, the Grand Canyon, Old Faithful, and blowing out candles at her eleventh birthday party. But then, no pictures. None—until the photo with Libby in her high school cap and gown delivering her Valedictorian speech. He flipped back several pages.

Where were the pictures from age eleven to eighteen?

Yes, Libby's mother died when Libby was eleven, but had her father not bothered to snap a single photo of his daughter for seven years? He perused the photo of Libby in her high school cap and gown and noted wariness in her eyes, as though the carefree girl who had screamed her way down Disney's Matterhorn had died along with her mother. In her place stood an older-than-her-years unsmiling high school graduate.

He flipped back and forth from the happy pre-teen girl to the somber high school graduate and wondered how seven years could have changed her so much.

Had her spark for life been buried in the casket with her mother?

Tears stung his eyes as he gazed at the motherless girl. The abject loneliness staring back at him gripped him to the bone. When he turned the page, he noted her college graduation picture. Then her medical school graduation picture.

Why hadn't her father taken any pictures? Even her graduation pictures were taken by a professional photographer and not her father.

Yes, the man had lost his wife, but he still had a daughter who needed love and attention—and a few photos for her scrapbook! A picture is worth a thousand words they say, but what if the father can't be bothered to *take* a picture? Anger boiled inside him against the negligent man who allowed Libby to limp through her teen years abandoned.

He flipped to a page after her medical school graduation picture and noticed a guy with his arm wrapped around Libby's shoulders. Jealousy slammed him when he saw a look of unbridled happiness on Libby's face. This must be the boyfriend she'd mentioned. Colin. Marcus couldn't help but check him out. The guy was good-looking, no question of that. Tall, sophisticated. Even his hair lay flat, unlike Marcus's unruly mop.

What had happened to end the relationship? Was Colin part of the past that Libby was so ashamed of? The past that had made her freeze up and recoil from him in the park?

Had she gotten pregnant and given up a baby for adoption? Had an abortion? Robbed a bank to cover her medical school debts? What did Libby not trust him enough to share?

He glanced up to see Libby spooning a large portion of lasagna on his plate. Whatever it was, she'd tell him when she felt emotionally secure enough to trust him. Trust could not be rushed — or forced. If they were meant to be together, God would orchestrate the timing, so he needn't harangue her to tell him.

When Libby entered the living room and announced dinner was ready, he offered up a prayer on Libby's behalf then closed the scrapbook. Something life altering — had happened to Libby.

What is she hiding from me?

CHAPTER 18

Between savoring bites of lasagna and ignoring Trixie's soulful eyes begging for table scraps, Libby and Marcus outlined a plan to ensure no other patient became poisoned in Libby's office. First, get the front door lock changed. Next, send every medication currently in her drug closet for toxicology testing to ensure other drugs weren't contaminated. Third, purchase a heavy-duty combination lock for the drug storage closet, and lastly, install a hidden motion-detector camera in front of the drug closet and in Libby's private office.

She stabbed a cherry tomato with her fork. "Should I get an alarm system, too?"

"No, we *want* the intruder to be caught on our video surveillance," Marcus said, forking up a bite of lasagna. "An alarm would just scare him off. As long as the chemo is secured, we want to catch him in the act."

Libby nodded. "Good point. Video footage would provide great evidence."

"Especially since we don't even know that the aflatoxin was added in your office. It could have been added by some nutcase at the Atlanta distributing factory."

"Better safe than sorry, though. If there's any chance someone tampered with the chemo in my office, I want them caught in the act." Libby buttered her roll with a vengeance.

What about fingerprints? Could she somehow keep the doorknob to the drug closet clean enough to lift uncontaminated fingerprints? If so, that would provide even more evidence. "Maybe I could wipe off the doorknob every night before I leave. That way, the cops could lift unadulterated prints if someone tries to open the drug closet."

"It's worth a try," Marcus agreed, shoveling a forkful of lasagna into his mouth.

Libby couldn't ignore the dread churning in her stomach. "How much do you suppose it's going to cost to hire someone to get those motion detector cameras up and running?"

Marcus's head jerked up. "*Hire* someone? Why would you hire someone when you have John Q. Handyman at your disposal?" He gestured toward himself.

"You've installed security cameras before?" She couldn't suppress her skepticism.

He averted his eyes. "Well, no, not exactly. But how hard can it be?" He raised palms as though the task were no harder than changing a light bulb.

Swell – Mr. Overconfident.

Knowing her luck, he'd end up electrocuting himself. "It's bound to be tricky," she said, hoping he'd take the hint and recant his offer.

Marcus lifted his fork as though it were a pointer. "I'll have you know, I won first prize at my junior high school science fair."

"And how many contenders *were* there for this illustrious prize?"

Marcus squirmed in his chair before admitting, "Four of us fought tooth and nail for that esteemed blue ribbon."

She burst into laughter. "Any more hidden talents I should know about?"

He leaned across the table and wiggled his eyebrows. "I have lots of talents I'd love to show you."

She stood up and extended a dirty dinner plate toward him. "Such as loading the dishwasher?"

He rose from the table and came to her, but instead of taking the dirty plate as she had anticipated, he wrapped his arms around her waist from behind and nuzzled her neck. He murmured in her ear, "Opera, installing security cameras, loading dishwashers, kissing beautiful doctors. There's no end to my talent." He marched a row of light kisses up her neck.

Her breath caught, and she arched her neck and giggled as his feather-soft pecks tickled their way toward her ear.

"I thought of nothing else but kissing you all afternoon," he whispered. "Couldn't focus on my work one bit." He continued his slow exploration of her neck. "You're a beautiful distraction."

He squeezed her shoulders gently and then glided his hands slowly down her upper arms. Her pulse quickened, and she released a soft moan. With the lightest of touches, he worked his way down her forearms to her hands.

He suddenly jolted and let out a gasp. He jerked back his hand, now smeared with pasta sauce from the dirty lasagna plate she'd been holding. Engrossed in Marcus's tender kisses and caresses, she'd forgotten all about the pasta-smeared plate in her hand. She groaned.

Talk about a mood buster!

Her cheeks warmed, and she rushed to the kitchen with the slimy plate and returned with a damp dishcloth and wiped the sauce off his hand.

"I am so sorry, Marcus. You distracted me so much I forgot all about my dinner plate."

Marcus raised an index finger. "Distraction — another of my many talents."

She rolled her eyes and tossed the dirty dishcloth into the kitchen sink.

He touched her nose and grinned. "That, my dear, was a lousy aphrodisiac. Next time, how about scented candles and soft music?" He then drew her to his chest and whispered, "Let's forget about the dishes for now, shall we?"

Before she could reply, his lips claimed hers, at first softly, and then with more passion. She raked her fingers through his hair and tugged his head closer. As he molded his body to hers, she felt his heart hammering. Thankfully, Gus and Trixie lay curled up together on Trixie's bed sound asleep. No doubt they were exhausted from their long hike.

Marcus kissed her neck and murmured in her ear, "Right now, I'm dying for dessert, and nothing is sweeter than your kisses."

She froze then pulled back to stare at him.

Seriously? How dumb does he think I am?

She shook her head and tsked at him.

"What?" he said, as though puzzled at her less than thrilled reaction to his sweet nothings.

Arms crossed she demanded, "Did that sappy line work with Brittany?"

He grinned sheepishly. "Every time."

She wagged a playful finger at him. "A lame line like that will not work on me, bucko."

Marcus's shoulders sagged in exaggerated despair. "I suppose I'll have to recite Robert Barrett Browning to win your favor, my lady?"

She grabbed his shirt and tugged him close. "A Shakespearean sonnet — in perfect iambic pentameter," she teased.

She fingered his chiseled chin and drank in the dark chocolate of his eyes.

I wish I could savor this moment forever.

Molding herself to him, her lips claimed his, until she had to pull away breathless and tingly all over. "You *are* a man of hidden talents," she whispered. "Your kisses make me weak in the knees."

Marcus grinned. "Hey! If I proved I can kiss, just imagine how good I'll be with security cameras and power tools. Vroom! Vroom!" He pretended to hold a chain saw.

She rolled her eyes, unable to suppress a chuckle.

Suddenly, the deafening crash of shattering glass imploded in the living room. Trixie and Gus leaped from their bed barking. Libby and Marcus ran into the living room, and their mouths dropped in shock. There, in the middle of the living room, lay a cement cinderblock. Glass fragments covered the couch, piano, and coffee table. Larger, sharp-edged shards of the broken window littered the hardwood floor and Oriental rug.

Marcus glanced out the window then dashed out the front door in hot pursuit of the perpetrator. Libby followed close behind. They scanned the parking lot to her townhouse but saw no one.

Whoever threw that cinderblock *had* to have been here only moments earlier.

Suddenly, tires squealed, and a white pick-up truck zoomed away. The perpetrator had purposely parked a distance away so no one couldn't catch a close-up of his face—or license plate. They chased after the truck but were only able to make out the first two letters of his license plate: T7. Libby did notice the driver's head nearly reached the roof of the truck, suggesting he was tall—like Roger. She yanked her phone from her pocket, dialed Metro police, and requested Julius be sent since he was familiar with the case. They hurried back inside to wait for the police.

Brandy must have heard the deafening crash because she pounded on Libby's door. "Libby, are you okay? What has that SOB done to you?"

Libby let her in, and they cautiously tiptoed around the broken glass to reach the kitchen. Marcus carried the dogs into the bedroom and shut the door, so they wouldn't cut their paws on the sharp shards of glass.

After introducing Marcus to Brandy, Marcus offered to clean up the mess while Libby filled Brandy in on what had happened. He grabbed the broom and dustpan and headed for the living room.

As the two women settled into kitchen chairs, Libby inquired, "Why didn't you call me after you and Julius returned from Chattanooga? I've been dying to hear with you found out."

"We didn't get back to Nashville until two in the morning, so I didn't want to wake you. I decided to wait until Julius uncovered something worth telling."

Libby's shoulders sagged. "Does that mean you didn't see any signs of Roger?"

"None."

"He wasn't living at his registered apartment in Chattanooga?"

Brandy shook her head. "No, and we checked the place three times over the course of the day just to be sure. No sign of him or his vehicle." She raised a finger. "And get this—his mailbox was crammed with unopened mail, some of it postmarked for six weeks earlier."

"Which suggests he left Chattanooga a while ago."

Brandy pointed at her. "Exactly, but when Julius called the parole officer, the guy didn't answer, and his voice mailbox was full. When Julius couldn't leave him a message, he called the guy's workplace, and they said Roger's parole officer had called in sick with the flu every day for the last two weeks."

Libby gripped the arms of her chair. "Which means he was too sick to check in with Roger and make sure he was staying out of trouble."

"Our thoughts exactly, so Julius rang up the Chattanooga Chief of Police, and the guy promised to look into it and get back to us. So far, we haven't heard a word."

"We?" Libby smiled. "So, you and Julius are a 'we' now?" Libby knew her friend was probably dying to tell all.

Brandy touched Libby's arm and grinned. "Girl, I hate that I met Julius because of your misery, but OMG, that boy is fine!"

Marcus entered the kitchen with a dustpan full of glass shards just as Julius's cruiser sped into a parking place out front.

Brandy and Libby met him at the door and ushered him in. After Julius inspected the crime scene and scribbled down the details of the smashed window, he snapped pictures and documented Marcus's description of the get-away truck.

Brandy asked, "Did you ever hear back from Roger's parole officer or the Chattanooga Chief of Police?"

"Parole officer?" Marcus turned to Libby with widened eyes. "Who is this Roger?"

Libby ignored Marcus's question, as she was desperate to find out Roger's whereabouts. "What did you find out, Julius?"

Julius shifted his weight and stared at the floor. "You're not going to like what I found out. Not at all."

"What do you mean?" Libby asked, already dreading his response. Since she already knew Roger had hightailed it out of Chattanooga and straight to Nashville—or more specifically, to her picture window—what could be worse than that?

Julius released a weary sigh. "When Brandy and I saw no signs of this Roger Anderson at the address he listed on the sex offender registry, and when his parole officer wouldn't return my calls, I called the Chattanooga Chief of Police."

"Sex offender registry?" Marcus whipped his head around to face Libby. "What's he talking about? What sex offender registry? And will someone please tell me who Roger Anderson is?"

Libby mumbled to Marcus, "I'll tell you later." She then gestured for Julius to continue.

"The Chief of Police obtained an emergency search warrant to inspect Anderson's apartment."

"And..." Libby said impatiently.

Julius adjusted his glasses, grimaced, then dropped the bombshell. "Unfortunately, he found Anderson's parole officer dead on the floor. Strangled."

Libby gasped, and her hand flew to her mouth. "What?"

"*What?*" Brandy's eyes grew bigger than moon pies.

Julius shifted his weight. "Not surprisingly, Anderson was nowhere to be found."

The blood drained from Libby's body, and she forced herself to sink onto the couch.

Julius continued. "No one has seen or heard a thing from Anderson in over three weeks. The parole officer's body was apparently already decomposing when it was found. The coroner places the murder around six weeks ago."

As Libby absorbed the news, her stomach heaved. Six weeks — just long enough for Roger to travel to Nashville, break into her medical office, and contaminate the chemo with aflatoxin. Anyone who would strangle his parole officer would not be above poisoning patients. Roger was behind the contaminated chemotherapy — especially since no other cases of aflatoxin poisoning had cropped up.

"Wait! Time out." Marcus created a "T" with his hands. "Would somebody *please* tell me who Roger Anderson is?" Marcus gazed back and forth between Libby and Julius.

Julius turned toward Libby with a startled expression that said, "You haven't told your boyfriend about Roger yet?"

Julius stared down at his feet and said nothing, clearly not wanting to be the one to divulge Libby's secret.

"Sorry, Libby. I assumed he knew," he mumbled.

Her face burned with embarrassment.

This is what I get for trying to hide my past from Marcus — busted.

Unable to look Marcus in the eyes, Libby stared at her nails and began to pick at a hangnail. "Roger Anderson is a guy from my childhood. He went to prison twenty years ago, but he was recently released on parole. Since I testified against him in court, he could be seeking revenge."

Marcus's eyes widened. "*Twenty years?* What did he do to you?" Then, as though subtracting twenty years from Libby's current age and combining it with Julius's comment about the sex offender registry, Marcus's voice softened with sudden understanding. "Oh, Libby." He reached for her, pulled her into his arms. "That's what you were trying to tell me when Mom barged in on us, wasn't it?"

She nodded, her eyes brimming with tears.

Marcus turned to Julius, worry lines creasing his forehead. "And now you're telling me this convicted pedophile has murdered his parole officer and gone AWOL?"

Julius adjusted his glasses. "Pretty much."

The room went silent as the unsavory news sank in.

Julius glanced around as though waiting until everyone had processed the unwelcome news before continuing with more details. "Turns out, someone *claiming* to be James called the parole office every day saying he was too sick to make it into work."

"Which we now know was Anderson trying to cover up the murder," Marcus surmised.

Julius nodded.

"Exactly," he said. "Anderson used a cheap pay-by-the-minute tracker phone, so there was no way to trace the call. When I spoke with the police chief to complain about James not returning my phone calls, he immediately became concerned because James was a top-notch parole officer who never missed work, and who never ignored phone calls — even when he was sick."

"What was James doing at Anderson's apartment?" Marcus inquired.

"According to James's last recorded computer entry, Anderson had not checked in for three weeks in a row, and he had ignored James's phone calls, so James became concerned and decided to go directly to Roger's apartment to see if he was there."

"Big mistake, that," Marcus mumbled.

Julius nodded. "You got that right. Since James was single and Anderson was calling the office every day with an alibi for why James was not at work, no one suspected anything."

Brandy dropped to the couch as though in shock. "So, the guy who just threw a cinderblock through Libby's window strangled his parole officer?" She glanced up at Julius and added, "I can't believe we went to his apartment three times, and the whole time that poor parole officer was lying there dead."

Julius said nothing, but his lips thinned, and a hint of tears glistened in his eyes. "James died because he went above and beyond the call of duty trying to keep the public safe."

Guilt settled in Libby's chest. James died trying to keep her safe.

"Does Anderson drive a white pick-up truck with a license plate that starts with T7, by any chance?" Marcus inquired.

"I don't know, but I can check." Julius pulled out his I-pad and quickly zoomed into the registry then pointed at the screen. "Bingo. T7R846."

He nodded grimly. "At least now we know where he is. Thirty minutes ago, I assumed he'd probably hightailed it to some remote corner of North Dakota or Wyoming to avoid arrest." Gesturing toward Libby's broken front window, he added, "This shows he's becoming progressively more unbalanced."

Swell! Any more cheery news to make my day?

Noting Libby's stricken face, Julius reassured her. "Don't worry. After murdering a parole officer, Anderson is enemy number one on the Tennessee Most Wanted list. We know his truck and license number, so if he keeps driving around, we'll catch him in the next few hours."

"I certainly hope so. If this guy has it in for Libby, he could easily break in and..." Marcus squeezed Libby's shoulder. "Well, we won't go there." He then informed Libby, "No way are you sleeping here tonight."

"Absolutely not," Julius agreed.

Libby snorted.

Sleep? Fat chance I'll ever sleep again — not with Roger skulking about.

Just the thought of him mere feet from her living room after murdering a parole officer, made her insides quiver.

A wave of nausea coursed through her. She sucked in a slow breath, determined to remain calm.

Julius gathered up his supplies and pointed a finger at Libby. "Do not enter this townhouse — not even to get fresh clothes — unless Marcus or I escort you in. Roger could sneak in here while you're at work and hole up in a closet or behind a shower curtain just waiting to nab you."

Libby's spine stiffened. She hadn't thought of that frightening possibility!

"If you see any sign of him, call me. Day or night," Julius instructed. He handed Libby and Marcus a business card. "I don't need to tell you Anderson is extremely dangerous. And volatile. I read his prison record, and he is still hostile about his incarceration. He sees himself as the victim rather than the perpetrator. We're committed to a full-press manhunt, but until we catch him, you must remain vigilant at all times."

"I'll keep a close eye on her. I promise," Marcus said.

After Julius left, Libby leaned her back against the couch, too numb to speak. A terrifying thought circled in her brain like a broken record.

Roger killed his parole officer, and now he's after you.

Meanwhile, Brandy called the landlord to report Libby's shattered window. She vacuumed up the smaller tidbits of glass scattered on the floor, couch, and piano, while Marcus picked up and disposed of another dustpan of larger chunks.

Paralyzed with fear, Libby couldn't muster the strength to stand, let alone clean up the mess.

Her legs quivered so much she wasn't sure they would support her. The broken record repeated itself in her mind:

Roger killed his parole officer, and now he's after you.

Marcus placed a cold rag on her forehead and handed her some ice water. "Drink this."

Like an obedient child, she took the glass with trembling hands and drained it. She handed the empty glass back to Marcus, still too traumatized to utter a word.

Once the living room was back in order, Brandy tried to reassure Libby. "Don't worry—Julius will track him down quicker than a dog can catch a rabbit." She hugged Libby and insisted, "Call me, day or night, for any reason, and I'll come running, I promise." She then left.

Marcus sank onto the couch next to Libby and pulled her into the safety of his arms. He held her close and rocked her gently, soothingly, until her trembling quieted.

She couldn't force herself to make eye contact with him.

A cacophony of fear swirled in Libby's brain. Marcus knew her secret. What did he think of her now?

Roger killed his parole officer, and now he's after you.

The ugly refrain swirled and churned in her brain, refusing to leave.

Marcus gently tipped up her chin and forced her to look at him. "Libby, if we're going to have a relationship, we don't need secrets between us. I need to know what you're feeling right now."

He gripped her hands. "I need to know about your past—not to judge you—but to understand you and to help you cope with all this."

When she said nothing, he continued. "You're clearly in shock, and what happened twenty years ago had a profound impact on you. If I don't know the traumas of your past, I can't guard your heart and minister to your future."

Her eyes pooled. Something about his tenderness uncapped her safety valve, and she released a gut-wrenching sob. He pulled her closer and rubbed soothing circles on her back. "It's okay. Let it out. I'm here," he whispered.

She soaked his shirt with her despair and clung to him, her head cradled into his neck. She finally squeaked out, "I didn't tell you because I thought you'd blame me—like so many other people did."

He caressed her cheek. "Libby, you were twelve-years-old, and you'd just lost your mother. You were vulnerable and lonely—the perfect target for a sexual predator. You have nothing to feel ashamed about because you did nothing wrong."

"I know that in my head, but in my heart, I still blame myself for not telling my dad sooner. I should have ignored Roger's threats and—"

"Shhh," he said softly, combing away the wet curls stuck to her face. "Give yourself a break. We all have 20:20 hindsight."

"But I *knew* what I let Roger do to me was wrong. I *knew* my mother wouldn't approve. But I did it anyway because..." She burst into sobs. "Because he manipulated me and got me emotionally dependent on him."

Marcus brushed the tears off her cheek and handed her a facial tissue from the box on the end table.

After composing herself and blowing her nose, she continued. "My dad worked crazy long hours to escape his grief, and my friends didn't know how to handle my sadness, so they just quit calling. I felt so alone and abandoned."

"I'll bet."

"I guess it's not surprising that when Roger befriended me and acted as though he cared about me, I was easy prey. Plus, in the beginning, he was nice to me."

"In a sick, desperate way, he filled a void left by your mother's death," Marcus commented

"Until it all went south." She clenched her jaw. "I can't believe I put up with his sleazy demands."

She twisted the Kleenex in her fingers. "I hated all the stuff he coerced me to do, but when I tried to resist, he blamed *me* for tempting him. He threatened to tell my father and all the kids in the youth group that I was a tease who had come on to *him*. He even threatened to report my father for neglect. Claimed I'd wind up in foster care."

He shook his head. "Right now, I feel like punching that guy into oblivion."

She dabbed her eyes. "You and me both."

"How'd you meet him?"

Her shoulders sagged. "Sadly, he was my church youth group leader, so I assumed I could trust him and his concern for me was genuine."

"These guys are master manipulators. He singled you out because your mother died, and you were lonely. He found his perfect target."

Libby picked at a hangnail, causing it to bleed. "I wasn't his only victim. He went after another girl in the youth group whose parents were going through a nasty divorce."

Marcus's lips thinned. "There's a special place in Hell for low-life like that."

"By the time the police investigation was over, five girls from my youth group confessed that Roger had inappropriately touched them or said things that made them uncomfortable."

His eyes widened. "Five?"

She nodded. "Unfortunately, he fully violated Kristen — the girl whose parents were going through a divorce." Libby's eyes pooled. "Marcus, she was only twelve when he coerced her into sex, and she's been a mess ever since."

"How so?" he asked.

"She's been divorced three times already, and she's spent several stints in rehab for heroin addiction." She twisted her Kleenex. "I'm glad I never let Roger go all the way with me. He wanted me to — pressured me to — but I wouldn't let him."

Marcus grabbed both her hands and squeezed. "Libby, even if you had, it wouldn't change my feelings for you. Roger preyed on your vulnerability."

"Colin said I should have told my dad and called the cops the first time he touched me. He implied I must have secretly *liked* what he did to me, or I wouldn't have put up with it."

"Then Colin doesn't understand pedophilia. Look, maybe you *could* have done things differently, but you didn't — because at age twelve you didn't have the emotional maturity to know how to stand up to a first-rate sexual predator."

She chewed her lower lip.

"You were a victim, and if Colin didn't get that, he's an idiot."

His lips tightened. "And a heartless cad, I might add." He tipped up her chin, forcing her to look him in the eyes. "You've done nothing to be ashamed of, and it's time you forgave yourself for not speaking up sooner."

She dropped her gaze to her hands. "That's what my counselor said, and most of the time, I believe it."

"Libby, do you think God *wants* you to live the rest of your life afraid to open up or trust people?"

She shook her head. "I'm sure He doesn't."

He squeezed her hands. "After I messed up with Brittany, I had to ask God to forgive me. Jesus died not just to forgive us, but to free us from *ourselves*—from our guilt, our false guilt, our shame, and our past mistakes."

"Hmm. I've never thought of it like that before."

"He wants you to move on with your life free from emotional baggage, so you can better serve Him."

"I know you're right, and I want to," she said, brushing the tears from her cheek. "Will you pray with me?"

He gripped both her hands and offered up a heartfelt prayer. Libby added a desperate plea for God to help her move forward in freedom. When they finished, Marcus hugged her close. "You did it! See! That wasn't so hard!"

She grinned, suddenly feeling ten pounds lighter. "You know something? I feel free for the first time in twenty years, which makes no sense at all with Roger out to get me."

He smiled.

She shook her head. "I can't believe I told you all that heavy junk from my past, and you're okay with it. Colin sure wasn't."

Marcus chuckled. "Since I nearly married an identity thief, I won't be casting any stones!"

Libby glanced at her watch. "It's way past midnight. Let me pack up a suitcase, so I can spend the night at the nearby Hampton Inn."

"Why don't you sleep on my couch?"

"Because Roger has likely followed me to your place, so he knows where you live, too."

Marcus rubbed his chin. "You probably do need to stay someplace new."

"Besides, if I stay at a different motel every night, it will keep him off-guard. Plus, he'll be less likely to hurt me in a public hotel — too many witnesses around to hear or see what he does."

"Good point. With any luck, the cops will track him down in the next few hours, and then this nightmare will be over."

Marcus offered to keep Trixie for the night so Libby wouldn't have to bring the addled pup to a motel room.

After loading the dogs into his Mini-Cooper, Marcus followed Libby to the Hampton Inn to ensure Roger wasn't trailing her. No sign of a white truck behind them.

It was well after one in the morning before Libby finally flopped into bed, though she knew her eyes would never close. Not until Roger was caught.

Please, God, keep me safe.

CHAPTER 19

Marcus lugged two security cameras and his toolbox out of the elevator and into Libby's office. After carting the unwieldy boxes through the waiting room, he plopped them onto a table in the business office. "I'll have these babies put together and running in no time," he insisted, with an air of confidence he hoped belied his total inexperience. "John Q. Handyman, at your service." He bowed at the waist.

Libby's eyebrow rose as though unconvinced. "You sure you know how to assemble them?"

He shrugged. "How hard can it be?"

Was that a smirk on her face?

Thankfully, she refrained from snide remarks. Instead, she opened the boxes and helped him pull out and arrange all the pieces embedded in Styrofoam.

Marcus stared down at the umpteen tubes and bolts and screws and unidentifiable pieces and tried to ignore his growing panic. He hadn't anticipated such a complex assembly process. He only hoped the salesman who sold him the cameras hadn't lied through his teeth when he insisted the installation would be a snap. He'd even snapped his fingers.

Marcus pawed around the boxes until he found the directions.

He handed the instructions to Libby and asked her to read them aloud while he assembled the camera.

Libby cleared her throat. "Using a Phillips-head screwdriver—"

He jerked his head up. "A *Phillips-head*?" He dug through his meager toolbox and held up his lowly one-pronged version. "This one won't work. What size bit do they recommend?"

She shrugged. "It just says, 'Phillips-head screwdriver.'"

Marcus snatched the instructions from her hands. "Give me those!" After skimming them, he sputtered, "Why doesn't it tell me what size bit to use? And why didn't that good-for-nothing salesman *tell* me I needed a Phillips-head screwdriver?" He eyed her pocketbook on the table. "Don't suppose you carry a Phillips-head screwdriver with bits of every conceivable size in there, do you?"

She laughed. "No, but *I* never claimed to be John Q. Handyman."

He wagged a scolding finger at her and chuckled. "Don't go there with me, missy."

He flung the worthless directions into the air. "No pictures, no diagrams, and they don't even say what bit size to use. I ought to sue whoever wrote these useless instructions." He lifted a long, narrow, plastic tube as though it were incriminating courtroom evidence. "What the devil is this thing? And where does it go?"

"Guess you should have brought your *Electronics for Dummies* book, huh?"

Hands on his hips, he released a frustrated sigh.

"That snake-in-the-grass salesman insisted a third-grader could install this thing, but I don't think Bill Gates could get it up and running."

He pulled out his cell phone and snapped pictures of all the parts. He then snatched up the instructions and headed toward the door. "I'm going back to the store to pick up a Phillip-head screwdriver. And to wring the neck of that salesman. Bail me out of jail, will you?"

She chuckled and wished him luck.

"Wait, you're coming with me."

"No, I've got way too much paperwork to get done. You'll be back in thirty minutes."

He frowned, not happy with her answer, but she insisted she couldn't waste time making another trip to the hardware store when she had charting to do.

"Make sure you lock the door the second I leave and keep your phone handy."

She raised three fingers. "Scouts honor."

* * *

Libby pitied the poor salesclerk who had to face a hotter-than-Hades Marcus Romano. Judging from his paltry toolbox, Marcus didn't have a home improvement bone in his body, though apparently, he'd be the last to admit it.

With Marcus gone, she locked the front door of her office then settled into her leather office chair to dive into the two disability forms she'd procrastinated completing all week.

She'd just finished the first form when she heard the front door open.

That's odd. I know I re-locked it after Marcus left, and it's too soon for him to be back.

She heard footsteps approaching.

It's probably just the janitor.

Her hammering heart wasn't convinced, however.

The footfalls closed in on her private office. It couldn't be the cleaning crew, or she'd have heard thumping trashcans or the vroom of a vacuum.

She wiped damp palms on her trousers. Someone had broken into her office. What now? Confront him or hide under her desk? Perhaps she could scare him away by making her presence known.

What if it's Roger, and he's brandishing a gun?

She grabbed her cell phone and pepper spray and crawled under her desk. With shaking fingers, she texted Julius a frantic message then dialed 911. She whispered her address to the dispatcher and pleaded, "Please hurry. If it's Roger Anderson, I'm in imminent danger."

What now?

A noise came from the hallway—like someone had opened a door.

Was he entering her chemotherapy drug closet?

Heart pounding like a kettledrum, she crawled out from under her desk and tiptoed to the doorway to take a peek. Peering around her door into the hall, she noticed the door to her chemotherapy closet was now open. She had left it closed. Someone had broken into her office, and now he had entered her chemotherapy storage room. If only Marcus's security cameras had been up and running...

Clutching her pepper spray with shaking fingers, she extended her arm in front of her as though it were a gun ready to fire. As she passed an exam room, she grabbed an IV pole. If she had to, she could wallop him with it. It wasn't much of a weapon, but it beat having nothing.

"Who's in there?" she shouted, failing in her attempt to sound commanding.

Silence.

"I'm armed, and I've called the cops, so you better leave right now."

No response.

She inched closer to the storage room then heard the slam of a closing back door. The intruder had escaped out the back door of her storage room, which exited into the main lobby of the building.

She dashed after him hoping to snap a photo with her cell phone. But she was too late. She heard feet galloping down the stairs as though escaping a burning building. Whoever it was clearly hadn't come to nab her, or he wouldn't have bolted. Which meant he hadn't counted on her being in the office at eight o'clock at night. He could only have come for one reason: to poison the chemotherapy — again.

What better way to get back at Libby than to poison her patients and make her take the blame for it?

Libby hurried back to her waiting room and locked the door behind her — though she didn't know why since Roger obviously knew how to pick a lock. She leaned against the door, her legs weak and trembly. She forced herself to sit down and suck in slow, calming breaths.

Stay calm. Julius and Marcus will be here any minute.

She gripped the arms of her chair and willed herself to stay conscious. Her heart thudded faster than a metronome gone berserk.

It has to be Roger.

The doorknob rattled.

"Who's there?" she hollered.

"Marcus. Who else would it be?"

She dashed to the door, unlocked it, pulled him inside, and relocked the door.

One look at Libby's face, and Marcus dropped his shopping bag and pulled her into his arms. "Libby? What on earth? You look like you've seen a ghost!"

She clutched his arms. "Worse. Roger."

"Roger?" His eyes widened in horror. "Roger was here?"

"I didn't see his face. I just heard someone rummaging around in the storage room. As soon as I informed him that I'd called the cops, he bolted."

Marcus's brow creased with worry. "How'd he get in? We locked up when I left."

"Same way he did the first time he poisoned my chemo. He picked the lock."

Marcus gripped her shoulders, his eyes beseeching hers. "You never actually *saw* Roger, correct? You just heard someone sneaking around?"

"I never saw his face. I just heard him prowling around the drug storage area."

Marcus raked a hand through his hair. "I saw a janitor out in the lobby emptying the trash. Wonder if he caught a glimpse of anyone suspicious in the building?"

Her shoulders sagged. "Carlos only speaks Spanish, so he can't help us."

Marcus grinned. "Hablo espanol con fluidez."

Her face lit up. "You speak Spanish?"

"Muy bien, Senorita."

Arms akimbo she asked, "Another of your hidden talents, I suppose?"

"Si."

"Then, let's go talk to Carlos."

They hurried to the lobby, and soon he and Marcus were conversing at such a rapid speed that Libby's two years of high school Spanish proved useless.

Marcus pulled out his wallet and handed the janitor a business card. Smiles, hand gestures, a pat on the back, and then Marcus said, "Muchas gracias, mi amigo."

She had to admit, she was impressed. As they wandered back into her office, she asked, "Where'd you learn to speak Spanish so fluently?"

"My dad sponsored mission trips to South and Central America every summer. I learned by immersion."

She smiled at him. "There's no end to your talents, is there?"

"Eso es correcto, Senorita."

She whacked his belly. "Quit being a show-off and tell me what he said."

Marcus released a heavy sigh. "Unfortunately, he didn't see anyone because he was cleaning the office next door, but he promised to keep watch and call me, hospital security, and Metro police if he sees anyone who fits Roger's description in or around your office. Carlos may be the best friend we have. He cleans your suite five nights a week, so I feel safer knowing he's in the building when you're here finishing up your charting.

He gave me his phone number for you to call if you see or hear anything suspicious."

She eyed the shopping bag Marcus had dropped on the floor. "Any luck tracking down the clerk who sold you the security cameras?"

Marcus scowled. "His shift conveniently ended right before I came back into the store."

"Either that or he was hiding in a bathroom stall fearing for his life."

Marcus chuckled. "You're probably right. I was ready to clobber him. Luckily, another clerk talked me through the assembly process."

Libby glanced at her watch and frowned. "What's taking Julius so long? I called twenty minutes ago."

"He's probably tied up with another case. He is one busy detective." Marcus headed into the business office, where the security camera pieces lay strewn across the table. He yanked the Phillips-head screwdriver from his bag and waved it at her. "Now that I have the proper tools, I'll have this thing up in no time."

She wrapped her arms around his waist and hugged him. "I have full confidence in you."

"John Q. Handyman will get this camera running before another villain comes to frighten my damsel-in-distress."

She rolled her eyes. "Please tell me you never used *that* pitiful line on Brittany!"

Marcus mumbled something unintelligible and tugged out the instructions for assembly from his back pocket. "If only I'd had this thing up an hour ago—we could have caught him red-handed."

Libby thumped her forehead. "Wait! We *did* catch him red-handed! Literally."

Marcus stared at her blankly. "We did?"

"Fingerprints! He left his fingerprints on the doorknob of the door entering the storage closet. Unless he was wearing gloves, Julius might be able to lift prints."

"You're sure you didn't touch the knob and contaminate the prints?"

"Positive. He left the door open, so I didn't need to touch it."

* * *

Twenty minutes later, Marcus gave up on installing the security camera. "This thing must be defective. Or missing pieces." His lips tightened with frustration.

Right! Libby chomped on the inside of her cheeks and said nothing. Marcus had aced the Bar exam and spoke fluent Spanish, but he couldn't follow simple written instructions. Pitiful! Not wanting to humiliate him, however, she played along that the camera must be missing pieces. Plus, he looked ready to punch a hole in her wall.

She'd just have to hire someone who knew what he was doing. Or, she could probably figure it out herself once Marcus was gone.

When Julius arrived, Libby wanted to hug him. She escorted him to the chemotherapy storage room and enlightened him on the events of the evening. Marcus stood beside her with his arm wrapped protectively around her shoulders. After hearing the story, Julius agreed it was most likely Roger.

"But we shouldn't rule out random drug addicts looking for narcotics," he added. "After all, you *are* a cancer doctor." He pointed to a wall cabinet. "You keep any pain meds in there? Oxycontin? Morphine? Percocet? Lortab?"

"None," Libby insisted. "Just chemo and nausea meds."

Julius thumped his pad and frowned. "I've had crooks break into doctors' offices to steal pain meds and petty cash. But chemotherapy? Ain't much street value for drugs that make you puke and lose your hair."

"Except an addict or drug dealer might *assume*, as you did, that a cancer doctor's office would be loaded with narcotic pain meds," Marcus pointed out.

"True," Julius said, rubbing his chin. "It's most likely Roger, but we shouldn't rule out anyone since Libby didn't actually *see* the face of the intruder.

Marcus turned to look at Libby. "Though if it had been Roger, he most likely would have..." Seeing Libby's stricken face, he added, "We won't think about what he might have done."

Julius twiddled his pen. "Whoever did this knows how to pick a lock. That suggests a professional and not some punk kid."

"Can you lift fresh prints from the doorknob," Libby asked. "I've cleaned the doorknobs every night after work so they would be free of contamination just in case he did break in."

Julius nodded. "If Roger's fingers gripped the knob securely, we might be able to lift some prints, and that would confirm he'd been here, which violates the terms of his parole."

He shook his head. "Not that his rap sheet isn't long enough already after murdering his parole officer."

Julius pulled out his cell phone. "I'll get the team up here to lift prints."

Libby felt Marcus's grip tighten on her shoulder. "The sooner, the better. Libby isn't safe until he's caught."

"No, she's not," Julius agreed, his face grim. "She shouldn't have been left alone in this office. Not even for a minute." Julius's lips thinned with displeasure. "I thought I made that clear."

Libby hung her head in shame. "Julius, I could have gone with Marcus — *should* have gone with Marcus — but I wanted to finish up some important paperwork."

Julius offered a scolding shake of the head. "And that worked out well, didn't it?"

"I guess I thought I'd be okay for the few minutes Marcus was gone."

"But you weren't okay, were you?" He pushed up his glasses and frowned. "Look, I care about you, and your life is in jeopardy. You must be cautious — paranoid even — or you might not live to *see* a next time."

CHAPTER 20

The murder investigation lived in limbo for over three weeks, as detectives searched in vain for Roger. "It's like he just up and disappeared," Julius lamented.

Thankfully, the toxicology report came back proving that all of the medications in Libby's drug closet were uncontaminated with aflatoxin. Melissa's husband, Doug, installed the security cameras in ten minutes flat. No pieces were missing. Libby had to smile at Marcus's handyman ineptitude, but she kept the ease with which Doug had installed the cameras to herself.

Marcus displayed his true talent by composing a scathing letter to Banderbaxy Pharmaceuticals about their abysmal customer service. He also wrote a certified letter to Dr. Patel, the current head of the CDSCO, requesting an unannounced factory inspection of the facility that produced his mother's chemotherapy. While he knew there was a greater chance that Roger, and not Banderbaxy, was behind the tainted chemotherapy, for the sake of other patients worldwide, he needed to eliminate factory contamination as the cause of the aflatoxin. He also kept in regular contact with Scott at the FDA.

Since no other cases of aflatoxin poisoning had been reported to the FDA, Scott still suspected an inside job at Libby's office.

Thankfully, Sophia's jaundice and itchiness were finally becoming a thing of the past. She now boasted, "You can't kill a tough old bird like me—not even with poison."

Libby eliminated her embezzling ex-employee, Cynthia, from the suspect list with a few inquiring phone calls. Cynthia, it turned out, had moved to Texas one month *before* the aflatoxin poisoning and was now gainfully employed again. Pity the new boss.

To relieve stress, Marcus and Libby trekked Percy Warner Park with Trixie and Gus after work each day. With enough doggie bribes, Trixie could now sit on command and even heel—when she chose to.

After their hike, Trixie and Gus tug-of-warred over a mutually desired knotted rope while Libby and Marcus enjoyed dinner together at Marcus's house. Libby then headed back to her new digs at the Hampton Inn.

One Sunday after church, Sophia invited them to enjoy her homemade manicotti. Over lunch, she regaled Libby with stories about the mission trips their church sponsored every year in the Dominican Republic. Libby nestled on the couch between Marcus and Sophia as they flipped through pictures showing the church, school, and orphanage in the impoverished community.

Another photo, snapped at a huge Romano family reunion, featured over fifty Romanos from four generations back, all laughing and smiling over plates of spaghetti. The black-haired, brown-eyed Italians shared a remarkable resemblance.

As Libby turned page after page of photos with Marcus and his huge extended Italian family, tears filled her eyes.

What I would have given for a childhood like that.

She couldn't imagine being enveloped by the love of a caring extended family.

A photo at the end of the scrapbook displayed Marcus with his arm wrapped around a gorgeous blond with huge, cornflower blue eyes.

She pointed at the buxom beauty cozied up next to Marcus. "That's Brittany, isn't it?" No wonder Marcus drooled over the woman — she was a regular Christie Brinkley.

Sophia jabbed a finger at the picture, her lips thin. "I should have burned that picture. I don't want anything that reminds me of that she-devil in my house." She thumped the picture again. "That Jezebel used her feminine wiles to seduce my son."

Marcus rolled his eyes. "Ma, it takes two to tango, you know." He peered over at Libby and must have sensed her insecurity, for he snapped the scrapbook shut and returned it to the bookcase. "I'm sure we've bored Libby long enough with all these family photos."

Libby protested and insisted she loved getting better acquainted with his family. But a cloud of sadness hung over her.

You have no family. You're all alone.

She scolded herself for her self-pity. She was blessed with good health, a wonderful boyfriend, a job she enjoyed, salvation, wonderful friends like Melissa and Brandy, and an adorable puppy.

Focus on all the blessings you do have.

As though sensing Libby's insecurity, Sophia insisted on snapping a photo with Libby, Marcus, and the two dogs curled at their feet.

"I'll get you a copy, and we'll replace Brittany's photo with this one in the scrapbook," Sophia insisted.

Around ten, Marcus drove Libby and Trixie back to her motel unit and walked them to the door.

Marcus touched her cheek with his hand. "After losing your parents, I could tell hearing about my large family rubbed salt in your wounds."

"I guess I do feel envious of people with large, loving families."

He chuckled. "Sometimes, I felt suffocated by all my noisy, meddling relatives."

They pointed fingers at each other and said simultaneously, "The grass is always greener on the other side."

* * *

Libby bolted awake to the sound of Trixie barking. She glanced at the clock. Midnight.

What is she barking at?

Jumping from the bed, she raced to the window where Trixie circled and barked frantically.

"What is it, girl?" She patted the addled pooch and yanked the drapes apart to peer out the window. "Did you hear something?"

Her heart hammered as she grabbed her phone from her nightstand just in case.

Trixie howled and paced and growled and scratched at the window. Libby eyed the parking lot outside her motel unit, but she saw nothing.

Only the hum of traffic and the chirp of crickets permeated the night air.

"Quiet, Trixie! People are trying to sleep."

Hoping to shush her boisterous canine before guests in the unit next door pounded on the wall and hollered at her to pipe down, she ushered Trixie onto her bed.

She double-checked her locks, dragged a bulky dresser in front of the door to act as a barricade, and lined her phone and pepper spray within easy reach on her nightstand.

Trixie spun in circles on Libby's bed for what seemed like an eternity before finally curling at the foot of the bed and sinking into slumber. Libby forced herself to lie down, but the pounding in her chest made sleep impossible.

What startled Trixie? Is it Roger?

She must have eventually fallen into a fitful doze because muffled voices and the slamming of car doors startled her awake. Trixie paced near the door needing to do her morning doggie duties.

Libby peeked outside the window, and seeing nothing suspicious, she removed her barricade from the door and hooked Trixie's leash to her collar.

After unlocking and opening her door, she cautiously eyed the parking lot again. Seeing no sign of Roger, she headed for the grassy meridian with Trixie. As she escorted Trixie past her car, she suddenly noticed all four tires were flat. Squatting to inspect them, her breath caught.

Large, jagged slash marks — as though someone had intentionally punctured all four tires with a butcher knife — terrified her.

Roger was outside her window with a butcher knife just hours ago.

She instinctively scanned her surroundings again, as though expecting Roger to leap out of the bushes and grab her.

That's why Trixie barked last night. She heard him stabbing the tires.

When Roger heard the barking, he must have hidden behind the car or in the bushes.

She then noticed a note tucked under her front windshield wiper. With shaking hands, she tugged out the note and read: **Payday is here.**

CHAPTER 21

Fingers of fear crept up her spine and settled into her chest, constricting her throat and threatening to suffocate her.

Don't panic.

She forced herself to inhale slow, steady breaths. She then dashed back into her room with Trixie and latched and locked the door behind her.

He's found me again. I'm not safe.

She collapsed onto the bed, terror coursing through her veins like an IV infusion of ice water.

She grabbed her phone off the nightstand and keyed in Marcus's number.

"I'm on my way," he said, once she clued him in. "Keep your door locked, and I'll call Julius."

Libby huddled with Trixie on the bed, counting the minutes until Marcus and Julius arrived. To think Roger had been right outside her door last night with a butcher knife!

As soon as Libby saw Marcus's car pull up, she ran outside and threw herself into his arms. He hugged her, and insisted, "You're okay," though the creases on his forehead belied his words. He inspected her car and snapped pictures of the lacerated tires with his phone camera. After skimming the ominous handwritten note, his lips tightened, but he said nothing.

Within minutes, Julius arrived wearing jeans and a T-shirt. "Sorry for the civilian duds." He gestured toward his Titans T-shirt. "I'm technically off-duty today, and I was eating pancakes at an IHOP when you called. I didn't want to take the time to go home and change."

"Julius, I'm sorry to call on your day off."

He raised a hand. "No, I'm glad you did. I've made it my mission to catch Anderson if it's the last thing I do." He shook his head in disgust. "And with that slippery eel, it may *be* the last thing I do.

After circling the car several times, he photographed the slashes and jotted down details for his report. He then inspected the window outside Libby's motel unit for signs of an attempted break-in. "Look here," he said, pointing to the window frame. "Crowbar marks and gouges on this side of the window. Since you had the door double bolted, he tried to break in through the window."

Libby's breath caught, and she gripped Marcus's arm. He must have felt her trembling because he wrapped a protective arm around her shoulders.

"That does it! You're moving in with Mom and me," Marcus said. "She's got a guest bedroom upstairs, and I'll sleep in my old room on the first floor. That way, I can keep watch over you both. You cannot stay by yourself — even in a motel unit — until Roger is caught. End of discussion."

"What if Roger isn't caught for weeks?" Libby protested.

Recovering from liver failure, the last thing Sophia needed was an uninvited guest — especially one being pursued by a psychopath!

She crossed her arms in protest. "I can't expect you and Sophia to hover around me like unpaid bodyguards. Plus, Trixie will destroy her remote controls, you know she will."

Marcus squatted down and scratched Trixie's neck talking to her in a sing-song-y voice. "Has Mama not broken you of your taste for remote controls? Well, that's okay, because you were a very good girl last night. You scared off that naughty Roger and protected your Mama. Yes, you did!"

Trixie licked his face, her tail wagging.

Ignoring Libby's protests that she'd be a bother, Julius said to Marcus, "I like your plan, man. Keep your woman safe."

Libby tapped her foot in annoyance. "Fine, but only if you get Sophia's permission first. I am not barging into her house, suitcase in hand, and announcing, 'Hi. I'm moving in.'"

Marcus raised a hand of surrender. "Fine! I'll clear it with Mom first, but I'm positive she won't mind."

Julius added, "When you drive to your mother's house, watch for any cars following you. You don't want to disclose where Sophia lives. We found Roger's white truck abandoned in a Wal-Mart parking lot last night, so he's most likely driving a stolen car now."

"Which means we don't know what kind of car to be watching for," Marcus said.

Julius pointed at Marcus with his pen. "Exactly. Watch for any car that seems to be trailing you. Take a zigzaggy route through wrong neighborhoods on your way to her house to try to put him off, just in case he's following you at a distance."

Libby's stomach clenched. "What do I do if a car *is* following me?"

His lips pursed, and he twiddled his pen. "Call me, put on your flashers, and drive straight to the nearest police station." He grinned. "I bet Roger won't follow you there!"

Libby chuckled. "I bet not! Great idea."

"I'll e-mail you the address of every police precinct in Nashville. You can print if off and keep it in your glove compartment, just in case."

He turned to Marcus. "What's your mother's address? I'll provide extra police surveillance around her house to discourage Roger from breaking in. If I were you, though, I'd notify all your neighbors about what is going on. Show them Roger's picture. That way, they'll be on the lookout when you aren't home. Neighborhood watch — one of the strongest crime-fighting tools we have."

Julius snapped more pictures of the gouges in the window ledge then typed a few more notes into his report. His parting words to Libby chilled her to the bone: "Libby, I've researched this Roger Anderson. He's a psychopath who blames you, not himself, for his past twenty years in prison. We don't know how far he'll go to punish you, but if stalking you, slashing tires, tainting chemotherapy, and attempting to break into your motel room are signs of his rage, you must *never* let yourself be alone until he is caught. I mean it."

Marcus gripped her arm and forced her to look at him. "Did you hear that, Libby? You cannot be left alone. Roger has tracked you everywhere you've gone."

Julius's eyes widened, and he thumped the side of his head with his palm. "Of course! Why didn't I think of it sooner?" He crawled onto his hands and knees and inspected the bottom side of Libby's car with a flashlight. "Bingo! Just as I expected! A tracking device."

Marcus and Libby squatted, and Julius pointed to a small tracking device that Roger had implanted on the bottom of Libby's car. "That's how he found you at this motel unit."

Marcus's spine stiffened. "Then he knows where *I* live, too, because Libby has eaten dinner at my place almost every night this week."

Julius rubbed his chin in thought. "Libby, have you driven your car to Marcus's mother's house? If so, you're not safe to stay there, either."

Marcus and Libby recounted their last several weeks. Luckily, they had only driven to Sophia's house in Marcus's car.

Marcus crawled underneath his car using his cell phone flashlight. "I better check my car too. I wouldn't put it past Anderson to put a tracer there, as well."

After disengaging the tracker from Libby's car, Julius crawled out from underneath the car and rubbed his palms on his jeans. "Check the bottom of your car every day to make sure Anderson hasn't attached a new tracking device while you're at work or sleeping. Get hospital security to keep an eye on your car while you're at work. Make them walk you to your car."

Marcus crawled out and brushed off the back of his jeans. "Nothing attached to my car."

Julius promised to get back with them as soon as he had any breakthrough in the case.

He shook hands with them both and climbed into his cruiser. He pointed a finger at Libby and admonished, "Do what I say, and I mean it."

* * *

Roger peeked between the drapes of a motel unit just two doors down from Libby's room and grinned.

Libby's dunce-of-a-boyfriend had missed the tracker device carefully hidden on the bottom of Marcus's car.

Think you can outsmart me? Think again!

He could track Libby down just as easily at the boyfriend's mother's house as here.

This was all just a teaser, anyhow.

He salivated in eager anticipation, as he envisioned the final, glorious show-down he had all mapped out— the final revenge that would make Libby pay for her betrayal once and for all.

Think I'm a psychopath? A slippery eel? Just you wait, pretty boy!

CHAPTER 22

Since it was a Saturday morning and not a workday, Marcus suggested they eat breakfast together and then buy four new tires. "We can take my car to buy the tires, then I'll replace them for you."

Remembering his disastrous ability at installing security cameras, she couldn't stop herself from asking, "You know how to change a flat?"

Marcus released a snort. "Seriously?" Arms akimbo, he demanded, "What kind of a wuss do you think I am? Just because I couldn't get that *defective* security camera to work, doesn't mean I can't change a tire."

She arched a brow. "Uh-huh. How many times have you done it before?"

He averted his eyes. "Well, to be honest, none. But how hard can it be? Jack up the car, loosen the bolts, pull off the tire, replace it with the spare, and tighten the bolts. Voila! Tire changed." He flung his arm with dramatic flair.

"If I remember correctly, that's what John Q. Handyman said about installing security cameras. 'How hard can it be?'" She etched quotation marks with her fingers and grinned across the table at him.

"Not the same thing at all," he retorted. "Changing a flat will be a piece of cake compared to installing those *defective* security cameras." He raised upturned palms. "Besides, think what you'll save in towing costs."

Libby made a mental note to drive straight to an auto shop after Marcus replaced her tires to ensure they wouldn't fall off in the middle of the highway. Brilliant, gorgeous, Vanderbilt-trained attorney? Absolutely. Handyman and grease monkey? Not so much!

They grabbed bagels and coffee at a diner across the street then scribbled down the exact make and model of Libby's car tires and climbed into Marcus's Mini-Cooper to head to the tire store. Still exhausted from her sleepless night, Libby ordered a coffee to go.

Merging onto the interstate, Marcus asked, "Libby, if Roger victimized five other girls and fully violated one of them, why is he only coming after you?"

"Because I was the only one willing to testify against him in front of a jury."

Marcus nodded and passed a slowpoke in the right lane. He reached across the front seat and squeezed her hand. "Can you fill me in a little more on what happened?"

Libby sucked in a breath, wishing she didn't have to dredge up the past. But Marcus deserved to know the truth. No doubt, it would all get dredged up anyway when Roger got apprehended. No doubt her name would end up plastered in the *Tennessean*.

She swallowed a sip of coffee, wishing the caffeine would somehow instill the courage she needed to divulge the whole story to Marcus and face the media circus.

"After I confessed to my dad what Roger did, the cops obtained a vaginal DNA swab from Kristen that confirmed Roger had fully penetrated her within the previous 48-hours."

"So the District Attorney now had definitive DNA evidence against Roger for statutory rape, but he wanted your testimony to prove there were multiple victims?"

"Exactly. He said my testimony would gain the sympathy of the jury and would land Roger a much longer sentence because it proved he was a serial offender and a threat to society." She swallowed another sip before adding, "Since none of the other girls were willing to testify in front of a jury, the prosecution proceeded with their case based on my testimony and Kristen's DNA evidence."

Marcus shook his head. "I can't imagine what that was like for you, having to testify in front of a jury at age twelve without your mother there to support you."

She offered a wan smile. "Actually, I was a mature thirteen by the time the trial rolled around." She picked at a hangnail, the memories of this unfortunate chapter of her life enveloping her. "Unfortunately, the trial wasn't the worst part."

Marcus glanced across the seat at her, brow furrowed. "What could possibly be worse than interrogation in a courtroom?"

She rolled down her window and flung out her now cold coffee, wishing she could pitch her painful memories as easily as her coffee.

After depositing her empty cup in the car's plastic trash bag, she sucked in a deep breath to bolster herself before continuing her story.

"After the trial, rumors circulated all around school that I had seduced Roger and slept with him like Kristen had."

"Oh, wow! Kids can be so cruel."

"Tell me about it. The guys at school made horrible, degrading remarks, and the other girls' parents didn't want their daughters interacting with me since I was now 'experienced' with men and might corrupt them."

"Oh, Libby! That's awful!"

"Most believed I should have reported Roger the first time he touched me, and because I didn't, I must have wanted it."

"Unfortunately, people just don't understand, Libby."

"I couldn't walk to the cafeteria without someone taunting, 'hussy.' I spent all of high school trying to prove I wasn't a slut."

She turned to face him, fearful of what his reaction would be. But instead of judgment, she saw compassion radiating back at her. He cupped her hand with his. "That does sound worse than a trial."

"Don't get me wrong. The trial was a nightmare. Roger's defense attorney treated me like I was some kind of Lolita who willfully seduced his client—like Roger was the victim of *my* manipulative scheming." She clenched her teeth, still livid at how the attorney had portrayed her. "Meanwhile, Roger sat in the front row glaring at me, his eyes full of hate. I suffered my first vasovagal spell on the witness stand after that defense attorney badgered me."

Marcus's eyes widened. "So that's why you fainted when I interrogated you about Mom's jaundice. Post-traumatic stress disorder triggered by attorney interrogation."

She nodded. "Ever since the trial, when I feel verbally attacked or really upset, I get one of my spells. It's so embarrassing."

"Why did the prosecution allow that defense attorney to get away with those kinds of accusations on a minor. It's completely illegal."

"Oh, he protested and insisted the record be stricken of all conjecturing and inappropriate questions, but once the words were said, there was no taking them back from the minds of the jury. They eyed me suspiciously to see if there was any truth to it."

"And your father was okay with you standing trial and facing all that? I don't think I would let my thirteen-year-old daughter endure abuse like that."

Libby nibbled on a hangnail and stared out the window. "Dad told me I didn't have to do it, but we both wanted Roger locked up as long as possible so he couldn't do this to other girls. We knew my testimony was paramount to the case, especially since Kristen was unwilling to testify."

They drove in silence for several minutes until Marcus exited the highway and inquired, "How did you find out Roger was also abusing Kristen?"

"In eighth grade, Kristen and I both auditioned for the lead in the musical *Annie*. Kristen assumed since she was pretty and popular that she'd get the role. When she found out I was chosen instead, she blew up at me." Libby gripped the armrest as the unsavory memory assailed her. "I will never forget the words she hurled at me. That's when my eyes were opened to what Roger really was."

"What did she say?"

"She got up in my face and screamed at me.

"You think you're so special because you got the lead in the school play? Well, let me tell you something. Roger says *I'm* the prettiest, smartest, and nicest girl in the whole youth group. He says *I'm* his favorite, and the only reason he gives you the time of day is because your mother died. He feels sorry for you."

Marcus's mouth dropped. "Ouch! She sure didn't mince any words."

"Her words walloped me because what Roger told Kristen were the exact same words that he used on me — that I was the prettiest, smartest, and nicest girl in the whole youth group, and I was his personal favorite. He told me he only spent time with Kristen because he felt sorry for her since her parents were going through a nasty divorce."

Even now, the pain of learning she'd fallen victim to a twisted manipulator cut like a scalpel, and her eyes welled with tears. Before she could stop herself, she began to sob as the insuppressible flashback overtook her.

Marcus pulled into the parking lot of the tire store, turned off the ignition, and drew her into his arms. "It's all over now, honey. You're not alone anymore."

Libby absorbed strength from the comfort of his arms. When she finally composed herself, she said, "I can't believe I was so easily conned."

"You never dreamed the one person you turned to for comfort after your mother died would violate your trust like that. Especially since he was a church youth leader."

Libby brushed the tears from her cheek with the back of her hand and blew her nose on a tissue she located in the glove compartment.

She offered him a half-smile. "I thought pedophiles were creepy old men who snagged little girls off the sidewalk. Not young, good-looking youth group leaders who had earned the trust of you and your parents."

"It's a common misconception. Most of the time, pedophiles *know* their victims. Uncles, grandfathers, live-in boyfriends, step-dads."

Libby twisted the Kleenex in her fingers. "Once I knew the truth, I hated him so much I wanted him to be punished. Because of Roger, I felt stupid and dirty and manipulated. I'd told him repeatedly that I didn't want to do his touchy-feely stuff, but then he'd get all pouty and mad and claim it was *my* fault for tempting him. Said he couldn't help himself because I was so pretty. He said if I ever told my father what we were doing, he'd tell my dad I was a hussy who came on to *him*. He claimed no one would take my word over his because he was the church youth group leader and the nephew of our pastor."

"Wow! He *did* know how to manipulate."

"I ended up giving in to his demands because I didn't know how else to handle it." She picked at a hangnail, causing it to bleed.

"You must have felt trapped."

She snorted. "Trapped? Try terrified—especially when he threatened to report my father for neglect. He had me convinced I'd wind up in foster care."

Marcus grabbed her hand and squeezed. "I am so sorry you went through all that."

She stared down at their hands, reliving the trauma. "That's why I auditioned for the lead in *Annie*. I wanted an excuse to not go home with Roger after school anymore. I wanted out."

Marcus brought her hand to his lips. "How did your father react when you told him about Roger?"

Her eyes welled with tears, and she sniffed them back. "He cried. He blamed himself for not being there after Mom died. Said he was a terrible father and begged me to forgive him."

"Is that when he called the cops?"

"He first called Kristen's mom, who pried out of Kristen that Roger had, in fact, cajoled her into sex on several occasions. Once the police were able to obtain irrefutable DNA evidence against him, they charged Roger with statutory rape and pedophilia."

Marcus gazed at her with such compassion and acceptance she wanted to tell him she loved him. But she didn't dare. Not yet.

When she first told her ex-fiancé, Colin, he initially seemed understanding and kind, but in the days that followed, he began to use her confession against her. He accused her of somehow enticing Roger and secretly *wanting* him to touch her.

"You could have told your father sooner," he insisted. "It's not like Roger tied you down and *made* you do those things, so at some level, you must have wanted it."

After weeks of enduring Colin's digs, Libby broke things off. Enough was enough!

While she regretted her choices at age twelve, she knew from her extensive counseling that she was the victim of a mastermind manipulator. She had learned to forgive herself for not speaking up sooner, and she didn't need Colin shaming her for the rest of her life.

Because of Colin's reaction, however, Libby shut herself off and never dared to date again.

Never dared to hope someone as wonderful as Marcus could love and accept her once he knew her past.

Now that he knew the truth, would he eventually view her as damaged goods, too? Would he blame her for not reporting Roger sooner?

She glanced over at him, dreading what his face would reveal. But instead of disgust, gentle eyes moist with understanding greeted her.

"You were a victim, Libby, and you weren't guilty of anything—except being too young to know how to handle a seasoned sexual predator."

Her eyes pooled again.

Marcus understands. He gets it.

As though to lighten the mood, Marcus smirked. "Besides, who am I to judge? I wasn't exactly a saint myself. We PK's are known for our wickedness."

"PKs?" she asked, raising a brow, grateful to have a break from wallowing in memory lane.

"Preacher's kids."

She laughed. "What diabolical things did you do as a PK?"

"Some friends and I used to call people in the church directory claiming we were from the Campbell soup company."

Her mouth dropped. "Marcus!"

He chuckled. "We asked them, in the most adult-sounding voice we could muster, to sing the famous Campbell soup jingle. We promised to send them a case of vegetable beef soup in return. Then, when they sang the jingle, we laughed and yelled into the phone, 'Sucker!' and hung up."

Her mouth dropped. "How old were you when you pulled that stunt?"

"Fifteen."

She burst into laughter. "Does your mother know about this?"

His eyes widened. "Of course not! As far as she knows, I was the perfect child." He jutted his nose in the air and blew on his knuckles. "Beyond reproach."

She rolled her eyes. "Like I believe that! What other bad things did you do?"

His eyes twinkled. "I was great in math, but I had this one persnickety calculus teacher who took points off for the flimsiest of reasons. She always accused me of not showing my work enough. So out of spite, I put a bag of rotting potato peels, eggshells, and dog manure in her mailbox with a note saying this was her booby prize from the Publishers' Clearinghouse."

Libby's hand flew to her mouth. "Marcus! You didn't!"

He grinned impishly. "Afraid so. Age seventeen this time."

She giggled. "I'm feeling better and better about myself. At least I cleaned up my act when I was twelve. Sounds like you were a menace all through high school!"

He shrugged. "They claim male brains mature more slowly than female brains. That's my excuse, and I'm sticking with it."

She grabbed his shirt and pulled him in for a kiss. "You make me look like Mother Teresa."

He kissed her firmly. "Trust me, you are far more beautiful than Mother Teresa. And for the record, I've given up all my wicked ways."

She tugged his head close and whispered, "I hope not, 'cause you're one wicked good kisser."

* * *

Libby and Marcus emerged from the tire store with four brand new Firestone tires. As she eyed Marcus's tiny car trunk, she inquired, "And how do you propose we fit these into a Mini-Cooper?"

He scratched his brow, then his face brightened. "We'll tie them to the roof."

Her jaw dropped. "You can't be serious. They'll end up all over the highway."

"Not if I secure them really well. Let's go buy some rope."

Thirty minutes later, they returned from Home Depot with a large roll of corded orange twine. After fitting only one of the tires into the trunk, he flopped the second tire onto the roof of his car and tied it securely to the rearview mirrors. He then tied the third tire to the second one until all three tires were piled atop his car like a giant plate of doughnuts. "Okay, let's get these babies home and on your car." He motioned with his hand for her to get in.

She eyed the unstable tower of Pisa. "Are you *sure* they aren't going to end up flying all over the interstate?"

"Of course not! I tied them really tight. We'll be fine."

She climbed in, snapped on her seatbelt, and offered up a prayer for the poor tires — and the other drivers!

The tires remained firmly in place while they puttered on the side streets heading toward the interstate, but once they were cruising at sixty-five miles an hour on the interstate, the top tire flopped backward, partially obscuring the top of the back windshield.

Marcus slowed down to forty-five and put on his flashers. Soon, the weight of the top tire pulled backward on the remaining two and knocked them all askew.

Libby stuck her head out the window to inspect the precarious heap. They looked anything but secure. "I think we should pull over and retie them. They're all topsy-turvy."

"Since we're only a quarter-mile from the exit ramp, let me make it off the interstate, and then I'll pull over and secure the ropes before they brea—"

The twine snapped, and all three tires flew and bounced and rolled in every direction. Several cars slammed on their brakes and swerved to avoid the flying rubber.

Marcus pulled into the emergency lane, and before Libby could utter a word, he raised a hand to silence her. "Don't even say it."

She chomped on the inside of her cheeks to keep from laughing. They jumped out to collect the rebellious tires now scattered all across the interstate. Libby tackled the one that had landed nearest the edge of the road and rolled it to the car.

Marcus dashed onto the interstate and grabbed a tire. Drivers glared, honked, and swerved out of the way.

Once all three errant tires were retrieved, they stood on the side of the road, debating what to do next.

"I'll just walk to the motel. It's less than a mile away. That way, you can load the tires into the passenger seat and drive them to the motel. Then you can come back and get me."

Marcus glared at her. "If Roger doesn't first. Forget it!"

He raked a frustrated hand through his hair and circled the car as though trying to come up with a solution.

She examined the rope. "Unfortunately, the twine is torn beyond repair, and we used the whole roll already. We'll just have to leave the tires on the side of the interstate and make multiple trips."

Just then, a scruffy man in overalls driving a beat-up truck slowed down and pulled over into the emergency lane.

"You folks look like you need some help. I know it ain't much to look at, but this here pick-up truck can cart them tires off the highway for you."

Sheri brightened.

A Good Samaritan! Thank you, Jesus!

After talking with the man for a couple of minutes to ensure he wasn't a nutcase, Marcus loaded the tires into the bed of the man's pick-up, and they decided that Marcus should go with the stranger, and Libby should drive Marcus's car.

Or *attempt* to drive Marcus's car.

Since she had never driven a stick shift before, her shifting skills matched those of a driver's education drop-out. Would she ruin his clutch? Or his transmission?

With grit and determination, she jerked her way back to the motel, rather pleased she'd only stalled out twice. Once parked, she wiped sweaty palms on her lap.

Thank God I didn't crash the thing...or hit somebody.

After unloading the three tires from the stranger's truck bed, Marcus tried to hand the man a twenty-dollar bill for his kindness, but the man shook his head and refused the money.

"Nah, I'm just doing unto others as I'd have them do unto me. How 'bout you repay me by doing something nice for someone else when you see them in trouble?"

"No one else would be stupid enough to tie three tires to the top of his car," Libby mumbled under her breath.

Marcus pulled a face. "That, my dear, was a low blow. My ego is bruised." He dropped to one knee and flung his arm to his forehead in a melodramatic pose. "However shall I recover from this deep wound? Woe is me."

Embarrassed but humored at his ridiculous display in front of a total stranger, Libby gestured with her hand for him to stand up. "Get up, you goose! Trust me, Shakespearean acting is *not* one of your hidden talents."

The Good Samaritan chuckled and waved goodbye. "Well, I'll be off now. You folks have a blessed day." He climbed into his truck and drove off.

Marcus located a crowbar and jack from his car's trunk. "You'll be driving again in no time," he enthused, as he began to jack up the car and pry a slashed tire off its rim with a crowbar. Rather, he *attempted* to pry a tire off its rim with a crowbar.

After twenty minutes of yanking, tugging, sputtering, and cursing under his breath, Marcus whacked the ground with his useless crowbar. "These tires are clearly defective."

Right. Just like the security cameras were defective! I think not!

Libby cleared her throat. "Look, I'm no mechanic, but don't you need a tire iron to pry tires off their rims?"

He stared at her with a deer-in-the-headlight gaze.

Swell! Did this guy fall off a rutabaga truck headfirst?

Sleep-deprived and sick of his shenanigans, Libby said, "Let's just call a tow truck and go to Bridgestone. They have special machines designed to replace tires."

His face puckered in horror. "Why pay for a tow truck and mechanic? Once I buy a tire iron, I'll have these babies replaced in no time flat. Easy peasy."

Yup! Marcus would sooner drink cyanide than admit he couldn't do something. Knowing it was futile to protest further, she went along with his foolishness.

After three, count them, *three* futile attempts to find a place that even carried tire irons, they finally located an auto store that sold them.

Holding up his prized tire iron as though it were a Heisman trophy, Marcus insisted, "Now that I have the proper tools, I'll have those slashed tires off in a flash."

Flash, my eye! Try ten thousand flashes!

Two hours later, Marcus had only *one* of the four tires replaced. Libby released a frustrated sigh.

At this rate, I'll be a member of AARP before he gets my car up and running.

Nerves frazzled, Libby yanked out her cell phone. "Enough! I don't want to be here for another six hours!" Against his impassioned protests that he was now skilled and could finish the job in thirty minutes, an hour max, she called the tow truck, and an hour later, Bridgestone had replaced and properly balanced all four tires.

As Libby pulled out her credit card to pay the hefty bill, Marcus scowled and insisted, "I could have done it and saved you all that money."

Not wanting to bruise his pride any further, she said, "I know you could have, but I didn't sleep worth a flip last night."

When he looked unconvinced, she continued. "I'm exhausted and just wanted the whole thing over with. It was worth every penny."

Marcus shrugged and retorted with the infuriating quip, "A fool and his money are soon parted."

She refrained from kicking him in the shins and chose instead to offer up a hasty prayer: *Lord, give me the patience not to clobber Marcus with a crowbar – or tire iron.*

Eager to move on with her day, Libby drove back to the motel and checked out. She loaded Trixie into her car and decided to stop by the townhouse to pick up some fresh clothes. Of course, Marcus insisted on coming with her to keep her safe.

Reaching the parking lot, Libby slammed her car door, but before she could get Trixie hooked onto her leash, Brandy dashed out of her townhouse and gave her a big hug.

"Julius filled me in. I can't believe he slashed your tires and put a tracer on your car."

"And attempted to break into my motel unit."

Brandy clicked her tongue. "That Roger is grating on my last nerve. Gives me the heebie-jeebies just thinking about it."

"You and me both." Libby tugged on the leash to keep Trixie from darting toward a nearby chipmunk. "I sure wish they'd hurry up and find him. I'm dying for a decent night of sleep."

Libby gestured toward her new picture window. "I see the landlord got it installed. That was quick."

Marcus chuckled. "He probably didn't want snakes and squirrels traipsing through the place, chewing up the woodwork and defecating everywhere."

Brandy grimaced. "Eww!"

"Unfortunately, I can't move back in until they catch Roger," Libby said, then released a frustrated sigh.

"With Julius on the case, it'll be any day now, you wait and see."

"I was impressed when he figured out Roger had wired my car with a tracer."

"I'm telling you, the man is brilliant. And so committed to his job. Metro is lucky to have him."

Libby nodded. "He seems like a keeper."

"He may well have saved your life," Brandy said.

"Julius and Trixie *both* saved her life," Marcus corrected, bending over to pat Trixie's head.

"If Trixie hadn't barked her fool head off, Roger would likely have broken into the motel unit with that crowbar and..." He stopped mid-sentence. "Well, luckily, he didn't."

Lines of worry etched Brandy's forehead. "Girl, I'm worried about you."

You should be.

Roger had proven himself clever enough to evade arrest despite an all-out manhunt. After murdering a parole officer, you'd think he'd be camped out in an obscure part of Wyoming to escape arrest, but no, he was obsessed with making Libby pay for testifying against him. Would the nightmare never end?

She packed a suitcase with a Sunday church dress and some clean clothes for work. Marcus hoisted the suitcase into her trunk and reassured her, "Mom's got the guest bedroom ready for you." Seeing Libby's anxious expression, he added, "And she's delighted to have you."

Libby loaded Trixie into the car, and then Brandy hugged her and said, "I hope you come home soon. It's lonely around here without my bestie to mess around with. I miss you."

Libby hugged her back. "I miss you, too." She smirked and lifted a brow. "Guess you'll just have to settle for Julius's company until I come home."

Brandy grinned impishly. "Come to think of it, I haven't missed you at all."

CHAPTER 23

After an uneventful night in Sophia's guest bedroom, Libby attended church with Marcus and his mother. Now that her secret was out and Marcus seemed okay with it, she felt, for the first time in two decades, like she had nothing to hide. What a delight to be free of the shame she'd hauled around her entire life. For the first time since Roger's trial, she felt liberated. And loved. And happy — which made no sense with Roger threatening her at every turn.

As she sat in the church pew cozied next to Marcus, she had trouble focusing on the sermon. Marcus knew every detail of her past, but unlike Colin, he wasn't ashamed to put his arm around her in front of his mother and the entire congregation. Her heart whispered, "You've found your forever love." Brilliant, handsome, quirky Marcus. He could be such an overbearing jerk when he was angry or upset. And his handyman skills rivaled a baboon's, but she loved him anyway.

Longing for more of his touch, she reached for his hand and weaved her fingers through his. Marcus glanced over and smiled at her.

She wanted to sing louder than the church choir.

This is what unconditional love feels like.

She inhaled deeply, savoring the joy and peace radiating inside her. She loved Marcus with every pore of her being.

Maybe so, but does he feel the same way about you?

Her spine stiffened. Where had that party crasher come from? She willed herself to ignore the intrusive thought.

You shouldn't get your hopes up. He's never told you he loves you. He's never mentioned a long-term future together.

We've only been dating a couple of months, she retorted to her inner doomsday crier.

How do you know he doesn't just feel sorry for you — or protective — because of Roger?

Shut up and leave me alone, she hissed to her inner tormentor.

She forced herself to focus back on the sermon.

After church, Marcus treated Libby and Sophia to a Sunday brunch at the local Olive Garden. Once home, Sophia yawned and headed toward her bedroom. "After a hearty meal like that, I need a nap." Marcus and Libby settled onto the couch to watch a movie.

Whether from the lasagna lunch or the mediocrity of the movie, they fell asleep with Marcus's arm cradled around Libby's shoulders and her head nestled on his chest. After an hour, they woke up warm and cozy. Their eyes met, and they smiled. Words seemed unnecessary.

She raked her fingers through his curls, and his lips found hers, tender and then more demanding. She caressed his jaw and released a soft moan as he marched a row of kisses from her lips to her neck and back to her lips again.

Waves of desire coursed through her as he pulled her closer and explored her mouth further. She reciprocated with a fervor that left her breathless.

Don't let this moment end.

* * *

Suddenly Marcus forced himself to sit up and pull away. "Libby, I need to stop," he whispered. He stood and stretched, though the desire to continue his exploration of Libby's mouth and body was almost insurmountable. The love shining up at him from her beautiful, trusting eyes attracted him like a hummingbird to his mother's potted petunias. He loved running his fingers through her curls and soaking in the sweetness of her eager mouth. He loved everything about her.

But he felt overpowered by a strong desire to explore further — as far as she would let him go. He had reached the point of no return, and it took every drop of strength and conviction he possessed to force himself to pull away. After his break-up with Brittany, he had made a promise to God that he would stay pure until his wedding night. This time, he intended to keep it.

He glanced down at Libby's hurt expression and realized she needed an explanation. She clearly thought he was rejecting her tender affection. He sat beside her on the couch and grasped her hand in his. "Libby, there's something you need to know." He hated exposing his past moral weakness, but Libby had been honest with him about her past, so she deserved to know his.

"When Brittany and I were engaged, I went all the way with her. Like, all the time."

Libby straightened, a startled expression on her face. "You did?"

Shame coursed through him, but he forced himself to continue his confession.

"I knew better, of course. I *am* a Baptist preacher's son. But I was so ensnared by passion and what I thought was love that I completely ignored my conscience and the voice of the Holy Spirit."

She nodded, but said nothing, as though willing him to continue the story.

"I somehow convinced myself since Brittany and I were engaged, and she would be the only woman I ever slept with, what we were doing wasn't all that wrong. Since I loved her and had already made a lifetime commitment to her in my heart, I was just jumping the start line a little."

"It sounded reasonable at the time, didn't it?"

He released a sigh. "Until the identity theft fiasco. Then the full impact of what I'd done hit me. I'd traded in obedience to Christ and God's Word for a woman I no longer even trusted."

She squeezed his hand. "You must have felt so betrayed and disillusioned."

"I know it isn't macho in today's world for a man to stay pure until marriage, but I want to honor God by demonstrating I *can* resist temptation this time. I need to prove to God—and to myself—that *He* is more important to me than sex." He studied her face to see if she understood. "Does that make sense to you?"

"Absolutely. Even though I was only twelve, I knew what I was allowing Roger to do was wrong. It always left me feeling dirty and ashamed."

She picked at a hangnail and added, "I so wish I had told my father sooner."

"We all have 20:20 hindsight. After I broke up with Brittany, I confessed to Jack, a deacon in my church. I committed to him that day that I'd learned my lesson and would never have sex again until my wedding night."

"How did he take your confession, you being the preacher's son?"

"He was disappointed in me, of course, but as a man, he fully understood the powerful drive that compelled me. He encouraged me to attend the Men of God support group that meets weekly at our church. I've attended ever since."

"Do you feel rid of the guilt now? Have you forgiven yourself?"

He smiled. "I do. One of the things Jack said that helped me move forward was this: if I believe what the Bible says when I use it to condemn myself for sin, I need to believe what it says about God's forgiveness and His willingness to cleanse me of all unrighteousness when I confess my sins to Him."

"Wow, that *is* powerful. In other words, we can't take the bad without the good, or it isn't balanced."

"Or scriptural. We're not meant to live in shame. Anytime I'm tempted to beat myself up for caving in with Brittany, I remind myself God has wiped my slate clean. He loves me unconditionally, and in His eyes, I'm pure again."

"That's something I need to hold on to. He's a God of clean slates."

"Exactly." He kneaded her hand with his thumbs. "With God's strength, I will stay strong, and nothing is gained by clinging to the shame of my past mistakes."

He noticed she still looked hurt. "Libby? What is it?"

She stared down at her hands. "Were you afraid I might try to seduce you—like Brittany did? Or that I would succumb easily in my desire for you?"

He jerked his head back. "No! That's not it at all. I didn't trust *myself*. When things reach a certain point, the temptation to go further and further is unreal. I had to nip it in the bud before I got tempted to seduce *you*."

Insecure eyes gazed back at him. "So, it's not my checkered past?"

"*Your* checkered past?" His eyes widened. "You were twelve and the victim of a pedophile. I was over thirty and the son of a preacher!"

She opened her mouth several times, then she stopped herself. Finally, she blurted out, "Was it good? The sex with Brittany, I mean."

He didn't want to answer. It would only intensify her insecurity, but he couldn't build a stable relationship with Libby on lies, so he plunged ahead and hoped she could handle it. "Truthfully? Yes, it was. That's why I didn't want to stop once we started. But I always felt convicted the next day. I knew I was disappointing God, and that made me feel really bad about myself. Sure, my flesh was thrilled, but my spirit was weeping."

She nodded but said nothing.

He gripped her hands. "With God's grace, we're free from our pasts, and with His strength, we'll be pure until our wedding night."

Her eyes widened. "Wedding night? Was that a proposal, Marcus Romano?"

His heart lurched. No, it wasn't! He said it as a guiding principle, not as a marriage proposal.

While he was fairly sure Libby was his soulmate, he needed more time. They'd only known each other a couple of months, and after the Brittany fiasco, he no longer trusted his own judgment. Until God made it one hundred percent clear that Libby was supposed to be his wife, he wouldn't propose, no matter how much he loved her or craved her kisses.

But how did he tell her that without hurting her feelings?

He needed to let her know he wasn't rejecting her like Colin had. But how?

Humor maybe?

He got down on one knee, and with a dramatic sweep of his arm, said, "I'm proposing we get to know each other better before we consider a lifetime commitment."

Her face flushed crimson, as though she wanted to crawl into a clothes hamper and die.

Okay, humor was a bust. Would an honest explanation work better?

He crawled back onto the couch next to her and reached for her hand. "Libby, ever since my breakup with Brittany, I've been afraid to jump into a relationship too quickly. I want to trust God to pick my wife, so I'm waiting to hear clearly from Him. This time, I won't be controlled by my feelings. I want to be sure this time."

She stared down at her hands then pasted on a fake smile. "I was only kidding about the marriage proposal, silly. After my disastrous track record with men, I'll probably never get married."

The tears in her eyes belied her words.

Look what you've done! She's trying to save face.

He had no idea how to repair the damage he'd caused with his careless words. "Identity theft did little to instill confidence in my wife-finding ability, either."

Libby released a stilted laugh. "Wife finding is right up there with your skill for securing tires on a car roof?"

He wagged a scolding finger. "That, my dear, was below the belt."

She laughed, this time a little less forced. "I only said that to make it easier for you to resist my feminine wiles, as your mother calls them."

She tossed him a saucy grin. "After all, I wouldn't want to become her newest she-devil."

"Speaking of my mother, she promised to make her infamous chicken cacciatore for supper."

Libby patted her belly. "I'm still stuffed from lunch. Maybe we should take the dogs for a long hike to build up an appetite." She jumped off the couch and stretched her arms overhead. He forced his eyes away from her soft, curvy physique.

Take captive every thought and make it obedient to Christ.

They trekked to the door and called for the dogs. A long walk was just what he needed to make his thoughts obedient to Christ—and to move the conversation away from awkward subjects—like marriage proposals.

* * *

Marcus and Libby completed their four-mile hike with the dogs and had just reached Sophia's driveway when Marcus noticed a silver BMW—identical to the one Brittany used to drive—cruising down the street.

The shock of potentially seeing Brittany's car—let alone Brittany—triggered such a visceral reaction, Marcus's heart hammered in his chest. He drew in several slow deep breaths and grabbed ahold of the mailbox to steady himself.

Chill out. Brittany isn't the only person who drives a silver BMW.

Libby placed a concerned hand on his shoulder. "Marcus? What is it?"

He pasted on a smile, desperate to appear calm. After his marriage proposal blooper, the last thing Libby needed was another reason to feel insecure.

But half-truths were no way to build a relationship, so he filled her in on what he'd seen—or thought he'd seen.

Libby's brow furrowed. "Why would Brittany want to see you? You two didn't exactly leave on good terms."

"I have no idea." He ran an agitated hand through his hair and glanced down the street where he'd seen the BMW. Hoping to appear nonplussed, he shrugged. "It probably wasn't her."

"Even if it was Brittany, there's no future there. She may have tarnished your past, but that doesn't give her the right to ruin your future." Libby kicked a rock off the driveway with a determined punt.

Yanking hard on her leash, Trixie bolted toward the flying rock. Gus, older and tired out by their four-mile hike, flopped onto the lawn.

Marcus couldn't let it go. *Was* it Brittany? Pricy BMWs were definitely not the norm in his mother's decidedly middle-class neighborhood.

It was Brittany. At the core of his being, he knew it. A sinking dread settled in the pit of his stomach.

What did she want? Whatever it was, it couldn't be good.

As though reading his mind, Libby said, "God wiped your slate clean. No matter what happens, don't let Brittany's chalk-filled erasers dirty you up again. Remember the promise you made to God."

He turned to smirk at her. "Chalk-filled erasers?"

She arched a brow. "Hey! There are worse things I could call her. She-devil and Jezebel come to mind."

Marcus stuck out his fingers to mimic cat claws and hissed.

Before Libby could respond, Sophia opened the door and hollered for them to come in and enjoy her chicken cacciatore. They polished off a plateful of pasta then lingered at the table over tiramisu and decaf. Before they knew it, it was bedtime. Libby said goodnight and climbed the stairs to the guest bedroom while Marcus hunkered down in his old bedroom on the first floor.

This way, he could keep her safe — or so he hoped.

CHAPTER 24

Libby slept in the guest bedroom of Sophia's home for three weeks with no sign of Roger whatsoever. Julius surmised he'd left the state to avoid arrest. Finally, she could relax and get a solid night of sleep — until last night.

Trixie had woken her twice in the night barking like a banshee. Each time, Libby jumped out of bed and glanced out her bedroom window, looking and listening for any sign of an intruder. Nothing. Her heart hammered, convinced Roger was back. When she saw no sign of him, however, she flopped back into bed, where she flip-flopped for nearly an hour before falling back to sleep. The second time Trixie jarred her out of sleep with her barking, Libby bolted out of bed and tore open the curtains. Again no sign of him — or anything else — that should have caused a barking frenzy.

Libby released a frustrated sigh. What set Trixie off? Had she heard a squirrel on the roof? If so, Libby would need to invest in a muzzle, or Sophia would be tempted to throw her — and her noisy canine — to the curb.

She patted the bed until Trixie jumped up and curled next to her. Unable to get back to sleep, Libby pulled out her Bible and read until she dozed off.

When her alarm clock buzzed at six a.m., Libby yawned not ready to face the day after her rotten night of sleep.

Too bad. Time to carpe diem, she told herself, as she tugged on jeans and a T-shirt. Time to take Trixie and Gus outside for their morning constitutionals. Still half-asleep, she plodded down the stairs and met Marcus in the front hall, already latching a leash on Gus's collar. After hooking on Trixie's leash, they grabbed doggy bags and headed out the front door, discussing what could have set Trixie off last night. As they climbed down the front steps and walked past Libby's car in the driveway, they froze.

Someone had spray-painted with fluorescent orange paint on each side of her car the word **TRAITOR**. They circled the car, mouths ajar, too stunned for words. Meanwhile, Trixie sniffed and growled and barked. Instinctively, Libby pulled out her pepper spray from her coat pocket and scanned the neighborhood. No sign of him.

Marcus circled the car looking grim-faced. He scratched his neck and demanded, "How did he find you again?"

"How should I know?" She pounded the roof of her car. "I cannot believe what that good-for-nothing bastard did to my car! I swear, the police won't have to lock him up for life, because I'm going to kill him!"

Marcus's eyes widened at her unexpectedly colorful language. "Tell me how you really feel, why don't you?"

She offered a half-smile. "I would, but you'd have to wash my mouth out with soap and water. Pardon my French."

He shrugged then released a weary sigh. "This means Roger hasn't left the state."

"We better let Julius know. He's been operating under the assumption Roger hightailed it out of Dodge."

While Libby tugged out her cell phone to call Julius, Marcus inspected around the house for any signs that Roger tried to break in.

"How did he track me here?" Libby asked, now more furious than afraid. "I've put your mother's life at risk — the very thing I didn't want to do!"

He inspected the bottom of both cars, and this time, he found a carefully concealed tracer hidden under his car. Disengaging it, he waved the offending device at Libby. "Voila!"

Her shoulders sagged. "I am so sick of living out of a suitcase, but there's no way I can stay here anymore if Roger has found me again."

Marcus agreed she'd have to come up with alternative lodging until Roger was apprehended.

She kicked her car tire in frustration. Just what she *didn't* want — more nights in a hotel room. More car expenses. She'd never get her medical school loans paid off at this rate.

Julius arrived and snapped pictures of the vandalized car then wrote up another report. He shook his head, lips thin. "I swear, the Loch Ness monster would be easier to find." As he opened the door of his police cruiser, he reassured Libby, "Don't you worry, we *will* track down his sorry hide — eventually."

Eventually. Not the word Libby wanted to hear. How about today!

Marcus glanced at his watch. "It's almost seven now. We need to leave if we're going to get your car to the autobody shop before work. We can worry about packing up your suitcase and moving out after work. Mom can watch Trixie today."

Libby stomped up to the guest bedroom to change into work clothes, sorely missing the shower she wouldn't have time for, thanks to Roger's latest shenanigans.

Marcus followed Libby to the auto body paint shop so he could give her a ride back to her office.

They dropped her car off at the autobody shop, and while Marcus drove Libby to work, they agreed the safest thing Libby could do was sleep in a different hotel every night and take a cab or Uber to and from work each day. That way, there would be no car for Roger to follow. Marcus would check his car for tracers every day before visiting her. She would get hospital security to do a walk through her office every morning before she entered. Marcus would speak to Carlos and remind him to keep an eye out for Roger in the evening hours after Libby left for the night. He would supply Carlos and hospital security with a copy of Roger's mug shot.

Libby released a weary groan. Back to living out of a suitcase again.

Roger may be the fugitive, but I feel like one, too.

Marcus parked his car and insisted on escorting Libby to her suite. Once she'd unlocked her office door, Marcus stared down at his feet as though not wanting to tell her something. He finally came out with it: "Libby, I need to tell you something." He shifted from foot to foot.

Here it comes. He's fed up with all my drama and wants out.

"What is it?" she said, bracing herself for rejection.

"Brittany has been trying to contact me," he mumbled.

"Brittany?" Her stomach tightened.

"That silver BMW that inched past mom's house three weeks ago? It was hers."

"I don't know how I know, but I do," he admitted. "Because we were engaged, she obviously knew where Mom lives." He glanced up and released a sigh. "Truthfully? She's been stalking me for a couple weeks now."

Her mouth dropped. *Why didn't he tell me sooner?*

She leaned against her office door feeling woozy.

"My secretary informed me yesterday that Brittany has called three times this week demanding to speak with me. Hillary refused to transfer the calls, of course, but Brittany is not giving up. Plus, I saw that same silver BMW cruise past my workplace a couple of days ago as I walked into work. I told myself I was paranoid—that it was probably just a car that *looked* like hers. But when her BMW inched past Mom's house, I got the sinking feeling that I haven't seen the last of her."

Libby shifted her weight and leaned against the door, trying to soak in the enormity of Marcus's words.

"After she stole your identity and said those horrible things to your mother in the courtroom, surely she knows there's no future with you."

Marcus shrugged. "You'd think so, but Brittany is narcissistic and probably thinks she can sweet-talk or seduce me into taking her back—if she wants something. When it comes to men, she doesn't like to lose."

Libby scowled.

Swell! First Roger, now Brittany. What next?

"She doesn't actually *want* me," Marcus insisted. "She either wants financial support, or she wants to punish me for not dropping the charges against her, and what better way to punish *me* than by vandalizing my girlfriend's car?"

"Wait! Are you saying you think *Brittany*, and not Roger, painted the graffiti on my car?" The idea seemed preposterous.

Marcus shrugged. "I'm saying I wouldn't put it past her. Plus, there was no handwritten note this time. Every other time, Roger has left you a handwritten note."

She snorted. "His note was in giant fluorescent orange all over the side of my car."

He nodded. "Perhaps, but criminals usually operate in a very predictable pattern, and his is to leave you a handwritten note each time."

Arms crossed, she shook her head. "I'm not buying it. This is Roger up to his tricks again."

"Obviously, we'll proceed as though Roger *is* the perpetrator, but it's possible Brittany would pull a stunt like this just to punish me. She's always had a nasty temper, and she's no doubt furious I'm dating someone else and refusing to take her calls."

"If she's furious with *you*, why trash *my* car?"

"Because you're my girlfriend. Brittany was always insanely jealous and competitive with other women. If I laughed at another woman's joke or smiled politely at a pretty waitress, she accused me of flirting. She once accused me of two-timing her, even though I never did anything to warrant such an accusation. For all her beauty, Brittany was incredibly insecure."

Libby gripped the doorframe and forced herself to inhale a deep breath. While Marcus *claimed* he wasn't interested in Brittany anymore, would he be able to resist if she relentlessly pursued him and poured on her charm?

Worse, had Marcus refused to see Brittany because, deep down, he knew if he *did* see her, he might cave into her seductive charms again?

Could some part of him still love her—*despite* the identity theft and betrayal? After all, he'd once loved her enough to not only propose marriage but to violate his own Christian values. A love like that didn't die easily.

Libby forced a smile. Marcus mustn't know how much this mastermind-of-male-manipulation left her feeling threatened. Marcus told her the sex with Brittany was great. How could Libby possibly compete with memories like that?

Marcus curled fingers under her chin and tipped up her head. "Libby, look at me," he whispered.

Slowly, she raised her eyes, hoping her insecurity wasn't obvious.

He cupped her face with his hands. "Listen to me. I'm not interested in Brittany anymore—not at all."

She gazed into his eyes, wanting to believe his words.

"Getting involved with her was the biggest mistake of my life, and I deeply regret it."

His eyes scanned hers, as though desperate to convince her. He caressed her cheek with his fingers. "Libby, I see insecurity written all over your face, but I promise you, you don't need to feel threatened by Brittany." He placed a gentle kiss on her lips, then confessed, "I love you. I just need a little more time before I'm ready to make a lifetime commitment, okay?"

She smiled. "I love you, too, Marcus." She wrapped her arms around his neck and hugged him close, grateful he'd finally told her he loved her. "I feel better now. Thanks for reassuring me."

Marcus promised to come after work and drive her back to the auto body shop to claim her car. He kissed her goodbye and left.

Despite his reassurances, cruel internal voices started a bully fest.

You're a bowl of oatmeal compared to a crème Brulée like Brittany.

It was easy for Marcus to stay strong when Brittany was locked away in prison, but if she poured on her charm and seduction and begged him to forgive her, would he be able to resist? Remembering the picture with Marcus's arm wrapped around the beauty, she had to ask herself: will he even *want* to?

She reminded herself Marcus had character and had even joined a men's support group to help him remain morally strong. He was committed to God and wanted to save sex for marriage now.

Plus, Brittany had totally lost his respect and trust with the identity thief episode. And Sophia couldn't stand her.

But he'd also told her the sex with Brittany was great. How could she possibly compete with memories like that?

Shut up, she commanded her inner tormentor. *Marcus said he loves me, not Brittany now. I'll just have to trust him.*

Her stomach twisted.

Face it – after Roger and Colin, trusting men is not your strong suit.

She headed to her desk intent upon distracting herself with paperwork.

No point dwelling on something I can't change.

If God wanted them to be together, He would make it happen. Borrowing trouble by worrying about Brittany would only ruin her day.

She offered up a prayer of surrender and felt at peace. Her life was in God's hands.

With the hustle and bustle of hospital rounds and patients coming and going, her day passed quickly in its usual hectic but fulfilling way.

Mrs. Garrison's breast cancer had shown no sign of recurrence. Larry Biggs's leukemia was now in complete remission, thanks to his successful bone marrow transplant. Results like these were the reason she had chosen oncology as her specialty.

By five o'clock, all her patients and staff had left for the day, and she dove into her final office notes with a vengeance.

How she wished she could wave a magic wand and have the two hours of tedious charting and paperwork behind her.

She heard footfalls heading toward her office. She assumed it was Carlos coming to empty her trash.

Except it wasn't Carlos.

CHAPTER 25

She recognized Brittany immediately with her flowing blond tresses, huge cornflower blue eyes, and hourglass figure, which she displayed to perfection in a low-cut fuchsia tank top and white shorts. Toned arms and a glowing tan perfected her California beach girl image. Full lips accentuated her perfect smile. Brittany was even more striking in person than in her photo. No wonder Marcus felt proud to claim her as his fiancée.

Once Libby recovered from the shock of Marcus's former lover standing in front of her, a wave of fear ripped through her.

Why is she here?

If Brittany was the one who had vandalized her car, was she safe? Libby moved her cell phone and pepper spray closer.

Forcing herself to sound calm and in control, she said, "Brittany? How'd you get into my office? My front door was locked."

Hand on her hip, Brittany responded, "I just told the cleaning lady out in the lobby that you and I were old friends, so she let me right in."

Swell. Must be Carlos wasn't on duty tonight, and the temp didn't know better.

Brittany cleared her throat and smiled as though she and Libby were long-lost friends.

Libby stared up at the beauty queen and resolved she wouldn't let Brittany intimidate her. This was her office, and Marcus said he loved her.

Arms crossed, Libby boldly met Brittany's eyes across her desk and demanded, "Why are you here, Brittany?"

Brittany offered a warm smile. "I was hoping you and I could have a little chat."

A little chat? Give me a break!

It's not like they had anything to say to one another.

Libby made an exaggerated gesture of eyeing her watch. "I've got a ton of work to do, so I'll give you five minutes, not a minute more."

Might as well let her know who is in control.

Brittany frowned, clearly put off by Libby's curtness.

Well, what does she expect — warm and fuzzy?

Anyone Sophia called "that she-devil" was no friend of Libby's—especially if she might be responsible for the spray-painted graffiti plastered across her car.

With the expensive autobody bill fresh on her mind, Libby snapped, "Did you vandalize my car last night with orange paint?"

Brittany's brow furrowed as though she thought Libby was crazy. "Why would I do that? I've never even met you before!"

Libby felt her face flush. She must sound paranoid. "Then why are you here?"

Brittany jammed her thumbs into her short's pockets. "I just thought you should know before you become any more intimately involved with Marcus that he and I conceived a baby together."

Libby's heart dropped ten floors.

"What?" Nothing could have prepared her for a bombshell like that. She stared at Brittany, too shocked to utter a sound.

"It's true." Brittany unzipped her Gucci purse and pulled out a photo and plunked it down on Libby's desk.

With a perfectly manicured index finger, Brittany pointed to an adorable baby girl who looked to be around six months old and dressed in frilly pink. "This is Amanda Rose, Marcus's daughter."

Libby stared at the picture feeling sucker punched.

Marcus and Brittany conceived a baby together? She forced herself to inhale. "Does Marcus know about this?"

Brittany gazed down at her nails and frowned. "Not yet. He broke up with me a month before I found out I was pregnant. He's blocked my phone number and refused to take my phone calls at work. My mail comes back, 'Return to Sender', and when I stopped by his office to tell him about the baby, his secretary refused to let me talk with him. She even threatened to call security if I didn't leave the premises immediately."

Libby picked up the photo with trembling hands and stared at the beautiful baby, unable to pull her eyes away. This was Marcus's baby. Amanda Rose.

The blond-haired, blue-eyed cherub was the spitting image of her mother, but Libby didn't see any of Marcus's features. At all. She eyed Brittany suspiciously. "You're *positive* Marcus is the father? She doesn't look a thing like him."

She lasered Libby with a glare. "Give me some credit. Marcus and I were *engaged* when this baby was conceived. What do you take me for?"

Libby shrugged. While Brittany seemed sincere, Libby didn't trust her. Not one bit. She crossed her arms and did her best to look cynical. "Marcus will insist on paternity testing. You lost all credibility when you stole his identity and rang up his credit cards. It took him months to repair the damage you caused."

Brittany's face flushed. "Trust me, I had three months in prison to think about all the harm I caused him. People make mistakes, you know. I tried to ask for his forgiveness, but as I said, he won't even take my calls."

Good! The less contact between the two of them, the better.

Libby steepled her fingers with feigned confidence. "That's because Marcus considers his relationship with you a huge mistake. The biggest mistake of his life, in fact."

Tears filled Brittany's eyes, and she brushed them away with her fuchsia-painted finger. "How can you call sweet little Amanda Rose a mistake? Look at her—she's perfect." She jabbed her finger on the picture.

No doubt about it, the woman was good. Libby glanced down at the photo and had to concede, "She *is* a beautiful baby."

Brittany gripped the edge of Libby's desk. "Look, I've totally changed in the last few months. I've repented of my sin and learned my lesson. Now I just want to make things right with Marcus—for little Mandy's sake." She chewed on her lower lip and added, "I know what I did to him was terrible, but Mandy deserves to know her daddy, don't you think?"

Libby felt the air drain from her lungs, and a sudden wave of nausea and faintness walloped her.

Do not pass out. Remember, Marcus says he loves you, not Brittany.

She sucked in two cleansing breaths and forced herself to stay conscious.

A baby would change everything...wouldn't it?

Maybe not. Amanda Rose might not even be his baby.

This could all be one of Brittany's tricks. After all, Marcus said she was a master manipulator.

But what if it is Marcus's baby?

A sinking dread settled in the pit of Libby's stomach. Marcus was the honorable type. If it was his baby, he might feel obligated to attempt reconciliation with Brittany—for the baby's sake. If he'd gotten Brittany pregnant, he might even feel obligated to marry her, if that's what she wanted. Even if they didn't become romantically involved again, they would have to interact regularly to co-parent Amanda Rose.

What if Brittany really *had* changed? What if three-months in prison was the wake-up call she'd needed to change her ways? If she *had* changed, and they had a baby to share, it would only be a matter of time before they got back together.

Which meant his relationship with Libby might well end as quickly as it had started. How could she possibly compete with a gorgeous woman who held out the baby trump card, especially if the woman was repentant of her past wrongdoing?

Marcus had slept with Brittany and said the sex was great—except for the guilt. Did he secretly cherish memories of their forbidden, sultry nights together?

If Marcus and Brittany were married, he could once again enjoy great sex, only this time, without the guilt.

And with a baby to pull them together, Amanda Rose would have a daddy—a wonderful daddy.

Besides, if Brittany *had* changed, who was Libby to keep them apart when there was a baby to think of? It would be selfish. Godless, even.

Libby stared down at her hands, hands sporting short, practical, unmanicured nails, unlike Brittany's inch-long immaculately polished nails that exactly matched her top. Libby's hands were designed for examining patients, playing piano sonatas, and bathing Trixie. Brittany's hands were designed for wrapping around a man's arm as his most cherished possession.

She eyed Brittany across her desk and wanted to vomit. She mustn't let Brittany see how devastated and defeated she felt. "Why are you telling *me* this? This matter is between you and Marcus."

"But Marcus won't talk to me." She chewed on her bottom lip before adding, "I found out through Facebook that Marcus is dating you now. I was hoping that you, as another woman, would understand and want to see little Mandy Rose reared in a loving, Christian home with both her mommy and daddy."

Libby's eyes filled with tears. How *she* had longed for a mommy and daddy growing up. She glanced down at the picture of baby Amanda.

How could she deny this beautiful baby a chance to be raised by her biological father?

If Marcus proved to be the father, and he felt compelled to pursue a relationship with Brittany, there was nothing Libby could do to stop it.

Ironically, she remembered telling Marcus that he would make a fabulous father because of how gentle and patient he was with Trixie. Little did she know, his chance to be a fabulous father would happen with Brittany instead of her.

She stared at the picture of the sweet, vulnerable baby, and her eyes pooled with tears.

If Marcus no longer wanted anything to do with Brittany — as he claimed — and the baby ending up in a single-parent home, it wouldn't be Libby's fault.

Marcus could still be a good parent to Amanda, even if he didn't choose to reconcile with Brittany. Parents did it all the time these days. Only Marcus could decide if he wanted to attempt a reconciliation with Brittany. If he did, the Christ-like thing for Libby to do was back off and let him try.

And the two shall become one flesh.

The unbidden scripture verse flashed through her mind and taunted her. Marcus and Brittany, technically, *had* already become one flesh when they'd consummated their love and conceived a baby together. Did they need to make things right in God's eyes and reconcile?

As though sensing Libby's defeated thoughts, Brittany strolled forward and went for the jugular: "Having a baby to love and care for has completely changed me. I'm no longer the self-absorbed woman Marcus probably told you about." Her eyes pooled with tears, and she insisted, "Now, I just want to be a loving wife to Marcus and a nurturing mother to Mandy." She hooked a lock of hair behind her ear and smiled through her tears.

"You know, I think God allowed this baby to happen to pull Marcus and me back together again. To change me into a woman of God."

Libby stared at the woman dumbfounded, too shocked to utter a word.

Brittany brushed a tear from her cheek and continued. "I know I blew it with Marcus, but God has forgiven me, and through this baby, He's giving me a second chance with Marcus. He loved me once, and I'm asking you — for Mandy's sake — to let me try to win him back."

Sudden weakness and nausea gripped Libby. She lay her head down on her desk to keep from vomiting. Tumultuous waves billowed and churned in her stomach like a rowboat in a tempest. Overtaken, she snatched the trashcan from underneath her desk and vomited.

Brittany instinctively recoiled.

So much for showing Brittany who is in control.

"Are you okay?" Her eyes widened with alarm.

Libby reached for her water bottle and rinsed her mouth. "I'm afraid your news shocked me to the core."

Brittany put a hand on her shoulder. "I'm sorry." She chewed her lower lip and added, "I didn't mean to upset you, I just thought you ought to know about the baby before you surrendered your heart to Marcus."

Too late. I already have.

Libby lifted her water bottle with shaky hands and forced herself to swallow another sip of water.

There was nothing more to say. Only Marcus could decide if a baby changed anything.

"Why don't I leave and let you recover?" Brittany said. She slung her designer purse over her shoulder.

"I'm about to go introduce Marcus to his daughter. This time, I'm going to his office *with* Mandy, and I'm not leaving until he agrees to meet with me."

She headed toward the door then turned around as though she'd had an afterthought. "Please don't call Marcus about this as soon as I leave. Let me talk to him first. He shouldn't learn he's fathered a baby with me from you. It wouldn't be right, don't you agree?"

Libby nodded, too numb to speak.

"I'm worried about how he'll take the news. Wish me luck." As quickly as she had come, she was gone.

Libby flopped back in her chair, still in shock.

Wish you luck? Not going to happen!

A dagger of despair pierced Libby's heart. She should have known this thing with Marcus was too good to last.

Perhaps just to punish herself further, she picked up the photo of Amanda Rose that Brittany had inadvertently left behind and stared at the blue-eyed cherub.

A punishing thought slammed her: *You'll* never have a baby with Marcus.

With Amanda's chubby cheeks and sweet smile, how could Marcus *not* want to marry Brittany and make things right? Amanda Rose was that cute.

If Brittany really had changed—and only time would tell if she had—Libby's future with Marcus was doomed, and she was in for another rejection.

Now that Brittany had repented of her past and recommitted her life to God, Marcus would likely insist on doing the honorable thing and marrying her, even if he still had feelings for Libby.

A few hours of great sex with Brittany, and Libby would become little more than a blip on his radar screen, especially since she and Marcus had only been dating a couple of months.

If Amanda Rose proved in paternity testing *not* to be Marcus's daughter, or, if Marcus still wanted nothing to do with Brittany, he knew how to contact Libby. He could call her, and they could continue their relationship.

She agreed with Brittany that Marcus should not learn he'd fathered a baby with Brittany from Libby. Thus, she had to avoid communicating with Marcus until after Brittany dropped her bombshell.

With that in mind, Libby texted Marcus she had finished work early and taken a cab to the autobody shop.

She forced herself to add she was too tired to get together tonight and would stay at a local hotel. She didn't tell him where so he couldn't track her down.

Marcus immediately called her, but she refused to answer the phone—he would not learn about his illegitimate baby from her, and she wasn't a good enough actress to act like nothing was wrong.

She glanced at her watch. Soon, Marcus would know he was a father, and he would gaze into the eyes of his beautiful baby girl for the first time.

When he found out Brittany had re-committed her life to the Lord and wanted to be a Godly wife and mother, he would most likely fall in love with her all over again.

Tears poured down Libby's cheeks. She'd told Marcus she loved him, but only he could decide if fathering a baby with Brittany was a deal-breaker for a lasting relationship with Libby. She brushed away her tears and released her anguish to God.

"I was sure Marcus was the one, but if he isn't, give me your strength to endure the let-down, Lord. Grant Marcus wisdom and discernment with Brittany. Help him make the right choice."

While her spirit sounded strong, her heart splintered into shards. She fingered the picture of baby Amanda, and a pang of wistfulness overtook her. Not only had she lost her mother, it now appeared she would never get to *be* a mother, either. Why had she permitted herself to dream of one day cradling hers and Marcus's baby?

She pleaded with God. "*You know how much I love Marcus. I don't want to lose him.*" Her shoulders heaved with irrepressible despair. "*God, I feel so alone and frightened right now.*"

But the ball was in Marcus's court.

The sudden thought gripped her that she needed to get Trixie and all of her clothes moved out of Sophia's house while Sophia was at Wednesday night church.

Otherwise, Sophia would take one look at Libby's face and know something was terribly wrong. Sophia sure didn't need to find out about Marcus's love child with "that she-devil" from her!

Libby should leave a note and some flowers thanking Sophia for her hospitality. She grabbed a pad of paper and a pen. What should she say? She twirled the pen in her fingers until the words came to her:

Sophia, Since *Roger has tracked me down at your house, I can no longer reside there without putting your safety at risk. Plus, Trixie is too noisy and destructive to remain a houseguest. I will reimburse the cost of purchasing a new remote control. I look forward to seeing you at your next doctor's appointment. I promise to be careful, so you mustn't worry about me.* ~Libby

Heartened, she folded the note, and called for an Uber.

Marcus had told Libby he loved her.

But would a baby change everything?

CHAPTER 26

Marcus would not have been more shocked if Satan himself had walked into his office. One minute, he was reviewing a deposition, and the next, he was face-to-face with Brittany—a Brittany holding a baby she claimed was his! She'd somehow squeaked past his secretary by claiming she had an appointment with Marcus to discuss visitation rights for the baby!

Swell! The office gossips will have a field day with this one.

His first reaction? Brittany had borrowed some other woman's baby in an attempt to manipulate him. But one glance at Amanda Rose and he knew it was Brittany's baby; Amanda was the spitting image of her mother. Also, the timing of Amanda's conception coincided with the months he and Brittany had been intimate. Nevertheless, he couldn't stop himself from hurling, "How could you have gotten pregnant? We used protection every time."

Brittany shrugged and looked away. "It happens, Marcus. No birth control method is 100%, you know."

Arms crossed, he demanded, "You're *positive* she's mine? If I demand a paternity test, it will unequivocally prove *I'm* her father?"

Eyes narrow, she pushed on his chest with an insulted hand.

"We were *engaged,* Marcus. Who else do you think I'd be sleeping with when I was engaged to you?"

Okay, it was a low blow to accuse her of sleeping with some other guy when they were engaged. Brittany may have been a shopaholic and a colossal flirt, but surely, she wasn't a two-timer.

Baby Amanda yawned with her tiny arms stretched heavenward. She glanced up at Marcus, and her perfect little mouth curled into an adorable, toothless grin. Mesmerized, Marcus said, "Can I hold her?"

Brittany handed the sweet bundle to him, and he gently swayed her in his arms, making cooing noises. He touched her cheek, soft as satin, and found he couldn't take his eyes off her. She curled tiny fingers around his pinkie finger. He lifted her to his chest and gently caressed her back until her head nestled into the crook of his neck. Soon, she was sound asleep.

Brittany beamed. "You're a natural, Marcus." She transferred the sleeping baby to the baby carrier and covered her with a pink blanket.

No question Amanda Rose was adorable, but an inner prompting warned him to be wary.

Don't forget who you're talking to, he reminded himself. He crossed his arms and demanded, "What do you want from me, Brittany?"

"Want?" Her eyes widened with innocence. "I just thought you'd want to meet your daughter."

He didn't buy it—not for a second. She wanted something. The question is—what?

Brittany strolled forward and insisted she had undergone a spiritual awaking while in prison. She claimed she now wanted to become the Christian wife and mother that Marcus and Mandy deserved.

Marcus must have looked skeptical because she quickly added, "Look, I know it will take time to repair the damage and hurt I've caused you, Marcus."

He glared at her. "I'll believe it when I see it."

She touched his upper arm. "Marcus, I've changed, and I'm willing to do whatever it takes to win back your trust."

She nestled her body close to his and gazed up at him with imploring eyes. "I never stopped loving you and dreaming about the life we could have had together if I hadn't messed everything up. I regret what I did, and I've repented before God. I've asked Him to be the Lord of my life—this time for real." She clutched his arm. "Marcus, I'm begging you to give me another chance—for Mandy's sake." She caressed the sides of his face with her fingertips and cooed, "We were so good together. You know we were." She curled a lock of his hair around her finger and whispered in his ear, "Remember that night in Gatlinburg by the fireplace?"

She tugged his head toward hers, her lips already parted.

Marcus felt his heart pound, in part from shock, and yes, in part from past memories triggered by Brittany's seductive words and willing lips. He caught a whiff of her perfume—a light, blend of jasmine and lilac—the one she always wore when they were intimate—and the scent triggered a thousand unwelcome flashbacks.

The rational part of his brain immediately waved warning flags.

Danger! Danger! Danger!

Brittany had talked the Christian lingo before. Look where that had gotten him. What had his mother said? Judge a tree by its fruit?

Besides, he had Libby now. Beautiful, smart, dependable, funny, vulnerable Libby.

He felt so comfortable and yet aroused by her. In the three months they'd been together, they had developed a level of honesty and friendship that a year with Brittany never broached. No way would he jeopardize Libby's trust—or heart— no matter how hard Brittany tried to seduce him.

He grabbed Brittany's arms and flung them away. "Stop it! I'm not going there with you again. Ever! If Amanda proves to be my child—and I insist on a paternity test to prove it—I'll support her, and I'll be a good father to her. But you and me? We're history. I'm in love with Libby now."

Her face contorted with anger. She stared down at her immaculately manicured nails.

"Oh, yes, Libby." She glanced up with a sneer on her face. "Turns out, Libby and I had a little chat before I came over here to talk with you."

"Why would you drag Libby into this? She has nothing to do with it."

He clenched his jaw.

She shrugged. "I needed to find out how involved you two were before I met with you today."

She strolled closer and raised a challenging brow. "Perhaps before you throw me to the wolves, you ought to hear what she had to say."

Marcus scowled. "I'm all ears."

"Libby told me if you'd fathered a baby with me, I could have you."

He rolled his eyes. "I don't believe that for a second."

She stamped her foot. "Well, it's true! She said she didn't want to get stuck raising some other woman's kid, and if you had gotten me pregnant, you should do the honorable thing and marry me."

Rage coiled inside him like a viper. She was trying to manipulate him again. He crossed his arms and snapped, "I don't believe a word you're saying."

Brittany strolled closer, her brow arched, and a smug sneer plastered on her face. "She doesn't want a thing to do with you anymore. But fine, if you don't believe me, call her yourself."

She tugged her cell phone out of her pocket and thrust it toward Marcus.

That threw him for a loop. If she were lying, why would she insist he call Libby?

She shook her hand, challenging him to take the phone. "Go on! Let her tell you it's over. She was so angry with you she barfed in her trashcan and nearly passed out. It was revolting."

Marcus's heart jolted.

Brittany would have no way of knowing about Libby's vasovagal spells unless she really *had* vomited. Libby only got vasovagal when she felt angry and upset, which meant Brittany was telling the truth.

More compelling, Libby *had* just sent him a cold text message informing him she didn't want him to come and pick her up at work. She then refused to answer his phone call even though he called her back immediately.

She'd also ignored his text messages. Now he knew why. She was so angry she couldn't stomach even talking to him.

Crushing hurt pummeled his chest.

How could Libby toss away all they had been through together? She'd told him she loved him.

That she'd be selfless enough to put the baby's needs ahead of her own, he could believe. But to not want anything to do with him just because he may have fathered a baby with Brittany? Ouch!

Brittany jostled her hand, holding her cell phone in his face. "Go on. Call her. Let *her* be the one to tell you she doesn't want anything to do with you anymore."

Marcus shook his head and leaned back in his chair, too upset to utter a word.

Brittany sat on the corner of his desk. "To be honest, I was surprised how easily she broke things off. I guess since you two had only been dating for a couple of months, she decided to cut her losses and run."

With all they had been through, it seemed so much longer than a couple of months.

Brittany waved the phone in his face again. "Call her — I insist. I don't want you doubting me."

Too hurt and mortified to face Libby's rejection in front of Brittany, Marcus mumbled, "No, that's okay. I believe you, Brittany."

If she were lying, she wouldn't have been so insistent on him calling Libby.

Brittany slipped her phone back into her short's pocket then clasped her hand on his arm. "You know, maybe Libby's rejection is God's way of telling you you're supposed to be with me."

Marcus instinctively pulled away and raked a hand through his hair. It didn't make sense.

Libby loved him—he was sure of it. How could she throw in the towel so easily?

Brittany grabbed his hand and squeezed.

"If you loved her, I'm sorry it didn't work out. Trust me, I know what it's like to lose the love of your life—the person you wanted to spend the rest of your life with. That's how I've felt for over a year now."

Marcus looked into her eyes and wished he had a woman's intuition. Was Brittany sincere, or was she manipulating him again? His gut said the latter.

As though reading his indecision, she massaged his hand gently with her thumbs. "I know it's going to take time to earn back your trust. I'm just asking you to give me a chance—for Mandy's sake."

Overwhelmed by Brittany's sudden re-appearance and Libby's equally sudden rejection, Marcus felt weak and shaky. He leaned his head into his hands on his desk and forced himself to inhale deep breaths.

Libby must have been devastated by the news. Her curt text message and refusal to take his phone call or respond to his text messages confirmed Brittany's claim. He clenched his teeth. Couldn't she have told him in person, instead of going through Brittany or stonewalling him? Didn't he at least deserve that? Why hadn't Libby given him a chance to explain? Or at least waited for the paternity test results to come back. Heck, Amanda might not even be his baby, though the timing of her conception did match the dates they'd been intimate.

Maybe Libby just needed time to calm down before she could face him. Maybe in a day or two, she'd call and say she wanted him back, even if he had fathered a baby with Brittany. Maybe all was not lost.

He released a weary sigh. If he *was* Amanda's father, the ball was in Libby's court.

Only she could decide if fatherhood was a deal-breaker. All he could do was wait and pray.

He turned to Brittany. "Look, this has come as a total shock. I need time to process all this—and to pray." Not fully trusting her, he added, "Before I make any decisions, I will insist on paternity testing."

Her lips thinned, and cold eyes glared back at him. "Fine! If that's what it takes for you to believe me, go ahead—do your stupid paternity test."

She grabbed a pad of paper off his desk and scribbled down her address and phone number. Slapping the pad in front of him, she snapped, "You may not want anything to do with me, but as a Christian man, I would think you'd want to get acquainted with your daughter. While you wait for the test results, why don't you come over to my place and visit Mandy? She ought to know her daddy, don't you think?"

Before he could answer, she grabbed the baby carrier and stormed out.

Marcus flopped back in his chair arms hanging like limp linguini.

What on earth just happened?

CHAPTER 27

Libby daubed on an undereye cover-up to disguise the bags and dark circles caused by endless nights of crying and bolting awake every time her motel room creaked, or Trixie barked. Sleeping in a different location every night had grown old. Really old. Car doors slamming, televisions blaring through paper-thin walls, mumbling voices, moans of romantic interludes, and heated arguments all blended into a cacophony of noise that made obtaining a good night of sleep a thing of the past.

By staying on the move, however, Roger had not tracked her down in over two weeks. The FBI had stationed an undercover agent outside her office building during office hours in hopes that Roger would try to stake her out at work. So far, he had either not shown up or eyed the agent and been too savvy to fall for their disguise.

Maybe he'd finally left town to avoid arrest. That's what Julius believed, though he'd been wrong about that before.

Unfortunately, with the Roger problem potentially gone, Libby had more time to dwell on losing Marcus.

Why hadn't he called her? If he loved her, shouldn't he try harder to pursue her?

Maybe since she'd refused his call the day Brittany showed up, he thought she was mad.

Maybe he was waiting for her to call. If so, should she?

Libby thrashed in bed at night, mulling over these questions.

When Libby toyed with calling Marcus, she forced herself to pull out the photo of Amanda Rose and stare at it until she felt convicted not to interfere. The baby should come first, and if Marcus felt obligated to try and make things work with Brittany for the baby's sake, it would be wrong of her to meddle. Only Marcus could make this decision.

Memories of her time with Marcus tumbled through her mind, unbidden and cruel. She rehashed every conversation, every kiss, his beautiful smile, his comforting arms, and his gentle way with Trixie. When she couldn't sleep, she journaled about their time together. If she couldn't be with him in person, at least she could preserve their memories.

Was Marcus missing her, too?

It sure didn't feel like it. From the minute Brittany entered the scene with baby Amanda in tow, Marcus had not called or even texted her. Not once. No goodbye. No good luck. Not even a, "Have a nice life." She found herself checking her phone constantly to see if he'd left a message. Nada.

For the first time, she understood why her father used work as a balm for grief. She found herself spending longer and longer hours at the office if only to clean her desk, prune the plants, or organize the pamphlets about chemotherapy and cancer. Anything to distract herself from an ache, a void, a longing so deep she sometimes wished she could curl up and die.

How could she have been so mistaken about Marcus? He was *the* one—she'd been sure of it. But now all she had was heartache.

Had her life degenerated into the lyrics of a bad country music song? Pitiful!

She met Brandy in Starbuck's one Saturday morning to catch up on all that had happened. Brandy insisted Libby should call him. "What if he's waiting for *you* to call *him*? What if he needs to know you can accept him, even if he *has* fathered a baby with Brittany?"

Brandy crossed her arms, frustration plastered across her face. "It's just a misunderstanding. You're being a stubborn bonehead. Call him, already!"

Brandy was right, of course. What did she have to lose? But Libby couldn't make herself do it. She'd dialed his number more times than she could count, but as soon as the phone was about to ring, she disconnected, telling herself she'd call tomorrow.

Truthfully? She couldn't face his rejection. Been there, done that with Colin, and she didn't want a repeat with Marcus. If she didn't call, she could cling a little longer to the hope things weren't really over with Marcus, and he just needed time. He would eventually call her.

The alternative was unthinkable.

Every day, she promised herself if Marcus didn't call by eight p.m., she'd send him a friendly text message asking how things were going. Nothing snarky or confrontational. She'd make it casual and friendly: "Hey, Marcus. How are things going? I've been praying for you."

But she couldn't make herself do it. What if he didn't reply?

Or worse, what if he did reply with a cold text message telling her things were over, so back off?

Since the landlord had replaced her front window, and there were no further signs of Roger stalking her in three weeks, Libby occasionally spent an evening at her townhouse practicing the piano and hanging out with Brandy.

She then spent the night sleeping on Brandy's couch—just in case Roger *was* still lurking around. The next night, she slept in a new motel to keep Roger off-kilter—if he was still in Tennessee. She checked her car for a tracker device twice a day, but thankfully, she never found one.

On the plus side, Libby was in the best shape of her life. She could run eight laps around the Vanderbilt track in the time it took Brandy to slog around it four times. Sprinting until she doubled over gasping for breath temporarily numbed her sadness.

Endorphins to the rescue.

Melissa suggested she take up scrapbooking as a creative way to fill in her lonely hours and preserve childhood memories. Desperate to distract herself from her misery, Libby drove to a local craft store and purchased enough colorful pages, ribbons, stickers, buttons, and crimping scissors to scrapbook ten lifetimes.

She had to admit, focusing on positive childhood memories—the crackle and pop of Girl Scout campfires, the inviting aroma of gingerbread Christmas cookies lovingly decorated with her mother, the bumpy ride on a burro to the bottom of the Grand Canyons, the whinny of her pony, Chestnut, and even her nerve-racking piano recitals—helped channel her raw emotions into something enduring. Something positive.

Tonight's photo was a favorite—a close-up from a happier time when hiking in Cade's Cove with her mother and father.

Mountain laurel enveloped the entire forest. She remembered the butter-yellow lady slippers, vibrant fire pinks, delicate blue phlox, and majestic white trillium that dotted the mountain trails as they traversed the Smoky Mountain paradise.

Will I ever know happiness like this again?

She touched the photo wistfully and admired her mother's dark auburn hair and large, turquoise eyes— eyes that matched her own. She tried to erase the memory of Marcus saying her eyes mesmerized him.

Don't think about Marcus. Think about hiking in the Smokies. Think about Virginia bluebells.

Remembering a favorite Scripture verse, she admonished herself to think about things that were pure and lovely and praiseworthy.

She adhered the crimped photo of the mountain vista to a cheery pink scrapbook page. After embellishing the page with stickers of wildflowers and Smokey the Bear, she added her completed page to her scrapbook and glanced at her watch.

Good—bedtime.

When she was asleep, she didn't have to paste a smile on her face and quote Philippians 4:8 to buoy her spirits. Or resort to Smokey the Bear stickers to maintain her sanity.

Brandy had fallen asleep on Libby's couch while watching a movie. Rather than wake her, Libby threw an afghan over her, turned off the television, and brushed her teeth.

Before padding to her bedroom, Libby's eyes drifted to the framed photo Sophia had taken.

The photo showed she and Marcus snuggled together on the couch with the two dogs curled at their feet. Happiness radiated from all their faces.

If only Brittany hadn't come along and spoiled everything.

Another week dragged by like an oppressive Southern heat wave — muggy and depressing. Time hadn't made a dent in her shattered heart, and she doubted it ever would. Even Trixie moped around as though missing her buddy, Gus.

At least she hadn't heard a peep out of Roger in over three weeks now, though she didn't dare believe he'd left for good. He was probably keeping a low profile to avoid arrest.

Surprisingly, his *lack* of contact proved just as nerve-wracking as his slashing her tires, as it kept her wondering what he'd do next — and when.

Sometimes, when she couldn't sleep, she closed her eyes and savored memories of Marcus. Even his bungling handyman and mechanical skills now seemed endearing.

Too bad he was so busy enjoying Brittany and Amanda Rose that he couldn't be bothered to give her a moment's thought — or a phone call to see how she was doing.

If he wanted to see her, he knew her phone number. The ball was in his court. Unfortunately, he wasn't dribbling in her corner.

Tomorrow she'd shoot him a friendly text...if she could just get up the nerve.

She knelt beside her bed and prayed Marcus would find happiness, even if not with her.

She thanked God that Roger had left her alone for another day.

"Dear God, give me the strength to make it through another day."

Another dreary, depressing day.

CHAPTER 28

Raised voices echoed from the lobby of Marcus's law office. He put down his computer mouse and tried to listen through his closed office door.

Wait! Is that Mom yelling at my secretary?

With any luck, Hillary would get rid of her by claiming Marcus was tied up with a client.

"I don't care if he does have a client in five minutes," Sophia snapped. I've been calling and calling him for three weeks now, and he won't return my calls. Libby left the house abruptly with just a vague note. When I called her to find out what was going on, she said I needed to discuss it with Marcus. So out of my way!"

She must have stormed past his secretary because the next thing Marcus knew, she was pounding on his office door and shouting, "Open up!"

When he didn't respond, she pounded even harder. "Marcus Daniel Romano, you open this door right now. I'm not leaving this office until you tell me what's going on with you and Libby."

Marcus groaned.

So much for Hillary getting rid of her.

He flung open the door and glared at his mother. Her fist was still mid-air as though ready to keep pounding until he opened the door. "Mother! Stop that! Your behavior is totally inappropriate."

His wide-eyed secretary stammered, "I-I'm so sorry, Marcus. I tried to stop her but—"

He raised a hand. "It's not your fault, Hillary. You couldn't have stopped her if you'd called in the National Guard. When Mom makes up her mind to do something, she's a force to reckon with." Glaring at his mother, he added, "A regular wrecking ball in a Faberge egg factory."

Sophia charged up to his desk and crossed her arms. "What happened between you and Libby?"

Noticing his secretary looked far too interested in the conversation, he gestured toward the door. "Thank you, Hillary. You can go now."

After closing the door behind her, Marcus turned and faced his mother head-on. "That's none of your business."

Her face puckered. "Of course, it's my business. Libby is my oncologist, and some madman is after her."

Okay, she had a point. That was the reason he'd initially been hesitant to date Libby.

He didn't want to tell his mother about the baby unless a paternity test *proved* Amanda Rose was his. If the test came back negative, he could tell Brittany to scram, and his mother would never be the wiser, thus sparing himself from endless diatribes on the evils of fornication and gold-diggers.

Sophia marched forward until she was in his face. "Out with it." She jabbed his chest with her index finger. "And tell me the truth because I know when you're lying. You can't fool a mother."

Marcus forked a hand through his hair, trying to buy time.

Eyes narrow, she crossed her arms, ready for a show-down.

"I'm not leaving until you tell me what's going on, so unless you plan to drag me out of here kicking and screaming, I suggest you start talking."

Kicking and screaming? There's a scene I'd rather my law partners not see.

Accepting defeat, he sank into his leather chair, released a deep sigh, and braced himself for a tirade.

Might as well just blurt it out and get it over with.

"Brittany is back."

Sophia's eyes widened. "Brittany? What does that good-for-nothing she-devil want?"

When he didn't answer immediately, she added, "I hope you escorted her to the door and told her, in no uncertain terms, to leave you alone, or you'll slap her with a restraining order."

Marcus gestured toward the wingback chair next to his desk. "Have a seat, Mom."

She'd better be sitting down when he dropped the baby bombshell. He turned until he was directly facing her.

Here goes...

"Brittany marched into my office three weeks ago and refused to leave until I talked with her."

She glowered. "What did *she* want? Another credit card to max out?"

"It's worse than that, I'm afraid." He sucked in a breath and released it slowly, already dreading his mother's verbal volcano. "She showed up with a baby and claims I'm the father."

Her mouth dropped.

"She claims she still loves me and wants us to make a go of it—for the baby's sake."

Face ashen, Sophia gripped the arms of her chair, but no words came out. After the news sank in, she exclaimed, "Is that even possible? I mean, I know she entangled you with her seductive charms, but surely you used protection. Please tell me you weren't a complete dunderhead."

Gee, thanks, Mom.

"We used protection every time, but no method is perfect, and Brittany insists the baby is mine."

She flapped her hand. "I'm sure she does."

"The date of the baby's conception coincides with the months we were intimate."

"Pffft. I wouldn't put it past that gold-digger to have a sugar daddy on the side."

Marcus's lips thinned. "Ma, be nice."

"I'm just say—"

He interrupted. "Look, I'm not naïve. I've ordered paternity tests, and the results are due back any day. If I'm not the father, I'll tell Brittany to buzz off. If I am the father, I'll have no choice but to pay child support and learn how to co-parent with her."

Sophia shook her head, scowling. "I always wanted grandchildren, but not with that she-devil as the mother."

"The baby *is* adorable," Marcus offered, hoping to soften her. He pulled out his wallet and extracted a photo then handed it to his mother. "Her name is Amanda Rose. Isn't she pretty?"

Sophia stared at the photo, and her wrinkles softened. "Amanda Rose. She *is* a beautiful baby." Examining the picture more closely, she commented, "She definitely favors her mother."

"Which is why I'm insisting on paternity testing. But in the very real possibility she is mine, I've been spending evenings at Brittany's with the baby."

Her head jerked up. "And not with Libby?"

"Exactly." He averted his eyes in a vain attempt to avoid dragging Libby into the discussion.

Like that will ever work.

Her eyes narrowed with suspicion. "But you and Libby *are* still dating, right?"

His throat closed off, and he wasn't sure he could get the words out. "No, Ma, we're not."

"Because..." Sophia gestured with her hand for him to explain.

"Libby broke things off because of the baby."

"What?" Sophia could not have sounded more surprised if Marcus told her he'd booked a flight to Jupiter. "That doesn't sound like Libby."

"Brittany visited Libby before she came to tell me about the baby. Apparently, Libby told her if I'd fathered a child with another woman, she wanted nothing to do with me."

Sophia scowled. "I wouldn't rely on the word of Jezebel. Did you confirm it with Libby herself?"

"I tried to, but she refused to return any of my phone calls or texts. She clearly doesn't want anything to do with me, or she'd call."

Undeterred, Sophia demanded, "Did you talk to her in person?"

Raising exasperated hands, he snapped, "I don't know where she's staying. Until Roger is caught, she's in a different hotel every night."

Glaring at his mother, he added, "And unlike you, I don't believe in accosting people in their workplace about a private matter."

She shrugged unapologetically. "Hey, if that's what it takes to get the job done."

"Right! You want me to barge into her waiting room in front of an office full of patients and demand to see her? That would go over big. If she doesn't hate me already, she sure would after a stunt like that."

Sophia leaned forward and squeezed his hand. "She doesn't hate you, Marcus. She's just confused about what to do with a baby and another woman in the picture."

His eyes welled with tears. "Truthfully? If she won't stand by me over something like this, then she's not the woman I thought she was."

Sophia nodded. "I'll admit, I'm disappointed in her lack of loyalty."

"You and me both. I thought she loved me." He looked away and added, "She *said* she did."

Hillary knocked on the door and announced his next client had arrived. Sophia stood and pulled her son in for a warm hug. "I'll be praying for you, Marcus. And Libby, too. Remember that God can work all things together for good for those who love Him and are called according to His purposes."

Marcus ushered his mother into the lobby and thanked her for her prayers.

"How about I cook up a pan of lasagna for lunch this Sunday?" She patted his cheek. "Everything will seem better after homemade pasta. You wait and see."

CHAPTER 29

Things weren't adding up. For starters, Brittany claimed she spent days at home caring for little Mandy, but the two times Marcus dropped by to visit the baby during his lunch hour, Mandy was with a babysitter. Brittany had no job, so how could she afford a sitter, let alone all her new clothes, purses, and shoes? The stench of the old shopaholic Brittany wafted into his nostrils like a pile of rotting mackerel. Even though the paternity test results weren't back yet, Brittany expected Marcus to pay for the baby's diapers and baby formula.

While Marcus made it clear he would never get romantically involved with her again, Brittany acted as though it were his job to support her every shopping whim—and they weren't even dating! Nor would they ever be. Marcus wasn't convinced Amanda was even his daughter, but just in case she was, he made a point to visit Mandy every day and to keep Brittany's house stocked with diapers and formula. As for money for shopping sprees? Forget it!

Thank goodness the baby was a delight. Her gummy grin and wiggly toes warmed his heart and lessened the pain of losing Libby. He loved cuddling the sweet bundle of pink and softness, but more times than he cared to admit, his thoughts drifted toward Libby.

Libby would love touching Mandy's soft cheek and downy hair. Libby could share Mandy's cute giggle with me. Libby could help me figure out why Mandy is screaming right now.

But Libby didn't want anything to do with him. She'd refused to answer his phone call and ended things with a curt text message. She'd made no effort whatsoever to call since she found out about Mandy three weeks ago.

He forced himself to stay insanely busy from sun-up until midnight. Work, run, visit Mandy, and work some more, then fall into bed exhausted. He signed up for a refresher karate class—something he hadn't done since law school—anything to get his mind off Libby.

If she truly loved him, she would have taken his call that night and at least made an effort to let him explain. She would have called to check how he was doing.

But she hadn't.

And then there was Brittany…

For someone who claimed she wanted Marcus back in her life, she sure didn't act like it. The minute he arrived to visit Mandy, Brittany tore out of her apartment to go work out at the fitness center.

"I've got to lose the five pounds I gained with this baby," she claimed. But three hours later, she returned, looking like she hadn't broken a sweat. Maybe she showered at the YMCA, but if so, shouldn't she be carting home a bag of dirty gym clothes?

In the few minutes they conversed before she dashed off, Brittany grated on his nerves.

Unlike Libby, with whom he could engage in meaningful discussions about politics, stressors at work, books, and his hopes for the future, Brittany had no interests outside shopping and trite reality shows.

Did she honestly think he cared which woman "The Bachelor" picked for a rose this week? Why had he never noticed how vapid she was when they were dating? When he brought Gus with him one night, she'd screamed, "Get that fleabag off my couch!"

Excuse me, but Gus did *not* have fleas!

Where were the results of that blasted paternity test?

He eagerly checked his mailbox every day. Nada. The company insisted he should receive them any day, but it had already been two weeks since he'd mailed in the samples—two long weeks.

It all came to a head the night Brittany broke a fingernail taking Amanda Rose out of her swing. "Shoot!" she whimpered, gazing at her torn nail. On and on, she lamented, as though her broken nail equaled a nuclear attack on New York City.

Sick of her bellyaching, he sputtered, "For crying out loud! It's just a fingernail! Get over it!"

Her eyes narrowed. "Get over it? You want me to go around with one broken nail when all the others are perfect? I'll look like a freak."

Marcus rolled his eyes.

Give me a break.

Brittany then had the audacity to cozy up to Marcus and plead, "I just need fifty dollars for a French manicure." She gazed up at him with forlorn puppy dog eyes and a pouty lower lip.

I can't believe I ever fell for this. Talk about manipulation.

He still had student loans to pay off, yet Brittany wanted him to squander money on a French manicure.

Forget it!

Before he could stop himself, he snapped, "Libby survived just fine without fancy French manicures."

Brittany glared at him. "What you ever saw in that vomiting nerd is beyond me. If I were a man, I wouldn't want her unless she had terminal cancer and a million-dollar life insurance policy."

If he had been the violent sort, he would have pitched a lamp at her — or better yet, a brick. But he contained his fury. "It's all about the money for you, isn't it, Brittany? You haven't changed a bit. You're still the same narcissistic gold digger you were a year ago."

Her eyes narrowed. "You know what? When all is said and done, what else is there? Everything else is just emotional fluff with no guarantees." She then stomped out of the house, slamming the door behind her.

Marcus stared at the door too shocked to move.

What did I ever see in the woman?

Thank God she *had* stolen his identity — otherwise, he would have married her and been permanently stuck with her. How could he have been so blind?

Yesterday, when Brittany didn't get her way by pouting, she attempted — unsuccessfully — to seduce him. As though he'd fall for her obvious attempt to manipulate him with sex again.

This time it didn't work. He'd made a covenant with God to stay pure until marriage, and he had no intention of allowing Brittany's desire for a new dress to spiral him into a sexual downfall with a manipulator.

In the past, she'd mesmerized him with her style and beauty. But now the time and money she wasted on keeping up her appearance was a turn-off. He far preferred Libby's wholesome beauty.

Libby could look just as beguiling running on a trail in gym shorts as she did in a fancy church dress. Natural beauty, that's what his mother called it.

Mandy began to whimper, so he picked her up out of her crib and nestled her into his arms. Poor Amanda Rose—stuck with such a self-centered mother. Too bad Libby wasn't her mother. He'd noticed how Libby lit up around the babies at church. She would have made a loving and attentive mother.

But Libby didn't want him. Libby had refused to answer his phone call and text messages. Libby made it clear as long as Mandy was in the picture, she wanted nothing to do with him. And despite how much he loved Libby, if little Mandy proved to be his daughter, he would not abandon her. He had his faults, but deadbeat dad wasn't one of them. Besides, if Libby couldn't accept that he'd fathered a baby with another woman, was her love for him really unconditional?

While Marcus wasn't a part of Libby's life anymore, he still wanted to ensure her safety until Roger was caught, so he checked in with Julius regularly.

Julius assured him Libby was keeping a low profile by staying in a different motel every night. The cops drove by her workplace and townhouse on a regular basis.

A hospital security officer walked Libby to and from her car and checked for tracers to ensure no one was following her. As a consequence, no one had heard a peep out of Roger in over three weeks.

Lounging on Brittany's couch, Marcus patted Mandy's back until she yawned, stretched her tiny arms, and drifted off to sleep. He tucked her into her crib then tip-toed back to the living room.

He defiantly patted the couch next to him, and Gus jumped up and flopped down next to him. Marcus stroked his shaggy neck. If Brittany didn't like Gus's dog hair on the couch, she could find herself another free babysitter!

Even Gus seemed depressed these days—always glancing toward the door as though expecting Trixie to pounce in at any moment. Marcus missed Trixie's antics, too.

He stood up and paced around Brittany's apartment, reminding himself to quit ruminating about Libby and her crazy dog.

You've got to move on. She doesn't want you anymore.

Except he wasn't sure he could move on. Libby was everything he ever wanted in a wife. But she didn't love him enough to accept he had made a mistake.

He wrote Libby more letters than he could count, begging her to reconsider and take him back, but then he shredded them. Libby didn't need another man manipulating her. She'd had that in Roger.

If Libby came back to him, it had to be because she loved him and couldn't live without him—even if Mandy came with the package.

In his last conversation with Libby, he'd told her he loved her and had no interest in Brittany.

The ball was in Libby's court—if only she wanted to play ball.

* * *

Another sleepless night. Libby glanced at the clock on the nightstand in tonight's motel room and groaned.

Three in the morning.

She fluffed her pillow and flipped onto her back. No luck. Her side? Less luck. Three-thirty a.m. At four a.m., she declared surrender and turned on the light.

Instinctively, she reached for the photo of Marcus next to her alarm clock. She had snapped the picture on a whim during one of their hikes in the park. His unruly curls and beautiful smile still gripped her heart. She stared at his dark chocolate eyes and felt the familiar longing and heartache. And then, while staring into those dark brown Romano eyes, it hit her like a sledgehammer.

Amanda Rose isn't Marcus's baby. She can't be.

Heart pounding, she straightened in her bed and stared at the picture again. Why hadn't she realized it before now? She'd aced Human Genetics and should have figured it out the second she saw the picture of Amanda Rose.

When she and Marcus thumbed through Sophia's photo album displaying pictures from a Romano family reunion, every single family member — and their spouse — for four generations back had dark brown eyes.

Nary a blue or green-eyed gene in the entire family tree. All dark-eyed, dark-haired Italians.

But Amanda had light blue eyes — a near impossibility if Marcus were the father.

Yes, Mandy would carry the recessive blue-eyed gene of her mother, but Marcus's four-generations of brown-eyed genes should have been dominant. If Amanda Rose were Marcus's daughter, she would have brown eyes.

Which meant Brittany was lying.

She grabbed her cell phone off the nightstand and made herself call Marcus — before she lost her nerve.

If he still loved Brittany and wanted to marry her anyway, that was his business. But he should know the truth before he made a commitment to Brittany out of some false sense of obligation. She wouldn't put it past Brittany to come up with forged paternity test results.

Deep in her heart, Libby knew Marcus still loved her. He had to.

CHAPTER 30

Jarred by the ringing phone on his nightstand, Marcus rubbed his eyes and eyed the alarm clock. Four a.m.

Who on earth was calling at this time of night?

Had his Mom been rushed to the hospital? Had Roger attacked Libby? Face it—phone calls at four in the morning were always bad news.

He grabbed his cell and croaked out, "Hello?"

"Marcus, it's me."

A shot of adrenaline coursed through him. Libby! "Are you okay? What has he done to you this time?"

"No, I'm fine."

Her voice trailed off as if she were hesitant to say more.

He gripped the phone, still worried. "What is it then?"

When she didn't respond, he couldn't ignore his annoyance. Here she'd completely ignored his texts and calls and then had the nerve to wake him up three weeks later in the middle of the night.

Unable to suppress his pique, he snapped, "What do you want, Libby?"

"It's about the baby."

His breath caught. Had she finally come to terms with him fathering Amanda Rose?

Maybe it had just taken her time to process everything.

He forced himself to say nothing so she could gather her thoughts and share what she was feeling.

Perhaps if she had come to terms with another woman's baby being a part of their lives, all was not lost.

"Amanda Rose is not your baby."

His breath caught. How could Libby possibly know that?

"Since the paternity test isn't back yet, you can't be sure of that."

"I can. Brown-eyed genes are dominant over blue-eyed genes."

He raked a hand through his hair, trying to wake up enough to process what she was saying.

"By six months of age, if Amanda Rose were really your daughter, she'd have to have brown eyes."

Unconvinced, he responded, "But couldn't I be carrying a blue-eyed gene from some long-lost relative, even though I have brown eyes?"

"Normally, I'd say yes, but for four generations back, no one in your family, including spouses and in-laws, have ever had blue eyes, right?"

He mentally pictured all the members of his extended family. "No, we're all dark-eyed Italians."

"Amanda carries the blue-eyed gene of her mother, but if she were your daughter, she'd have to have brown-eyes because the brown-eyed gene you would have given her is dominant over the blue-eyed gene of her mother."

"So you're saying Brittany lied about me being the father?"

"Not necessarily," Libby conceded.

"What do you mean?"

"She may not *know* you aren't Amanda's father. Maybe she only cheated on you one time, and she figures the odds were far greater *you* were the father and not the other guy since you two had sex all the time."

As the unsavory news percolated through him that his ex-fiancée had cheated on him, Marcus wanted to throttle Brittany for needlessly putting them through all this angst for nothing.

He chastised himself for so easily falling for her superficial charms. He'd only seen what he wanted to see. Talk about gullible! And stupid.

While furious at Brittany for two-timing him, Marcus couldn't ignore the relief flooding through him. Thank God! He would no longer have to entangle himself with Brittany co-parenting a baby that wasn't his. The mistakes of his past could remain in the past. It also meant there might be a chance to reconcile with Libby.

"Libby, now that Brittany and the baby will be out of the picture, is there any hope for us?" He held his breath as he waited for her response. While still hurt that she'd abandoned him when he needed her most, just hearing her voice made him realize deep at his core, he still loved her and couldn't imagine life without her.

"That's totally your call, Marcus. I thought you didn't pursue our relationship because you were trying to make things work out with Brittany. Since there was a baby involved, I didn't think I should interfere. The ball was in your court."

"*My* court?" Marcus moved the phone to his other ear. "I called and texted you a dozen times that day. You never responded. I thought you were furious and didn't want anything to do with me."

"I didn't respond because I didn't think you should hear about fathering a child with Brittany from me. Hardly my place to dump that on you. Plus, Brittany *asked* me to let her tell you first."

Hmm. Libby *had* sent her curt text message and refused to take his phone calls *before* Brittany showed up with the baby.

"Why didn't you call me after Brittany broke the news to you?" Libby said accusingly. "I was waiting for you to call me."

"Brittany said if I fathered a child with her, you told her you wanted nothing to do with me."

"And you *believed* her? I never said that," Libby snapped.

He shifted in the bed and switched the phone to his other ear. "What else was I to believe when you never called me back or responded to any of my texts? I thought you were furious with me."

She mumbled something under her breath that he couldn't make out. "That low-down she-devil! I can't believe she told you I wanted nothing to do with you. That's a total lie." She released a loud fume. "So basically, you've been waiting for me to call you, and I've been waiting for you to call me?"

He shook his head in disgust. "Yup." Why had they endured three miserable weeks apart for no reason? "I guess we both get an F in communication skills, huh?"

She chuckled. "More like an F-minus."

"What do you say we get together for breakfast this morning? I can't wait to see you again."

She readily agreed and ended their call.

Marcus shook his head, still trying to process all that Libby had told him.

I'm not Amanda's father!

He had wondered why the paternity test had taken so long. Now he suspected Brittany swiped them from his mailbox so he wouldn't learn the truth. Just like she had hidden the credit card bills with his name on them by having them sent to *her* address. That way, he wouldn't uncover the thousands of dollars she rang up on her fraudulent acquired credit cards.

How could Brittany stoop so low as to lie about Amanda's paternity? Worse, since Mandy was conceived while they were engaged, it meant Brittany had cheated on him. No wonder she didn't want him to know the paternity test results—he wasn't the father!

She no doubt thought she could seduce him back into her good graces until he forgot all about *wanting* to see the paternity test results. It certainly wasn't for lack of trying on her part.

Brittany's claim that Libby wanting nothing to do with him was all a lie. Libby had been as miserable and heartbroken as he these last three weeks. She hadn't answered his call and text messages because she hadn't wanted to be the one to break the news about Amanda Rose, and all this time, he'd thought she had rejected him because of the baby.

Too agitated to sleep, he plodded to the kitchen and fixed some coffee. He needed to spend serious time in prayer so he could handle Brittany like a man of God instead of a screaming maniac. Right now, he wanted to throttle her!

He gulped a swig of coffee and wrapped up in an afghan with Gus nestled next to him. He bowed his head and surrendered the whole mess to God, praying for wisdom and self-control.

He was jolted out of his prayer by the chime of his doorbell. His heart exploded with joy when he opened the door and in leaped Trixie.

There stood Libby dressed in flannel pajamas and slippers—her hair disheveled, her eyes sleepy. But she had never looked more beautiful.

"I hope it's okay I came," she said, hooking one of her luscious auburn curls behind her ear. "I couldn't sleep, and I figured after the news I just dumped on you that you weren't sleeping too well either." She chewed on her lower lip then glanced up at him shyly. "I know it's early, and I look terrible, but I couldn't wait to see you again."

Before she could utter another word, he pulled her into his arms.

She clung to him and whispered, "I've missed you so much."

Her words were more melodious than an aria from *Carmen*. For three weeks, he'd prayed she'd come back to him, and now she had.

He pulled back to drink in every feature of her beautiful face. He was rewarded by a happy glow radiating back at him. He caressed her cheek and confessed, "I've been miserable without you too, Libby. Absolutely miserable."

Her eyes pooled with tears. "I didn't realize how much I loved you until I thought I'd lost you."

He gently wiped a tear from her cheek with the pad of his thumb. "You never lost me, Libby. I told you that day outside your office that I loved you and only wanted you. I don't say words like that lightly."

"I love you, too," she whispered.

He kissed her then, desperate to convey his overwhelming love for her. Diving his fingers into her curls, he tugged her head closer, intoxicated by the slight quiver of her lips.

Her arms wrapped around his neck, and her mouth met his with such need, it left him breathless. A soft moan escaped her lips, and his heart hammered.

After three weeks of drought, she was back in his arms—where she belonged. He pulled back to soak in every detail of her—and to convince himself it wasn't all a dream. He gazed into her eyes and wanted to melt in the love he saw radiating back at him.

She rewarded him with a contented sigh. All tension gone, they settled onto the living room couch with steamy mugs of coffee, their legs entwined under an afghan.

Marcus updated her about all that had transpired in their three weeks apart. "Being around Brittany only confirmed what I already knew: you're the one I want to spend my life with. I think God *allowed* that identity theft not to punish me, but to rescue me from marrying the wrong woman."

She beamed. "And all the while, I thought she had ensnared you back into her lair."

Marcus shared his suspicion that Brittany was hooking up with some other guy under the guise of working out at the gym while Marcus babysat Mandy at night.

"If the paternity test results weren't back yet, why did you agree to babysit?" Libby inquired.

"It seemed like the right thing to do."

"Why?" she demanded.

He shrugged. "I honestly didn't think she'd cheat on me when we were engaged, so if Mandy *was* my daughter, I didn't want to lose any more time with her. Plus, I needed to take on my financial responsibility and care of her."

"I'll bet Brittany is meeting up with Amanda's real father. Why don't you follow her the next time she supposedly goes to the gym and find out where she goes?"

He swallowed a sip of coffee and mulled over her suggestion. "I think I should just cut my losses and tell her we're through. If I'm not Amanda's father, there's no future between us, so why confront her about the other guy?"

"Why?" She slammed her mug onto the coffee table so hard its contents sloshed out. "Because Brittany *needs* to be confronted. Don't forget, she marched into my office claiming you were Amanda's father. She claimed she was a changed woman and begged me to let the two of you reunite—for Mandy's sake." Angry eyes bore into his. "Brittany told you I didn't want anything to do with you—which is total hogwash."

He nodded. "Right, but is it worth the bother of a confrontation?"

"If you let her get away with manipulating people like that, she's never going to change. She needs to face consequences."

Marcus chuckled. "You sound just like my mother."

She smirked. "I consider that a compliment."

He pursed his lips as he considered his options.

"Tell you what, how about I follow Brittany tonight when she supposedly heads to the gym? I can text you with the location, and we can confront her together."

She crossed her arms, her lips tight. "You do that. I want to give that lying piece of she-devil a piece of my mind!"

"Getting in touch with your feline nature, are you?" Marcus exposed his claws and hissed.

Her eyes narrowed, and she pointed a finger at him. "Don't even go there, buster! I'm still mad at you for not calling me these last three weeks."

O-kay! Maybe time to lighten the mood!

"Want to take the dogs for a walk this morning before we head into work, my feisty little calico?"

She smirked, and without missing a beat, said, "Sure, my roving tomcat."

CHAPTER 31

Marcus hunched over his work desk, reviewing the pile of snail mail his secretary had heaped into his mail bin. After tossing the bulk of it into the recycling, he sipped his coffee and bit off a chunk of his blueberry scone. When his cell phone rang, his caller ID informed him it was the Food and Drug Administration. Marcus perked up.

Scott.

Three weeks had passed since they'd last spoken, so Marcus was eager to hear the results of their investigation.

After exchanging pleasantries, Scott said, "You won't believe what has transpired since I last spoke with you."

Marcus swallowed another sip of much-needed caffeine. "What's happened?"

"After you sent those scathing letters to the CEO of Banderbaxy and Dr. Patel at the CDSCO, Dr. Patel called to inform me he would personally oversee an unannounced inspection of Banderbaxy's factory. I think after last year's broken-glass-in-the-atorvastatin debacle, he wanted to assure me he demands high standards."

Nice to know my letter accomplished something!

Marcus shifted the phone to his other ear and located a pen and writing pad. "What did his inspection reveal?"

"He found the factory in deplorable condition—rats running around the storage unit, moldy ceiling tiles, workers not wearing gloves or hairnets, inadequate sterilization of the vats, altered quality control reports, you name it."

Marcus's heart lurched. "This is the factory that produced my mother's generic Taxotaphen?"

"I'm afraid so, and the news only gets worse. In an effort to save money, Banderbaxy used grossly outdated cornstarch as its inert ingredient. The burlap bags of cornstarch were also housed in a moldy storage facility. Dr. Patel found evidence of aflatoxin in the cornstarch. That's how the aflatoxin made it into your mother's chemotherapy—contaminated cornstarch."

All of his mother's suffering was needlessly caused by sloppy manufacturing. Marcus gripped the phone wanting to choke someone.

Since he hadn't heard a word from Scott in three weeks, Marcus concluded Roger had broken into Libby's office and tainted the chemotherapy. Now he knew differently.

Scott continued. "Because intravenous chemotherapy is mainlined straight into the bloodstream, it only takes a minute amount of aflatoxin to do drastic damage. It's a miracle your mother didn't die of fulminant liver damage."

"She nearly did," Marcus said, scribbling down the details. He then asked the all-important question. "What has Dr. Patel done to correct the problem?"

"He completely shut down the factory in Paonta Sahib and told them he'll keep it closed until they pass every manufacturing standard."

"That's good to hear."

"He said he was tired of Banderbaxy's slipshod manufacturing practices."

"That makes two of us."

"Apparently, he waved your letter in their face and said their dangerous manufacturing standards jeopardized the reputation of all Indian generics."

A slow grin spread across Marcus's face. "Wow! To be honest, I figured my letter would be read by some low-level flunky and tossed into the rubbish bin."

"The fact that you're an attorney and sent the letter certified to the FDA, as well as to Dr. Patel, no doubt made them think you were serious."

"I *was* serious. If Banderbaxy wants a chunk of the eighty-billion-dollar-a-year generic pharmaceutical business, they need to adhere to strict industry standards."

"Thanks to you and Dr. Patel, I think Banderbaxy is finally getting the message. Besides shutting down the factory, Dr. Patel slapped them with the largest financial penalty allowed by law."

Marcus penned down the additional details trying to assimilate all the pieces of the puzzle. Things still didn't add up. "We've been investigating the case here in Nashville as though it were an inside job. If the entire batch of Taxotaphen was contaminated at the factory in India, why haven't other patients besides my mother developed liver toxicity?"

"Didn't I tell you?" Scott's voice rose an octave. "Over two thousand cases of liver toxicity worldwide have now been reported."

"Two thousand?"

Marcus scribbled the statistic onto his notepad. "Most were in Germany and France," Scott added, "but twenty cases have so far cropped up here in the States. Interestingly, your mother's case was the only one in Tennessee, even though dozens of vials with the same batch number were sold to oncologists across the state."

The letter Libby faxed to all the oncologists in Tennessee – it worked!

Marcus filled Scott in on the warning Libby had written and faxed.

"Any deaths?" Marcus asked.

"Ten worldwide – all in heavy drinkers whose livers couldn't handle the added strain of aflatoxin. Most, like your mother, just got severe toxin-induced hepatitis, but survived."

He twiddled his pen while trying to come up with all the questions he should be asking. "I assume a worldwide recall was issued?"

"Of course."

"And has every doctor with vials of Taxotaphen with this batch number been notified?"

"As of today, yes. Since the recall notice, we are receiving retroactive reports of patients who developed liver toxicity, but the oncologist hadn't run toxicology tests to figure out that contaminated Taxotaphen was the culprit. Dr. Holman was the only physician in the world to put two and two together and run the toxicology tests."

Twirling his pen between his fingers, he voiced his thoughts. "So, in reality, there are probably even more *unreported* cases from doctors who haven't gotten word of the recall yet."

"Exactly. The doctors no double attributed their patient's jaundice to other causes. Unfortunately, the recall will lead to a major worldwide shortage of generic Taxotaphen since Banderbaxy is the world's largest producer."

"Trust me, tainted chemotherapy is far worse than a shortage. My mother stayed jaundiced for a month. In the beginning, we weren't even sure she'd survive."

"Toxin-induced hepatitis is no picnic in the park," Scott agreed.

Marcus couldn't help but add, "Unless the park has serious poison ivy. Mom nearly clawed herself to death due to her high bilirubin level."

After a pause, Scott said, "I want to thank you for writing such a persuasive letter to Dr. Patel. Without it, he might not have ordered the impromptu factory inspection that led to a worldwide recall. No telling how many lives you saved."

Marcus beamed with pride. Nice to see his hard-earned law degree amounted to more than fodder for bad lawyer jokes. "Hopefully, a factory shut-down and exorbitant fine will convince Banderbaxy to play by the rules. And if they don't, they'll get shut down again."

"This is the first time, to my knowledge, the CDSCO has performed an impromptu factory inspection and immediately shut down a factory. That was some letter you wrote."

"Well, I *am* an attorney," Marcus said. "Writing persuasive letters is my job."

"Please thank Dr. Holman for me, as well."

"Will do."

"Because of her tenacity in solving your mother's case, the problem was uncovered before thousands of lives were lost."

"She's an excellent oncologist, and my mother is lucky to have her."

"I've mailed a formal letter to both of you summarizing all of our findings, but I wanted to personally give you an update on how seriously the FDA took your complaint."

"Thanks, Scott. It's good to know my tax dollars aren't *all* wasted on squabbling politicians in Washington."

"Every member of the FDA investigation team takes the job seriously. After all, it could just as easily have been one of our mothers instead of yours poisoned by aflatoxin."

Marcus thanked Scott again for his dedication and ended the call, still shaking his head. He had assumed Roger was behind the tainted chemo.

So Libby's original hunch that this mother's chemo was tainted at the factory panned out.

Marcus drummed his fingers on his desk, trying to incorporate Scott's update with the other facts of the case. If the chemo was tainted in India, and not by Roger, as he had concluded, then who snuck into Libby's office and then bolted as soon as he heard Libby coming? Surely it had to be Roger, but if he wasn't there to poison the chemotherapy, why was he there?

If he'd wanted to attack or murder her, why didn't he do it that night? She was in the office alone and defenseless. If the intruder were a common thief, why hadn't he rummaged through drawers looking for petty cash?

Had he been looking for narcotics to sell on the streets?

Without the fingerprint report, they had no proof the intruder was Roger.

Marcus rolled his neck and massaged his tight neck muscles. Instead of clarifying things, Scott's phone call raised more questions than it answered.

Who broke into Libby's office — and why?

Since Libby would likely be swamped with afternoon patients and wouldn't have time to talk with him, Marcus decided to wait until their hike after work to give her Scott's update. No point upsetting her in the middle of the day. Besides, Marcus needed to do some investigating of his own before he talked with her.

He glanced at his watch. He had an hour before his next client, which left just enough time to run over to the police station. With any luck, the results of the fingerprint analysis would finally be back, and that might clinch the mystery of whether Roger was the one who broke into Libby's office that night.

* * *

Julius was sitting at a metal desk completing paperwork when Marcus arrived. He offered Marcus coffee, and over Styrofoam cups of the bitter brew, they pulled up Roger Anderson on the computer.

Even in his mug shot Roger Anderson was handsome. Marcus could understand how a vulnerable, pre-teen girl might fall victim to his beach boy good looks, especially if he were doting.

"Have they made any progress in tracking him down," Marcus asked, leaning over Julius's shoulder at the computer.

Julius frowned. "No sign of that slippery eel anywhere. Not since he vandalized Libby's car in your mother's driveway. The man just up and disappeared." He clicked on a different computer site and added, "If he has a brain in his skull, he's left the state to avoid arrest. Killing a parole officer while out on parole? We're talking life in prison without parole—maybe even the death penalty."

Marcus tried not to make a face with every sip of coffee strong enough to kill a Tyrannosaurus rex. "What about the fingerprints we sent over? Any results from them yet?"

"I checked yesterday, but they weren't back. Unfortunately, thanks to recent budget cuts, there's a backlog."

"You'd think with Roger guilty of murdering a parole officer his prints would move to the front of the pack."

"You'd think! I flagged it as a top priority, so let's see if it's come in today." Julius clicked and scrolled and then pointed at the screen. "Bingo!"

Marcus read the results, and his heart jolted.

The fingerprints belonged to Roger.

Marcus ambled the small office rubbing his chin. "Roger broke into Libby's office, but he didn't attack her, even though she was there alone and defenseless. He didn't poison the chemo, so what was his agenda?"

Julius raised upturned palms. "No telling what that psychopath had up his sleeves."

The words did little to calm Marcus's nerves.

"Anderson has it in for Libby, so it's a good thing she scared him off," Julius added.

Until Roger was caught, Libby's life was in jeopardy, and short of hovering over her 24/7 with a loaded gun, there was little Marcus could do to protect her.

He glanced at his watch. His next client was due in the office in ten minutes, so he had no time to discuss things further. He thanked Julius for his time and promised to update Libby about the fingerprint results.

* * *

As Libby and Marcus trekked their favorite trail in Percy Warner Park with Trixie and Gus, Marcus updated her about Roger's fingerprints and the aflatoxin contamination in India. The news hit Libby like a bludgeon, and she stopped dead in her tracks. "So it *was* Roger who broke into my office that night, but he wasn't the one who contaminated the chemo?"

Marcus placed a reassuring hand on her back. "Julius promised to pull out all the stops to capture him."

"When he does, I now have proof that all the handwritten notes left on my car and on the gifts were from Roger."

"How can you prove it?" Marcus asked, stepping over a tree root.

"Last night, I remembered that on my twelfth birthday, Roger gave me a copy of *The Lion, the Witch, and the Wardrobe*. He wrote a note on the title page, wishing me a happy birthday, and he signed it. Since I've always loved C.S. Lewis, I kept the book and pulled it out last night."

"And —. "Marcus gestured with his hand for Libby to continue.

"It confirmed that Roger's writing on the title page exactly matches the writing from the notes."

Marcus gripped her shoulders and gazed into her eyes. "Libby, promise me you'll be careful. This guy knows where you live, where you work, and what kind of car you drive. He knows how to pick locks and attach tracers. Julius says he's a hard-core psychopath."

"Tell me about it. Last night, every time the motel room creaked, I bolted awake, thinking it was Roger breaking in. And a couple of nights ago, I jumped out of my skin when Carlos entered my office to empty the trash. I let out such a loud scream I nearly gave him a heart attack. Talk about embarrassing!"

He grabbed her hands and squeezed them. "Make sure you carry your pepper spray and cell phone at all times. Get security to walk you to your car."

"Trust me, I do."

They completed their hike and loaded the dogs into their cars. Sophia promised veal parmesan for supper.

After three weeks without Sophia's cooking, Libby looked forward to it.

CHAPTER 32

It was Friday night, but Libby was determined to stay at the office until her desk was clear. After getting back together with Marcus, she had dashed out of work the second the last patient left the office so she could spend as much time with him as possible. The net result? Hours of neglected paperwork and computer documentation demanding her attention. But she couldn't put it off any longer.

While she was alone in the office, Libby wasn't worried. More than a month had now passed since the car graffiti incident, and Julius was convinced Roger had fled the state to avoid arrest. Plus, Carlos would be in to clean her office any minute.

Thus, when Libby heard the front door of her office open and close, she assumed it was Carlos coming to vacuum the carpet and empty the trash.

She glanced at her watch.

Eight o'clock. He's right on time.

She reminded herself not to scream and give him a heart attack when he entered her office. Focusing her attention back on her office note, she didn't give Carlos another thought.

Until she heard a hauntingly familiar voice.

"Hello, Libby."

Adrenaline shot through her like a rocket. She instinctively gripped the edge of her desk.

There in the doorway stood an older version of her childhood nemesis.

"Roger! What are you doing here?" Her heart thudded wildly.

Roger strolled forward and stood inches from her desk—arms crossed, eyebrow arched, a demonic glint in his eye. "Long time no see, kitten."

"How did you get in?" she asked stupidly, already knowing the answer.

He smirked. "Twenty years in the slammer, thanks to you, and I learned a few things—like how to pick a lock." He rounded the corner of her desk and stepped even closer, as though intent on maximizing his intimidation.

Don't let him know how much he frightens you. Show him you're an adult now.

She crossed her arms defiantly and said with a commanding voice, "It wasn't thanks to me, Roger. *I* was just a child. You took advantage of my vulnerability and reaped the consequences of your own poor choices."

He slammed his fist onto her desk, his neck veins engorged with rage. "You're gonna blame *me* when *you* seduced me?"

Her mouth dropped. "Seduced you? I told you repeatedly I didn't *want* to do your touchy-feely stuff—it made me uncomfortable."

He offered her a hint of a smile. "Ah, but that was our ritual, wasn't it? Our little game. You act all hard-to-get, and I wear you down until your 'no' becomes 'okay.'" He closed in on her—an intimidating mass of muscle and height.

Her legs turned to rubber, and her hands shook.

Remind him you're not a kid anymore. Tell him to leave!

Before she could utter a word, he gripped her shoulders with such force she winced. "We *both* played the game, Libby, but only *I* got punished. That wasn't right."

His face flushed crimson, and his eyes bore into hers with equal measures of hatred and rage. "You got all the fun, and I got the prison sentence. You turned on me."

She flung his hands off her shoulders and tried—unsuccessfully—to push him away. "Get your hands off me!"

How dare he blame me for his incarceration!

A sudden wave of nausea and dizziness gripped her. No! She could not faint. She had to show him he couldn't intimidate and control her anymore.

Roger reached for her hair and fingered a lock between his fingers. "I always loved that red hair of yours." He smirked. "Always wanted to see it down here, too." He reached for her crotch with a lusty glint in his eyes. "But you never let me get that far, did you?"

She slapped his face so hard it sounded like the crack of a whip. "I want you to leave. Now." She shoved him with all her might, and he staggered backward, but he grabbed the edge of her desk to keep from falling.

He grinned as though enjoying what she had just done. "You're such a tease. You always were."

She had to make him see she meant it and wasn't being a tease. Unfortunately, her pepper spray was in her purse hanging from a hook on the back of her office door—just out of reach.

Her only hope was to stall him until Carlos came in to empty the trash.

Keep him talking. That will buy time.

She forced herself to meet his eyes defiantly. "I never liked what you did to me, and when I found out what you did to Kristen, it made me so mad I reported you for statutory rape."

His eyes locked on hers, and he nodded knowingly. "That's why you ratted on me, isn't it? You were jealous because Kristen got what you secretly wanted. I did it with Kristen before I did it with you. That was my mistake." He shook his head as though disgusted with himself. "I should have forced myself on you. Clearly, that's what you wanted, wasn't it, kitten?"

What?

Her mouth dropped in horror. Is that what he thought? That she *wanted* him to *rape* her? The man truly *was* a psychopath.

Her insides began to quiver, and her knees turned to Jell-O.

Roger continued his deranged monolog. "Sure, you would have put up a fuss, but deep inside, you *wanted* me to do it. You wanted me to introduce you to womanhood, and when I didn't, and you found out about Kristen, you turned on me."

Horrified at his perverted interpretation, Libby snapped, "I reported you because what you did was illegal. And morally repugnant."

He stepped forward and gripped her face with such force she grimaced in pain. His eyes penetrated hers like laser beams, terrifying and crazed.

"I'm here to finish what we started twenty years ago. I've spent two decades in prison, thanks to you, so I intend to get my due."

Julius's words flashed back to her: *He's a psychopath who blames you for his incarceration. He's intent on revenge, so never be alone with him.*

Her heart hammered so hard she felt dizzy.

Lord Jesus, help me! I'm about to be raped.

She had to stay calm and act like she was in control. Pointing toward the door, she commanded in a loud authoritative voice, "I want you to leave. Now!"

He crossed his arms and smirked. "Ain't gonna happen, kitten."

Panic welled up inside her. Should she make a run for it? Scream?

She glanced toward the door. Surely Carlos would enter her office to clean any second.

She had to do something—but what? Roger misinterpreted every protest as some kind of sick cat-and-mouse game. A deranged ritual.

She pointed to the door. "Roger, this is not a game for me. Now get out!"

His eyes went wild with desire, and he laughed sardonically. He gripped her hair and yanked until her face was just inches from his. "Your protests only whet my appetite. I've been dreaming of this moment for two decades."

Her cell phone rang.

Marcus.

He was calling her with Brittany's location. This was the night they were supposed to confront Brittany about her deception.

She dove for her phone, but Roger grabbed her wrist. "We won't be needing a cell phone for what I've got planned."

He yanked on her arms and forced her out of her chair. Jerking her to his chest, he hissed, "Payday is here, sweetheart."

CHAPTER 33

As soon as Brittany sped off for her supposed gym workout, Marcus dashed to his car with Amanda in tow. He hooked the baby into her car seat and followed Brittany from a safe distance. Sure enough, she drove right past the fitness center and cruised into the wealthiest section of Nashville. She parked her BMW in the driveway of a castle-sized stone estate. Marcus parked a short distance down the street to avoid detection but close enough to witness Brittany entering the house.

A tall, blond man met her at the door, and the two shared a kiss. They entered the house and closed the door.

Marcus clenched his teeth furious he'd fallen for her lies — again.

Fitness center, my eye!

He glanced into the back seat to check on Amanda Rose. Good — she'd fallen asleep.

Who was this guy? With his blond hair and light coloring, he was most likely Amanda's biological father. Judging from the wrought iron gate, multiple turrets, and flowing fountain in the driveway, he could easily afford a wife and baby, so why wasn't Brittany pursuing that guy for child support?

Marcus pulled out his cell phone and dialed Libby's number to notify her of the address. After the fifth ring, it went straight to voice mail.

That's odd.

Libby insisted she wanted to confront Brittany, and she promised to come as soon as Marcus provided her with the address. She knew tonight was the night Marcus was following Brittany, so why hadn't she answered her phone?

He shot her a text message with lover boy's address and then leaned back against the headrest to wait for Libby's reply.

When ten minutes passed and she still hadn't responded, a seed of worry planted itself in his brain. It wasn't like Libby to ignore his messages at eight o'clock at night, especially when they had agreed upon a strategy to confront Brittany. Even if an emergency at the hospital had cropped up, she would normally have texted him a hasty reply.

Why isn't she responding?

He shifted in his seat, trying to ignore his unease.

It was probably nothing. She was probably admitting a patient to the hospital.

Marcus called Carlos in hopes he could enter Libby's office and reassure him that Libby was okay. But the phone call went straight to Carlos's voice mail. He shot off a text message to Carlos, but since his spoken Spanish was a lot better than his written Spanish, he wasn't sure the message made sense.

He straightened in his seat and drummed his fingers on the steering wheel, trying to quell his rising panic.

She's probably fine. Roger has been AWOL for over a month now. Don't borrow trouble.

Marcus startled when Brittany exited the house with her mystery man just thirty minutes after she arrived. They kissed on the front porch, and then the guy handed her a wad of cash.

Brittany sashayed down the stairs, waved good-bye, and strolled toward her BMW. The guy shut the front door, and Brittany unlocked her car door with her fob.

Marcus jumped out of his car and stomped over to Brittany. "Did you enjoy your time at the fitness center? I'll bet your pelvis just got a fantastic workout."

Her eyes widened. "Marcus? What are you doing here?"

He crossed his arms and gestured his head toward the mansion. "I might ask you the same thing. Thought you were going to the gym to work off baby fat."

Acid bubbled up his throat. *How dare she deceive me like this.*

She stared at the ground and tapped her foot, as though trying to trump up a plausible excuse. Finding none, she threw up her palms. "What can I say? Busted."

"If you wanted a rich guy who lives in a castle, why were you pursuing me?"

She shifted her weight and glared up at him. "You wouldn't understand, Marcus."

His lips tightened. "You think? You claim you want things to work out with me, yet you're screwing around with whoever that rich blond guy is."

He pointed with his thumb toward the mansion.

She stared at him speechlessly, as though too dazed at being caught in the act to come up with a plausible explanation.

No way am I letting you off the hook!

"You claim you want things to work out for us. You demand I give you money for diapers and formula then dash off to meet up with some other guy under the guise of working out at the gym? But I'm supposed to understand? Enlighten me."

She averted her eyes and tapped her foot again, as though stalling for time.

He crossed his arm, refusing to back down. "I deserve an explanation, Brittany. And how about the truth this time because I'm not going to believe any more of your lies."

She flung back a lock of hair. "Alright! I lied because I knew you wouldn't approve of me seeing Jake."

"Because..." He gestured with his hand for her to continue.

She examined her nails, clearly not wanting to confess. Finally, she mumbled, "Because he's married."

"Married?" Marcus's shoulders dropped. "Oh, nice, Brittany! Wasn't it bad enough you broke up Libby and me? Now you're a homewrecker, too?"

Her head jerked up, and her eyes bore into his with rage. "I am not a homewrecker. Jake's wife is a total witch, but he can't divorce her because she's threatened to take him to the cleaners if he contacts a lawyer. They already live in separate houses, so I'm not wrecking anything."

Marcus gestured at the massive estate in front of him. "This isn't his only house?"

Her face lit up. "Actually, Jake owns four homes. One in Nashville, one in Palm Beach, one in Stowe, and one in Vail."

Marcus pointed to the wad of bills in her hand. "I see Mr. Moneybags is feeding your shopping addiction."

"A baby costs a lot of money," she replied defensively.

"As do your fancy shoes and French manicures." He shook his head in disgust. "I always knew you liked expensive stuff, but I never thought you'd stoop so low as becoming a call girl to get it."

Eyes seething, she slapped his face. "How dare you! I am *not* a call girl! Jake loves me. He just can't divorce his wife."

Marcus couldn't help himself. "Can't, or won't?"

"Can't! Not without losing half his fortune."

Marcus snorted. "God forbid he have to settle for only *two* mansions."

Brittany glared at him. "He'd be an idiot to lose half his fortune, so he'll never divorce her. She refuses to grant him a divorce because she's Catholic and doesn't believe in divorce." A tear formed in her eye, and she brushed it away. "Because of her, I can never marry him."

Marcus softened slightly. "Then find somebody else, Brittany. Somebody single. Somebody available."

She sashayed forward and caressed his arm. "I have—you." She gazed up at him with a smile she no doubt thought would leave him weak in the knees. Instead, he wanted to kick hers! "I still want us to get married, Marcus. That way, Mandy will have a daddy."

His mouth dropped, too shocked to utter a word.

Is the woman delusional?

She gazed at him imploringly. "If you agree to marry me, I'll ditch Jake, I promise. You're the only one I've ever really loved."

He shook his head in disgust. Did she seriously think he'd marry her after the kissy-faced display with Jake he just witnessed? Did she think he was that stupid—or desperate? Did she think she was that irresistible?

Too livid to respond to her ridiculous request, he unlocked his car door and unhitched Amanda's car seat from the back seat and transferred it to Brittany's car.

He turned to her, barely able to contain his fury. "Don't ever call me again. I want zero contact with you." He formed his hand into a giant circle. "Zero."

She clutched his arm. "Marcus, wait! I told you I'd give up Jake. You're so good with Mandy. She needs you."

He pulled away from her clutch. "Forget it!"

She dug a finger into his chest. "How can you abandon your own daughter when you claim to be a Christian?"

Rage pummeled through him. "Because Amanda Rose is not my daughter—she's Jake's. Libby says it's not even possible for me to produce a blue-eyed child since everyone in my family has been brown-eyed for four generations."

Arms akimbo, she snapped, "Well, how would I know that? I haven't gone to medical school."

"Maybe if you'd stayed faithful to me when we were engaged, you'd *know* who Mandy's real father is without me needing paternity tests to prove it."

He eyed her suspiciously. "Where *are* the results from that paternity test, anyhow? I sent them off three weeks ago, and the company says I should have received them by now. Did you steal them from my mailbox?"

Brittany's face flushed, and she flung a strand of hair off her shoulder with a flip of her hand. "As a matter of fact, I did."

"It's a felony to steal people's mail, you know."

She shrugged. "Whatever. I didn't want you to get them because I thought the lab made a mistake."

Marcus snorted. "Right! You didn't want me to get them because they proved I'm *not* Mandy's father, didn't they? But you weren't going to tell me! You were going to soak me for free babysitting and diaper money for as long as you could get away with it. You were going to try and seduce me into taking you back again."

She stomped her foot. "Okay, I admit it! I lie. I steal. I manipulate. You know why? Because I *have* to. It's the only way to get ahead in this world."

Marcus scowled. "That's ridiculous."

"Is it? My mother was a nice Christian wife and mother. You know what that got her? Ditched by my father when she was forty. Disillusioned, depressed, scraping to get by. Stuck raising three kids all by herself. Thanks, but no thanks." She glared up at Marcus. "My father dumped her for a woman half his age who was beautiful, sexy, put-together. So you tell me? Where did 'nice' and 'Christian' get her? Alone and dirt-poor, that's where."

He almost felt sorry for her with her cynical worldview.

"Not every man is as unprincipled as your father, Brittany. My father stayed faithful to my mother their whole marriage, and I would have stayed faithful to you if we had ever married."

Her eyes suddenly pooled with tears. "Don't you think I know that? Why do you think I crawled back to you and wanted *you* to be Mandy's father, not Jake? I wanted Mandy to have a better father than I had." She brushed the tears from her cheeks. "I knew you'd provide stability for her." She looked away and added softly, "And me too."

Marcus scratched his temple. "If you wanted things to work out with me, why were you fooling around with Jake? That doesn't make any sense."

She shifted her weight and stared down at her nails. Finally, she confessed, "Jake was my insurance policy."

"*Your insurance policy?*"

She released a sigh. "Look, I could tell you were in love with Libby by the way you were sulking and always talking about her. I didn't dare to put all my eggs in your basket until I was sure I'd won you back for good. I couldn't risk calling things off with Jake and ending up high and dry like my mother." She glanced up at him. "You weren't supposed to find out about Jake."

He shook his head in amazement. "Doesn't it exhaust you — leading such a double life? Feigning you're a Christian mother around me and a femme fatale around Jake?"

She shrugged. "I'd rather be exhausted than powerless and broke like my mother."

He forced himself not to roll his eyes.

"As long as I keep my looks, I'll always have a man to pay my bills and buy me nice things." She glared up at him. "All you men want is sex and a beautiful arm ornament, anyhow."

"Not all of us, Brittany," he retorted. "Might I remind you I've turned down your insulting attempts to seduce me three times now?"

Her lips narrowed, and she put her hands on her hips. "I don't get it. You used to adore making love to me."

"Sex *is* great, but following God is more important to me now. This time, I'm waiting until marriage, when the sex between Libby and me will be better than great because it will come with God's approval and a lifetime commitment."

Brittany stared back at him skeptically. "After my screwed-up childhood, I don't even believe that's possible." She added wistfully, "I wish I did."

She opened her car door and turned around to face him, eyes pooled with tears. "Good luck with Libby, and I really mean that. You're a great guy, and she's lucky to have you."

He mumbled goodbye and climbed into his car, one regrettable chapter of his life finally behind him.

* * *

Marcus dialed Libby again. No luck — it went straight to voicemail. No response from Carlos either. As Marcus left another message on Libby's voice mail begging her to call, a disturbing premonition settled over him.

Something is wrong — terribly wrong.

His phone rang. He glanced at the caller ID.

Thank God! It was Carlos.

Thank God!
Marcus's chest tightened.
Why hadn't Libby responded to his calls?
Was she still alive?

CHAPTER 34

With shaky fingers, Marcus pushed his car's call button to connect his call with Carlos.

Please, God, let her be okay.

Turns out, Carlos hadn't received Marcus's first message because he'd been vacuuming and hadn't heard the phone ring. As he stepped off the elevator to clean the medical suite adjacent to Libby's, he happened to notice a tall blond man loitering outside Libby's door. Although he could only see the back of the man's head, Carlos thought it matched the mug shot that Marcus had shown him. Carlos then witnessed him picking the lock.

Since Carlos didn't speak English, he wasn't sure how to confront the guy. Worse, what if Roger was armed? If he scared Roger away, the police would lose a prime opportunity to capture him once and for all. Thus, Carlos tiptoed away unseen and immediately called 911.

The dispatcher possessed more snarky attitude than Spanish aptitude and couldn't understand Carlos's broken attempts to communicate in English. He hung up thinking he might get further with hospital security. Unfortunately, they couldn't understand him either. He then called Marcus.

Marcus's gut tightened. "How long has Roger been in her office?"

"Just a couple of minutes," Carlos reassured him. "Do you think I should barge in and confront him? If you think I should, I will."

"Have you heard any screaming or sounds suggesting he is hurting her in any way?"

"I snuck into the waiting room, and I could hear them talking in her office. I couldn't understand most of what they were saying, but I did hear him say payday is here."

Marcus gripped the steering wheel, trying not to panic.

Dear God, keep her safe until I can get there.

Heart pounding, Marcus stepped on the accelerator desperate to rescue Libby before Roger...No, he mustn't let his mind go there.

Carlos continued. "If I'd heard screaming or thuds or gunshots, I would have charged in, but if Roger just shoots me and runs away, how will that help? We'll miss the chance to catch him, and I end up dead. That's why I called 911."

"You did the right thing, Carlos, " Marcus reassured him.

He gripped the steering wheel, his knuckles now white, as he raced toward Libby's office. "I'm less than five minutes away. I'll call 911 and make sure they send back-up. Hopefully, they've already dispatched someone based on your cell phone coordinates. Stay hidden, but where you can hear what's going on."

"What if she starts screaming?" Carlos asked, his voice shaky.

"If he's hurting her, barge in and demand he stop. Libby has pepper spray. It's either on her desk or in her purse. Spray it directly into his eyes — that will slow down his escape."

"What if he has a gun?"

"If he has a gun, run for your life. I don't want *you* getting killed, too."

"Me either," Carlos agreed. "I have four children who need their father." His voice became frantic. "Please hurry."

Marcus ended his call and commanded Siri to ring 911. Thankfully, the snarky operator had already dispatched cops to Libby's office based on the GPS coordinates on Carlos's phone.

"I couldn't understand a word he said, but I've done this job long enough to know desperation when I hear it. I dispatched cops and an ambulance as soon as I got off the phone with him," she reassured Marcus.

He sighed in relief. The police were on their way.

But would it be too late?

He next called Julius, who promised to beeline it straight to Libby's office.

Marcus turned on his flashers and sped to Libby's office like a contender in the Indianapolis 500. When he came to a red light, he glanced both ways, blasted his car horn, and sped on.

Here's hoping I don't get pulled over for reckless driving.

When he reached Libby's office building, he dashed up the five flights of stairs two at a time, not wanting to waste time waiting for an elevator.

Gasping for breath, he charged into Libby's suite and bee-lined toward her office.

Please, God, don't let it be too late.

Relief flooded through him when he saw Carlos hovering in the hallway outside Libby's office.

They dashed inside with Carlos carrying his vacuum cleaner overhead like a club.

Adrenaline surged through Marcus at the sight of Libby on the floor, mouth gagged, hands tied above her head, and her blouse ripped open with her bra exposed.

Luckily, her undergarments and skirt were still on, suggesting Roger hadn't raped her — yet.

Dressed only in tight-fitting underwear from the waist down, Roger displayed the sickening evidence of a fully aroused sexual predator. Rage the size of Texas coursed through Marcus, and he charged toward Roger wanting to kill him.

At the sight of Marcus and Carlos, Roger attempted to dart around them and escape.

You aren't going anywhere, dirtbag — except back to prison.

With a fury he could barely contain, Marcus shoved him back into the room and socked him in the jaw.

Carlos blocked the doorway holding his vacuum cleaner overhead.

Roger shoved Marcus out of the way and stampeded toward the door.

Whack! Carlos walloped him on the head with the vacuum cleaner.

Stunned, Roger staggered backward and fell against the wall.

This allowed Marcus time to get his bearings. He charged at Roger and knocked him to the ground then attempted to yank his arms behind his back. With one desperate lunge, Roger broke free and charged toward the door.

Too late. Carlos had located the pepper spray in Libby's purse. He aimed and fired it directly into Roger's eyes.

Roger cried out in agony. Though blinded, he still fought desperately to escape. With a quick twist of his torso, he freed his right arm and walloped Marcus in the jaw.

Marcus instinctively grabbed his injured jaw.

Oww! That hurt!

Furious, he retaliated with a couple of quick moves he'd learned in his karate class. He slammed Roger in the solar plexus then walloped him in the groin with his knee.

Moaning, Roger attempted to stand, but Carlos slammed him on the head with the vacuum again. He crumpled to the ground.

With Carlos's help, Marcus forced both of Roger's arms behind his back, and they tied them together with the roll of twine lying next to Libby. Now for his legs...

Roger kicked, bit, lurched, and tried desperately to escape, but he was no match for a livid, martial-arts-trained Marcus, and a janitor armed with pepper spray and a vacuum. As though finally accepting he was outnumbered and would only get clocked for resisting further, Roger finally gave up fighting, and they tied his legs at the ankles.

It took every ounce of self-control Marcus possessed not to pummel the guy into oblivion, but not wanting to land in a prison cell next to Roger, he resisted and instead rushed to Libby's side.

He tugged the gag out of her mouth and untied her wrists.

With quivering fingers, she buttoned her blouse and burst into tears.

"Thank God you came. Roger said he was videotaping the whole thing, and after he raped me, he was going to strangle me—like he did that parole officer. Said I deserved it."

He cradled her in his arms and stroked her hair. "It's all over now, honey. You're okay."

She clung to him. "You and Carlos saved my life."

Within a minute, Julius and a horde of Metro's finest charged in and handcuffed Roger.

The nightmare was finally over.

CHAPTER 35

Julius stayed behind to gather evidence from the crime scene and to question Libby, Marcus, and Carlos while everything was still fresh in their minds. While he obtained their statements, the rest of the team snapped photos and secured the evidence. They finally solved the puzzle on why Roger had barged into Libby's office weeks earlier but then bolted without attacking her.

The night he broke in, he'd come to install hidden cameras so he could later videotape himself raping and strangling her. Since he'd painstakingly planned her rape and murder down to the minutest detail, having Libby startle him before his cameras were up and running did not fit into his scheme. In a panic, he'd bolted when he heard her voice and resolved to come back when no one was there. Obsessed with completing his final act of revenge to the minutest detail, Roger must have come back to Libby's office later that night when she wasn't there, picked the lock again, and completed the installation of his hidden cameras.

When interrogated by Julius about the hidden cameras, Roger confessed he wanted video footage of Libby "getting what she deserved." After raping and murdering her, he'd planned to hightail it to a remote part of Wyoming to avoid arrest. The gruesome video footage would provide later entertainment.

The hidden cameras now provided the prosecution everything they'd need for a slam-dunk case, especially since Roger stupidly bragged to Libby about strangling the parole officer and promising to do the same to her. Roger would land himself in prison for life without parole — if not the death penalty.

After completing their interrogation and crime scene investigation, the cops dragged Roger to a waiting police cruiser for transport to jail.

Libby, Marcus, and Carlos were now free to go. They thanked Carlos profusely for his help and invited his whole family to dinner after church on Sunday.

Libby gave Julius a bear hug. "Thanks for all you did. You've been great to work with."

Julius shrugged. "Just doing my job. I told you we'd catch that slippery eel, but man, he sure made me earn my paycheck."

Libby suggested since he and Brandy were dating, perhaps the four of them should plan on a dinner and movie night out together when things settled down. Julius heartily agreed. "I'd love that. After cracking this case, it's time for a little R and R."

Libby and Marcus waved goodbye then drove to Libby's townhouse.

Finally! She could move back home!

Once there, Libby doctored Marcus's swollen jaw with an ice pack. As though sensing his pain, Trixie licked his hand in sympathy. They snuggled together on the couch, wrapped in a quilt while sipping decaf. Trixie curled up on the sofa beside Marcus.

"I didn't get to ask you earlier, but what happened before I got to your office? Besides the obvious."

Libby grinned. "I used a weakness of mine to my advantage and outsmarted him!"

Marcus's brow furrowed. "What do you mean?"

"I faked one of my vasovagal spells to buy more time."

His eyes widened. "You *faked* passing out when someone was about to murder you?"

She scratched Trixie's neck and grinned. "I'm not a bad actress if I do say so myself. By feigning unconsciousness, it delayed Roger's scheme for a good five or ten minutes."

"How? I would think an unconscious woman would be easier to rape and murder than one who is fighting."

"Normally, that would be true, but I figured out Roger needed me to fight and resist his advances, or he wouldn't obtain the thrill he felt he deserved after his twenty years in prison. By fainting, it derailed his rape and murder plans long enough for Carlos to arrive and call you."

"How'd you know Carlos would come."

"I didn't know for sure, but he usually cleans my office between eight and nine, so I prayed if I could stall Roger a few minutes, Carlos might come in to empty my trash and rescue me."

Marcus beamed. "I told you Carlos would be our strongest ally. I couldn't have apprehended Roger without his help tonight."

"I've decided to study Spanish so I can be better friends with Carlos and his family. Really, I owe him my life."

Libby snuggled closer and pressed her ear over Marcus's chest, savoring the steady beat of his heart and the warmth of his arms.

Marcus raised her hand to his lips, and then winced in pain. "Ow! I don't know how I let that punch of Roger slip by me."

"Where'd you learn all those self-defense moves, anyhow?" Libby asked.

His eyes widened. "Did I never tell you I earned a brown belt in karate?"

She arched a brow. "Another of your hidden talents, I suppose?"

"I enrolled in karate all through college and law school as a stress reducer. The moves sure came in handy tonight."

"You got that right! I was impressed."

He gripped her hands, his eyes penetrating hers with a serious expression. "Impressed enough to marry me?"

She smirked. "Is that another one of your rhetorical question, or an actual marriage proposal this time?"

He chuckled. "I supposed I deserve that. I'd get down on one knee and do it properly, but Roger slugged me so hard, I'm not sure I could get back up."

He gripped both of her hands and gazed into her eyes. "Libby Holman, I love you with all my heart. Will you do me the honor of becoming my wife?"

Joy infused her body like sunshine on a balmy April morning. She squeezed his hands and exclaimed, "Yes, a thousand times, yes!"

He kissed her gently to seal the deal. "I had more than a hunch we belonged together, even that first day we met."

She pulled back and stared at him. "You mean that day you raked me over the coals for nearly killing your mother?"

He chuckled sheepishly. "Yeah, that day."

"I thought you were going to *sue* me."

He raked his hand through his hair. "Truthfully? The thought *did* cross my head, but I came around soon enough."

She laced her fingers with his. "Who'd have thunk a bag of contaminated chemotherapy would bring a doctor and a prosecuting attorney together—in a *good* way?"

He shrugged. "Stranger things have happened."

"We made a good team, don't you think? We forced a drug manufacturer to clean up its act, and then we caught a fugitive."

"No telling how many lives you saved by running that toxicology test. You followed your hunch, and in the end, you were right." He pulled an errant lock of hair from her face and tucked it behind her ear. "Despite all the stress and heartache, it's been worth it because it led me to you."

She smirked. "Your mom will be delighted you aren't marrying that 'she-devil' Brittany."

"That makes two of us." His eyes glinted devilishly. "Besides, I've found a new 'she-devil' to marry."

She whacked him playfully in the belly. "Just like I've found a new handyman and car mechanic?"

He wagged a finger in her face. "Hey, I knew karate, when duty demanded."

She placed a soft peck on his non-swollen cheek. "Yes, you did, my knight in shining amour. And for that, I'll be eternally grateful."

"As well you should!" he said with a grin. "In fact, I'll expect a lifetime of groveling as due compensation for services rendered."

She crossed her arms and offered an unconvincing scowl.

"Would Counsel settle for a lifetime of love and affection instead?"

He eyed Trixie gnawing on the remote control. "Stir in one ill-behaved Labradoodle puppy, and you have yourself a deal!"

BOOKCLUB QUESTIONS

1. The majority of all generic drugs and protective medical equipment, such as face masks and gowns, are now manufactured in China and India. How did this affect the COVID-19 pandemic?

2. Given the current adversarial trade relations between the United States and China, how safe is it that so many of our medications and medical supplies are produced in India and China? What potential threats does this pose? What are the pros and cons of living in a global economy?

3. Libby endured sexual abuse as a child and was reluctant to open up about it as an adult. Why was she an easy target for a pedophile, and what preconceived notions did she carry about pedophilia? How can we empower children not to become victims? How do we help adult women who are victims of sexual abuse?

4. Early in the novel, Libby hid her past from Marcus. Is it wrong for a woman to keep secrets (sexual abuse, a baby given up for adoption, a previous divorce, an abortion, a criminal record, drug abuse, etc.) from a steady boyfriend or future husband?

At what point in a relationship should a couple confess the unsavory details about their past? What harms might come from total honesty? What harms could come from *avoiding* full disclosure?

5. Did Sophia meddle too much in Marcus's life? How involved should the mother of an adult child be?

6. Marcus had a character flaw of lashing out impulsively when he was upset or angry. How do you handle anger? How does your husband or family handle anger? What does the Bible teach about the proper way to handle anger?

7. Roger was allowed out of prison five years early due to "good behavior" in prison. Is this a sound practice or merely a way to minimize prison overcrowding? Is release on parole appropriate for pedophilia?

8. Libby lost her mother at age eleven. What impact did her mother's death have on her life? (Career choice, relationships, health?) If you have lost a parent, how did it impact you?

9. Marcus sued doctors for malpractice as part of his job. Is suing, instead of forgiving, unchristian? In what circumstances is it *not* unchristian to sue someone?

10. At times, Trixie could be a remote-control-eating menace. Tell the group about your most memorable pet. What made this animal special? How do pets enrich our lives?

Here is the first chapter of Sally's first **Ladies in Lab Coats** novel called *Can You Lose the Unibrow?* If you like what you have read, the book is available in either paperback or e-book format from Amazon.

Or, if you prefer, you can obtain it off my website: www.sallywillardburbank.com

Can You Lose the Unibrow?

"How sharper than a serpent's tooth
it is to have a thankless child."
~William Shakespeare~
King Lear

Chapter 1

Tall, dark, and handsome—that's what twenty-year-old women want. By age thirty, they lower their standards to tall and dark. Age forty? *Please, God, let him have a job.*

Sheri Morris scrolled through the unsavory characters displayed on her laptop and grumbled to her mother, perched behind her like a vulture waiting for roadkill, "A year's subscription to *Losers Looking for Love.* You shouldn't have, Ma."

Linda Morris harrumphed. "Excuse me, but the website is called *Christian Professionals Looking for Love.* It's time you found a husband."

She wagged a scolding finger. "Now that you're forty, you can't afford to be too choosy."

Choosy?

Sheri eyed the cigarette dangling from the lips of one morbidly obese contender. "I'll need an oxygen tank to keep this one alive." She gestured toward the screen. "Look at these guys. Duds, all of them."

Linda brushed her off with a dismissive wave. "Nonsense. You don't need a whole battalion—just one nice man."

One nice man? In your dreams, Ma.

Sheri heard enough stories about online dating disasters to write a book—a very depressing book. Talk about an ego-busting, budget-bloating demoralizing waste of time—and that's if she didn't wind up dead in a dumpster.

Oblivious to Sheri's musings, Linda prattled on. "I've always dreamed of a Christmas wedding." Her eyes grew dreamy, and she extended her arm. "Picture it, Sheri. You in an elegant velvet wedding gown. The bridesmaids in festive cranberry red. The church adorned with fragrant evergreens, holly berries, and flickering white candles. Poinsettias will circle the altar, and the shimmering lights on a Douglas fir will make the church magical."

Sheri snorted. "You're planning my wedding when I haven't even had a first date?"

"With all the men to choose from on this website, you'll have a husband in no time." She snapped her fingers.

Right. Her mother made finding a husband sound as simple as ordering a Weed Wacker off Amazon.

Not wanting to hurt her feelings, however, she forced herself to say nothing—until her mother insisted, "Cupid is computer savvy these days."

Sheri rolled her eyes. "Shakespeare says, 'Some Cupid kills with arrows and some with traps.'"

Linda waved a scolding finger. "None of your Shakespeare foolishness with me, young lady. You can laugh all you want, but website dating is how it's done these days."

"Except I wouldn't marry any of these guys. Look, I know you meant well, but honestly? I wish you'd just bought me a terry-cloth bathrobe and slippers instead of this line-up of lunkheads."

"I was trying to be nice. A year's membership for this website was expensive, and you don't seem very grateful for my generosity." Her eyes pooled with tears, which she made a point of brushing away dramatically with the back of her hand. Then, to drive in her nail of shame, she reached for a tissue and blew her nose with the volume of a foghorn. "I try so hard to be a good mother to you and Tess, and what's my reward? Ingratitude, that's what."

Here we go again: guilt, gift-wrapped with a giant bow. Happy birthday to me.

Her mother picked up the framed photo of Sheri's sister standing with her husband, Colton, and son, Jacob, from Sheri's desk. "Tess and Colton are so happy, and they have little Jacob to boot." She dabbed her eyes with a tissue. "I just wanted you to be as happy as your sister. Is that too much for a mother to ask?"

Sheri was about to apologize when she heard Tess trill from the living room, "Did I hear my name?"

Mrs. Perfect-in-Every-Way breezed into the study and hooked a blond curl behind her ear. She eyed the puffing-smoke-stack-of-a-man displayed on the screen and snickered.

"Is that future lung cancer victim the guy Ma picked out for you?" She elbowed Sheri. "Just the man any doctor would want to marry—a smoker."

Thank you, Tess.

One glance at her mother's crossed arms and thunderous glare, and Sheri forced herself to say, "I'll keep browsing, Ma. There's bound to be one decent guy."

Just not this one or the last thirty I checked out.

She grabbed her mug of coffee and gulped a hefty swig. She'd need all the caffeine she could get to whittle through this sorry passel of deadbeats without wanting to inject herself with cyanide.

Please, God, let there be one tolerable man in the bunch.

Somewhere out there was a smart, funny, and principled man—her soulmate—and she wouldn't settle for less, no matter how much her mother cajoled her.

She clicked to the next candidate and groaned. Definitely *not* said soul mate—a sixty-seven-year-old banker seeking a forty-year-old woman.

Tess skimmed the man's profile over Sheri's shoulder. "Gross! What gives that old geezer the right to play in the sandbox? He's old enough to be your father."

Sheri scooped up another bite of cake and ice cream and stuffed it into her mouth. Surely stress would burn off the calories. Besides, it was her birthday.

She clicked to the next guy—Jeremy—a forty-year-old heavy metal guitarist with scraggly hair and enough tattoos to cause a worldwide ink shortage.

Jeremy wanted a supportive helpmate. Sheri shook her head in disgust. "Interpret that to mean he needs someone to pay his electric bill."

Tess laughed and nudged her, but their mother's sour expression suggested she wasn't amused.

Sheri clicked to the next screen. A guy with five ex-wives.

Next.

She spooned in another bite of carrot cake and wiped the luscious cream cheese frosting from her lips.

She clicked onto an attorney who bragged about how many lawsuits he'd won in the last ten years. One of those "1-800-BAD-DRUG" sharks. Wait! Hadn't she seen this guy's picture plastered all over Nashville's buses? Just the man every physician wanted—a lawyer who got rich suing doctors.

"Face it, Sheri," Tess said. "While you were slaving over textbooks in college, medical school, and residency, the rest of us snagged up all the decent guys like bargains at a Macy's Midnight Madness sale. Looks like you're left with the dregs."

Sheri squelched the temptation to asphyxiate her sister with cake. The cruelty of Tess's words, however, rang true.

"Theresa Morris Peterson, you take that back this instant," her mother demanded, jabbing a finger in Tess's direction. "That was mean and uncalled for, and I won't stand for it."

Sheri suppressed a smile. You'd think they were still squabbling six-year-olds from her mother's reaction.

Tess raised upturned palms. "Just saying…"

Sheri had always told herself she'd find a husband once her internal medicine practice was up and thriving. Her mantra? Focus on your studies and worry about hunting for a husband later. Unfortunately, "later" had come and gone nine years ago, and now, her twelve-hour workdays left little time to meet a smart, likeable guy the natural way.

Hence, her mother's birthday gift.

How degrading to expose her picture and profile to hundreds of strangers as though she were some worn-out nag at a horse auction one step from the glue factory.

After eight years without nary a date, she needed to kiss her pride goodbye before she wound up dying in a nursing home all alone.

Resolve renewed, she ignored Tess's barb and clicked to the next man on the website. A CPA named Greg Palmer.

Hmm. He might prove useful around April fourteenth.

Friendly brown eyes stared back at her, and his smile would make a dentist do a happy dance. At least the guy wasn't morbidly obese or holding a Marlboro. Even better? No boastful display of a shotgun and dead deer carcass draped around his shoulders like two previous contenders.

Before she could comment on the encouraging lack of mutilated animals, her sister pointed at his eyebrows — or eyebrow — to be specific. "Get a load of that unibrow! It's as bushy as a squirrel's tail!"

"Those eyebrows could easily be fixed with a simple tweezing," her mother pointed out.

Tess jabbed Sheri with her elbow. "Just think — you could spend your first date plucking his eyebrows."

Sheri burst into laughter until her mother's scathing glare made her clamp a hand over her mouth.

"Bushy eyebrows are no reason to reject an otherwise acceptable man," Linda insisted.

Tess's eyes nearly fell out of their sockets.

"Acceptable? Are you kidding, Ma? Look at that butchered haircut and those awful horned-rimmed glasses."

Tess pointed at the screen. "And check out the nerdy bowtie." She snorted. "He'd be as much fun as a tax audit."

Sheri's heart momentarily stopped. *Tax audit?*

"Speaking of tax audits, what if he works for the IRS? Would he audit my tax returns before agreeing to take me out?"

"Don't be ridiculous," Linda snapped.

"I don't know, Ma," Tess countered. "Accountants are known for being neurotic about minutia."

"So!" her mother hissed, arms akimbo.

"So what if the guy finds some obscure mistake Sheri made on her tax return and then reports her for tax evasion?"

Tax evasion? Yikes!

She hastily mashed on a key to exit the man's profile. *Why chance it?*

Sheri glanced at her watch then up at Tess. "I thought Jacob had a two-o'clock T-ball game."

Tess eyed the wall clock and jolted. "Holy moly, we're supposed to be on the field in thirty minutes." She dashed out of the study hollering to her husband and son to hightail it to the car—and make it snappy.

Never one to miss her grandson's games, Linda grabbed her purse and bolted toward the front door. "Meet you at the ball field, Tess." When she reached the door, she turned and shouted back to Sheri, "Good luck with the husband hunting," then dashed out.

Sheri signed off the website, drained and demoralized from her depressing exploration of available men.

She attempted to distract herself from the misery of husband hunting by tackling her favorite piece — the Moonlight Sonata — on the piano.

When Beethoven failed to cheer her, she ambled to the bedroom and grabbed an overflowing basket of dirty clothes. Even laundering dirty socks beat rummaging through a hopeless line-up of men she'd never want to meet, let alone marry.

Have I waited too long to find love?

About the Author

Hi!

Thanks for reading *More Than a Hunch*. I hope you enjoyed reading it as much as I enjoyed writing it!

By day, I run a primary care internal medicine practice in Nashville, Tennessee. By night, I escape into the imaginary world of other women doctors and write contemporary Christian romance novels.

Why would a busy doctor take up writing? Dreaming up and then penning stories has provided a delightful diversion from the aggravation that all too often comes with electronic medical records and insurance hassles.

A bit about me: I grew up on a dairy farm in Derby, Vermont, graduated from Montpelier High School, and Texas Christian University.

After earning my medical degree from the University of Vermont, I moved to Nashville with my musician husband, Nathan, to complete my internship and residency.

We are the proud parents of two wonderful adult children — Steven, an industrial engineer in Denver, and Eliza, a future veterinarian.

My first book, *Patients I Will Never Forget,* is a collection of humorous and inspiring stories from my thirty-year career as a primary care doctor. In addition, I recently released a non-fiction book, *The Alzheimer's Disease Caregiver's Handbook: What to Remember When They Forget,* to assist the families of patients with dementia.

I am currently writing a five-book romance series called **The Ladies in Lab Coats**. All five books feature women physicians. *Can You Lose the Unibrow?* is the first book in the series, and *More Than a Hunch* is the second. I am working on my third book in the series called *Hearts Heal in Haiti.*

Sign up for my email list to be notified of every book release or to request autographed copies.

My website is www.sallywillardburbank.com

Thanks again for reading *More Than a Hunch.* If you enjoyed it, please pen a 5-star review on Amazon and Goodreads to let other prospective readers know how much you enjoyed the book.

~Sally~

Made in the USA
Middletown, DE
26 August 2021

46134223R00186